# The Feminist EarthMother PartyGirl

## Joni Page

Potato & Leek

Potato & Leek, Australia

Potato & Leek
potato&leek.com



Published in 2025 by Potato & Leek, Australia

ISBN:        978-1-7638011-0-3        paperback edition
             978-1-7638011-1-0        eBook edition

A catalogue record for this book is available from the National Library of Australia



Typeset in Garamond 12pt by Potato & Leek
Cover artwork by Potato & Leek
Printed and bound by Ingram Spark

*Potato & Leek respects the traditional custodians of the Kaurna lands upon which it operates.*

A catalogue record for this book is available from the National Library of Australia

# Author's Note

I have a keen interest in psychological theories and assessment. They have often been a guide and a comfort when I needed to get clear about a problem.

The assessment tools described in *The Feminist EarthMother PartyGirl* do not exist beyond the scope of this book. This is a fictional story and to do justice to the journey, fictional assessment tools were necessary.

They were created from an amalgam of my imagination and my understanding of the underlying principles behind a wide variety of psychological assessments. Resemblance to any existing psychological assessment tools is unintended.

For

Sam

*Hip hip hooray!*

# 1

In times of the most catastrophic of catastrophes, the only place one can start is with the known knowns.

But what is known?

Start from scratch, Candice.

1. I'm not a girl. I Am Woman.

2. I'm over the age of eighteen, permitted to vote thanks to the efforts of the suffragettes, well past the years of growing tall and the perils of puberty and ready to pay full fare should I need to take public transport.

3. I'm not a virgin. I've had my heart broken more than once.

4. I live in my own flat with the lease in my own name.

5. I hold down a good job gained after years of slogging away at school and university.

6. I'm not reliant on a man for my future or fortune. I don't go by Miss. I'm not in the least bit interested in getting married. I don't even want to think about pregnancy or child rearing or choosing schools or being somebody's housewife.

I do want it. Someday. Just not now. Except the housewife bit. Is there an agency where you can hire a housewife so you can have all the good bits of marriage and none of the bad?

I digress.

7. I'm happy. I'm healthy. I'm well liked.

I'm a little egocentric, wouldn't you say?

If that was all there was this story wouldn't be very long. You'd think: *That was boring. Inane. Pointless. And not worth the effort I've put in to start it.*

Which brings me to the story of my life and where I am at this moment. All those things - boring, pointless, inane and not worth the effort I've put in to start it - unfortunately describe my current situation.

I think back on all the chances that had to happen for me to be here - all the lucky escapes, the miracles, the meetings, the opportunities, the full-term pregnancies that delivered generation after generation so I could exist, typing into my computer keyboard, the technology that was invented, the food industry, the health industry, the laws for equal rights and … well, paper and ink, and education, all of the absurd, implausible, improbable events that brought me to this point - obviously they'd be for nothing if I'm not going to take my life out for a spin.

Which is not what I've been doing. Step after step, pace after pace, plod after plod with no thought for where I'm heading. I have a job, a flat and a boyfriend … Whoops, I haven't mentioned him, have I? And he'd pull out his Sad Face if he knew.

My boyfriend of two months (let's call him Gene for privacy's sake, although his real name is Godfrey Channing) is a sweet guy. He has a kind demeanour and a well-paying job and a loyalty unsurpassed by my other boyfriends. I'm hoping he's not The One. Because I'm not ready for The One. I want to experience. I want to know myself and the world, I want to revel in the wonder of being here.

I know what you're thinking. *You should've thought about that before you got yourself a job where they're counting on you, before you took a lease out on your flat and, worst of all, you should've thought of this before you got into a relationship.*

My defence is I didn't. I only know this now because yesterday, during a personal development day at work, the facilitator gave us a personality test.

Which, unfortunately, I failed.

I'm apparently rule-driven rather than creative. A wallflower rather than the life of the party. Brain instead of heart. Reality not ambition. In other words, an introverted, rule-driven pragmatist who lacks emotional dexterity.

I have something important to say here, so listen up.

## THIS IS NOT ME!

Anyone who's ever spent time with me knows this isn't a valid description. And now it's plainly apparent I've well and truly misplaced myself.

Last night Gene worked a shift so I was home alone, pacing like a ghost, forgetting to eat dinner, seeking sense in my Self.

Today I need to get back in touch with my emotions. My gut needs to tell me more than just Time to eat. I need to break some rules. Be that lively, vivacious, spirited being of my youth.

Let's face it: school goes on for an interminably long time then is over in an instant. Now my twenties are about to do the same.

There's a Me out there somewhere and I need to find her, to break free from the well-worn road, to strike out anew.

To Liberation!

I'm going to follow my inner voice!

Damn it, there's the doorbell.

# 2

Gene wants to move in.

"Sure. That would be great," I tell him. "I need to sublet my flat while I go in search of The Truth."

He looks at me in that uncomprehending way he has as he stands at my front doorstep. He's got a dazzlingly handsome face but not a lot goes on under his trendy blonde haircut.

"Sublet? What? Uh, I don't get it?"

I smile. "I'm going on a journey." My heart lifts with every word.

His pretty blue eyes reflect the sky. "You're going on a holiday? I'll come, too? Sounds like fun?"

As always, he's unsure of himself. Dear Gene. He's sweet and compliant and a head turner. Kind of a Trophy Boyfriend. Yep, you're right: it's a world gone mad. *She's talking about him like men used to talk about women, dating him because he looks good without any intention of committing.*

Ah, my first Truth. Women, having complained mightily that our marketability as a partner was based on looks and whether we'd support our men without making a fuss about our own lives, are now free to do the same thing to men. And although I'm glad the score is even, Chaos Theory has romped straight in. Change one little thing and the whole system goes belly-up.

Maybe I wouldn't be so flustered about the passage of my life if I was married and spending my days proudly keeping my house clean and teaching my daughters how to cook. Maybe I wouldn't be so freedom-fixated if my life depended on finding someone to marry me so I wouldn't end up begging or selling my goodies on street corners. Feminism has brought with it freedom, but such liberation has called our lives into question. Now we have a choice: career or motherhood, or career and motherhood. I wonder if things are easier or a whole lot more complex.

Gene is waiting for an answer, his brow furrowing and creasing and bending askew.

"Not a holiday. A journey," I repeat. "Still planning it. I'll get back to you." I step back to close the door.

He holds it open. "Can I come in?" He blinks, his long lashes pathetically attempting to wipe the confusion from his brain.

I push it again. "I'm busy."

He peers past me, holds it open firmly. "Do you have a-a-a visitor?" His lip begins to wobble.

Damn it. He thinks I'm cheating. "Just busy."

"Are you okay?"

Still with the questions. Wasn't I the one who was asking them? What were they again? They flash their grubby hands across my brain and I see instantly only an introvert would push a lover out the door.

Gene leaves half an hour later, satisfied I'm not having an affair, and in other ways, too. On his way out, he's turned his clinical attention to hygiene, and the remnants of our conjugation now lie imprisoned in latex in the bin, where they belong.

I lay in bed alone, thinking about life, my knickers elsewhere, the skirt of my dress upturned against my chest. Boyfriend satisfaction level: well, he's cute, like I said. And out to prove a point today. A tick on my Physical Union Self-Satisfaction Indicator. I have a job I love, a roof over my head, a supportive family, fabulous friends.

And an aching desire to find the truth about Who I Am.

I revise the scant things I remember about Chaos Theory. I started out studying Science to save us from a climate crunch with my amazing physics, but wound up merging into English Lit because, as my mother says, *Words can be powerful.* Now it seems this wasn't me Following My Heart as I claimed, but instead veering crazily from one road to another. Chaos Theory in applied form.

Again, I digress.

I close my eyes and think of the many paths before me. When I choose one it will change me, which will decide my next path, which will change me again and decide my next path, and so on and so on catapulting me through a giant feedback system into eternity or as close to it as I can humanly get.

Which sounds like a recipe for getting completely lost. In other words, where I am now.

Time to think logically. If I call the present A and my future Z, how many Zs are there? And which Z do I want? And how can I get there, when making a decision may shoot me down entirely the wrong path?

Again, like where I am now.

Perhaps I need a Z Register. Yes! First, I need to consider all my Zs! I jump out of bed and hunt absentmindedly for my knickers while my brain races across the likely outcomes of my life.

Oh, knickers be damned, I need to get this down on paper. Get back to you later.

# 3

*Z Register.*

1. Single, CEO of large organisation, marvellous inner-city apartment, regular dinner and drinks with fashionable intellectual friends, a personal trainer and weekend spas to keep me looking fabulous.

2. Single, still working where I am, never doing anything different, middle-age flab, lonely nights over reheated soup I cooked on the weekend to busy myself, catch-ups with friends who haven't made it either.

3. Single professor at posh overseas university where I'm coveted by peers for my interesting accent and off-cultural ways, regular travel to other countries, soaking up ambience and cuisine.

4. Newspaper item in a paper in fifty years: Crazy spinster woman ordered to offload her 250 cats by council. Health inspectors condemn property.

5. School newsletter item in thirty years: We also want to thank this incredible mum for helping in the library for no reward other than her love of books. Now she's retiring, her children long left school. Thank goodness she didn't find anything better to do.

6. Mother, six children each born a year apart, popping them out like it's routine, running a household smoothly and still looking delightful with a cocktail in hand when hubby gets home.

7. Mother of two, cocktail in hand after school drop-off, hubby working so hard he doesn't notice the quiet desolation of my life.

8. Single mother, like Mum once was

Hyperventilate.

Maybe what I'm looking for is not so much where I end up but what I'm looking for. What I'm looking for is: What I'm Looking For!

It's a vision quest. A Vision Quest.

I pace, lost amongst the debris of futures I haven't yet lived. That I don't even want. That I haven't ever aimed for. The future me is already out there, dragging me towards her. I may as well grab myself a bottle of wine, a pizza and several chocolate bars, and wait for her to come get me.

Hyperventilate again.

Maybe I need to *see* who I am. When was the last time I looked at my Self? I always look in my full-length hall mirror to make sure nothing's wrong before I step out, because I once saw a woman walking in a mall with the back of her dress tucked into her tights.

I eagerly skip to my hall mirror. Well! My new yellow-and-white-check cotton sundress is gorgeous! But I'm a little ruffled from Gene. Still without knickers. I swish my dress and settle my hair.

What about my face? Hmm, lips a little dry. I press closer, oh, too close. I see everything, all the good and the bad. And the ugly.

I frown. Ouch, that makes things worse! I manoeuvre my face into something pleasant, focus on each bit. Nice eyes: on the green side of brown. Nose: slightly too stub, but nevertheless manageable. Quite cute really. Eyebrows: ugh, need a pluck! How long have I had that line of extra hairs under the regular arch of my brow? I pull up my fringe and look closely at my forehead. No wrinkles. Not bad for twenty-eight. My hair, straight, fine and blacker than a moonless night, brushes over my shoulders. My legs, long and lean, have a posture of their own making.

I giggle. I still make a good superhero. Actually, this is exactly who I am, a woman whose superpower is wondering. This is the first time

I've looked at myself so intently since I goofed off with silly faces as a kid and practised how to look serious and intelligent as a teenager.

I stand back and evaluate the whole me. I was doing three aerobic jazz classes a week before Gene came along, so I'm in a decent enough shape, not for a model, obviously, but then who is, except for models? I try to make my breasts sit up like the model's beach-ball boobies on the billboard on the way to work, which look like they're suspended by some unknown force, upright and erect against her teeny-weeny-kini.

Further investigation is required. Time to strip completely. Whoa! Naked! The sight makes me quiver. And not in a good way. *Breathe!*

I'm so frail, this delicate patching of muscles and bones and skin. I'm relying on everything to keep working in unison, largely ignored by me, taken for granted, without recognition or acknowledgement. Frightened, I start to cry. I take a deep breath and push my fingers into my neck, expecting to be reassured by my pulse. It's silent. I pinch myself hard on the hip, hoping that I'm still a going concern.

And I am.

So here is *me*, gloriously naked and vividly alive. No trappings. Nothing to lean on. Nothing to shield me from misfortune. I'm at A, and can take this flesh and blood to the Z of my choosing.

But where and what is my Z?

The mirror reveals my knickers sitting on top of the television.

I pull them on, flip on my bra, tug on my dress, slip on my yellow sneakers and head out the door.

I'm off to find my Z.

# 4

I take off out of the flats' driveway and into the street where the heat hangs in the air like a clear fog.

Mrs Feeble's two orange trees are overwhelmed with fruit. Mr Red's azaleas are thriving under his tidy porch. Mrs Snitch's fake turf looks decidedly pale.

Those are not their real names, of course. Mrs Feeble is elderly, so the optimism of her orange trees is appealing. Her son, Ernie (real name) sits with her on her verandah or takes her for a stroll in one contraption or another. His frequent visits hearten me as much as her orange trees.

Mr Red's red-brick house is two houses away from Mrs Feeble's. Everything about him is red apart from his pretty azaleas: his hair, his house, its roof, his car. His skin's also red, because he's a brickie. I often think about popping some sunscreen into his letterbox, but that would make me as judgmental as his neighbour, the disagreeable Mrs Snitch.

Mrs Snitch watches the world through eyes that expect the worst. Any time I've stopped to chat she's begun bitching about this loud party or that untended garden or those kids playing cricket on the road. I always remember an appointment that I'm late for. This happens two minutes in; I never get away this side of fifteen.

I turn left at the corner. The pub looms ahead on the main road, with its tall ochre walls and curious roof ornaments, standing haughtily as if lord of the tiny houses below. I hesitate, realising I don't know where I'm going. So symbolic of my life. But the pub is where I'm headed, at least for the moment. Hopefully not in life. I set off at a steady trot until I find myself at the corner sign: *Sports Bar*.

Wait, what? Why am I here? I hesitate, my heart booming, confusion running riot in my head. Yet the door sits temptingly in focus. I reach for the ornate handle, slowly, hesitantly, see my hand wrapped around the lever as if I'm holding onto my life, take a calming breath.

Someone jerks the door out of my hands from the other side and abruptly I'm on all fours! An omnipresent hush sweeps through the room, each drinker admiring the knickers now abandoned by my lovely dress, which sits over my head.

I right myself, pull down my dress, sit back on my haunches. "Nothing to see here!"

A hand grabs my arm, pulling me effortlessly to my feet. "Plenty to see, and all of it fabulous."

The owner of the hand is quite delicious. Deep brown eyes that stare unblinkingly into mine. A surprisingly kissable mouth. Taut arms peeking out of a short-sleeve ocean-blue freshly-ironed shirt. Nicely pressed navy trousers. At odds with a bar of t-shirts and tats.

"Thanks." I yank my arm free and stride purposefully to the bar, every eye still upon me, and every brain reverberating with the memory of my knickers. I seem to have been disastrously detoured by a distinct deficiency of direction, a common thread between my life and my Vision Quest. Why am I even here? I've never visited this pub before. My suburb is extremely mediocre and there are much better pubs within a short distance. The tug of my Quest urges me on. I lean on the bar. "Tequila," I growl.

Here's another odd thing: I don't drink tequila, have, in fact, never tried it. Its name popped out of my mouth before I could drag it back in. More of my old science lectures return. Methinks my Vision Quest has invoked Newton's third law of motion: *For every action, there is an equal and opposite reaction.*

Currently the Opposite Reactions team is winning.

The barman cocks a bushy eyebrow at me. He bangs a tiny glass onto the bar, pours a viscous, vicious liquid into it. "For you, on the house." He cocks his eyebrow again.

I decide not to give him a mouthful when he's been so kind in giving me a mouthful and besides, perhaps it's a tic and he can't help it. I turn to see everyone, including HeroMan who helped me up at the door, watching me intently. I hold the glass up. "Cheers!"

"Cheers!" they reply in unison.

My throat explodes as the firestorm hits my tonsils. "Right," I choke, "That's done," as though it was a box to tick on my Vision Quest. Which clearly it wasn't.

I march to a door that will lead somewhere less male-dominated, although I still have no idea where I'm headed. Or why.

I push the door cautiously this time, making sure there's nobody on the other side. A large expanse opens before me. I take in the stunning room in astonishment. In one corner there's a small water feature, in another there's a wide, lush atrium with sunshine streaming in from a giant skylight. The atmosphere is more congenial than the masculine mood of the sports bar. Appetising aromas fill the air.

The tables are set for dinner. A few laggards from lunch are ordering more wine and more beers and more desserts. Most customers are groups of oldies or couples with varying numbers of children. There's one large party with a few vacant seats and a balloon that proclaims *21 today!* spiralling lazily above a dainty blonde who looks like she's still in primary school. Across at the bar must be the absentees from the vacant seats. Young men, foot on the rail, beer in hand, quietly watching a game of soccer on the large screen.

Six men roost in a corner at a curving high table, drinking champagne and eating hot chips. Plenty of Zs there. Maybe here is the Equal Reactions team. I shake my head. Methinks that is hormones calling, the Vision part running roughshod over the Quest. Remember, this isn't a Husband Quest, but a Quest to locate Me.

Nevertheless, questions must be answered. Why champagne? Red wine and beer are what Men drink, isn't it? And why hot chips? Not Steak or Hamburger? I pause for a short break from my Quest; a dozen eyes eagerly watch me approach. "Hi," I smile. "Is this the right table for The Champagne and Chips Appreciation Society?"

The closest man fetches a bar stool, sets it next to him, pats it.

I sit down as one of the men says, "Our wives (the word stabs me) met when our kids were at kindergarten but we were all going to different schools. They decided to meet Saturdays from one till four. They don't all make it every week but it's a standing commitment."

I grab a small chip and chuck it in my mouth. "So you decided to do it too? Where are the kids? Looking after themselves?"

"Once a month we meet instead of our wives," another continues. "They were always going on about their champagne and chips, so we thought we'd see what all the fuss was about."

"We found it very nice," the guy next to me smiles, as if he finds me very nice too. "Rules are made to be broken, you know?"

I do. But mine are different rules to the one he's implying. My mobile rings. Damn it: Gene. I move away to avoid Gene hearing a cacophony of male voices in the background.

"That was nice," he breathes insipidly.

Ugh. I'm tiring of nice. "What's up?"

"Am I coming around tonight? We didn't make any plans."

Typical. I'm on a Vision Quest and he's asking about a Saturday evening's frivolities. I'm more eager to spend it on My Quest. Ouch: that sounds like introversion. No! Must remember my diagnosis is not the boss of me. "Actually, I could do with a night off."

"Shall I come around about nine-thirty?"

*What, just in time for bed?* "I mean a night to relax on my own. You know, I can be a bit introverted." The word is acid on my tongue.

"Oh, absolutely you should do that! I'll have a night at the club." He's rubbing his hands in glee, a free man on a free night where he doesn't have to worry about a girlfriend. "I love you," he simpers.

I hang up quickly, turn to find the Chorus of Husbands watching.

"He's a goner." The man I was sitting next to pulls me back.

"Planning your wedding yet?" asks the man at the far end.

I laugh. "Hasn't even entered my mind!"

"Uh-oh," says a man who hasn't spoken yet. "That's the beginning of the end." He raises his champagne. "Hallelujah."

The others follow. "Hallelujah!"

The man next to me speaks again. "When a girl finds a man she likes, she starts planning her wedding. If you're not, I give it a week."

Yikes! I stand up and brush myself down as I did when I stumbled into the Sports bar. The memory of HeroMan's hand returns to my elbow. I shut my eyes. I can almost feel his hand upon me.

"Where've you been all my life?" asks a warm voice.

Yikes, now the Question has a voice! I open my eyes to find HeroMan standing next to me. "My hero," I sneer, more to flatten my own fascination than his.

"Don't be like that." He steers me away. "Sorry guys, she's mine."

"Spoiling our fun," says the man who was next to me.

"Remember the wedding," says another.

They all raise their champagnes and smile. "Hallelujah!"

# 5

"The wedding?" HeroMan asks.

"Their little joke."

We arrive at a table next to the water feature. He sits down; I remain standing. I realise I'm frowning, remember my mirror work, smile. Our table is far from any other.

"This is cosy. Intimate." I lower myself into my chair carefully, ensuring my dress follows all proper social conventions.

"I've ordered us some mixed entrees," he says rapidly, as if I'm about to flee. "And pinot gris."

"Pinot gris?" I glance towards my Husbands, but they're immersed in their own chatter.

"This one's a particularly nice colour. There's a range, depending on how and where it's made. The colour of this one suits you perfectly."

I snap my attention back. He's grinning.

"This is a little presumptuous." I devour the glint in his eyes far too hungrily. "Thinking I can be wooed with food."

The waiter appears with a board of food and two glasses of the palest of pink wine.

"What's this again?" I hold my glass up to the light and twist it, examining its beautiful colour.

The waiter rearranges our table to fit the board. "Pinot gris. Very tasty." He winks at HeroMan. "It *goes down* very quickly."

"Hey, none of those stupid boy's club signals."

The waiter bows his head. "I didn't mean to offend. I hope you have a nice meal."

*Grrr. Nice.* Doesn't anyone have a vocabulary anymore? I scan the board, set for two, dips in the middle, a serve of pita triangles on each side, a duo of lamb skewers snuggled up at the end, a handful of calamari rings on each side of a tiny bowl of dipping sauce.

HeroMan speaks. "I was wondering what my afternoon might bring, and now I know. It wasn't what I expected, but just what I needed!"

I know what I need: to walk away. I've allowed myself to follow someone else's path, to head towards a different Z than I expected. Than I predicted. Than I intended. But the calamari looks tasty. And the lamb skewers juicy. And I skipped lunch in favour of the mirror.

I pick up a calamari ring and dip it into the sauce silently. What if I say nothing? This might be an effective research tool. Because what am I if not a scientist, experimenting with Life, hypothesizing towards a fresh theory on Men And Their Place In My Life? Oh, and uh, the purpose of my life. My subject smiles as I chew the rubbery ring.

"I like a girl who has no regard for manners." He sips his wine.

*Grrr. Girl.* I mutely masticate and make a mark on the mental checklist I've started to devise, courtesy of the data I'm collecting.

"I know you can talk." He sips his wine.

I turn again to my Husbands. The one on the end raises his champagne to me. I hide my smile and take a gulp. Mmmm. The wine is delicious. I pick up a pita, slough it through the tapenade.

"A healthy appetite. Nice."

*Ugh.* I hold my glass against my warm cheek. "What do you think's happening here?"

"Fabulous Guy asks Intriguing Woman to spend time getting to know him." He takes another sip. "So she sees he's a Fabulous Guy."

"What makes you think I'm intriguing?"

He sweeps my face, my shoulders, my cleavage. "Isn't it obvious?"

I pick up more pita. "I don't know I'd describe you as fabulous." I probably would but I'm not confessing that. "You are intrepid, though." I keep my eyes brazenly on his.

"I like a girl who uses big words."

I pause, swallow. "I'm above legal age, which means I'm a woman."

He sits back and sighs. "Sorry. Didn't know you'd be like that."

"Like what?" I take another swig of wine.

"Such a word tyrant. Girl, woman, they're interchangeable in our society." He looks hurt.

I want to soothe, instead I grimace. "Next you'll be calling me baby."

He grimaces back. "I meant no harm. You don't like being called girl? Or baby?" A smile creeps onto his face. "Baby's nice. It conjures up an image of someone sweet and innocent." He glances again at my cleavage. "And cuddly."

I'm playing but I can't help myself. "You like innocent?"

"Are you innocent?" He takes another drink.

I can't read his expression. I gulp down the contents of my glass, rise to return to my Vision Quest. He pulls me down, signals to the waiter to bring over a bottle. The waiter leaves without comment.

HeroMan refills my glass. "Please, stay. I only want to spend time with someone who's interesting."

I lean forward. His eyes light up at the reveal of my cleavage.

"If you think you'll loosen me up with food and drink, I'm happy to vacate my seat so you can find someone else." I say this gravely, although the wine's gone straight to my head and the attractive qualities of HeroMan seem to have gone straight to another part. I mentally note evidence supporting the Fairy Tale hypothesis of knights in shining armour being a turn-on, as HeroMan appears to have readied me for fun with a capital F, if you know what I mean.

At this point, don't judge me. I know an hour ago I was underneath Gene, and here I am getting my kicks from a stranger. I know society is not yet so advanced that this behaviour doesn't invite an unattractive name for me as a woman. If I were a man, you'd be lapping this up and egging me on.

"Things never used to be this difficult." HeroMan smiles pathetically. "Would you like it if I asked you on a date? Dinner, the movies, tickets to the football, you name it, I'm there."

I pause. He has the most beautiful eyes, large and brown like a deer. His coffee-coloured hair tips up from his head at varying angles. His dress is neat and not ostentatious, his expression frank, honest, free of any unspoken inclinations. I pick up a skewer. "Keep talking."

He smiles as I push each cube off the skewer onto a plate. "It's just, look at you. You radiate thrill. Zap my instincts. Call to my Truth."

"Truth, eh?" I point a cube of meat at him. "Define Truth."

"What's your opinion of love at first sight?" He refills his wine.

I put down the cube. "That's what you think this is?"

His face is engulfed with sadness. My guilt runs high. Who am I to play around with this guy, seemingly kind, who's on his own Vision Quest? I realise he's speaking, almost to himself. I lean in closer.

"-and then I was leaving when you fell at my feet. The thought that was running through my head the instant before that happened was Give up. You're wasting your time. You may as well be happy on your own." He looks up at me. "I only checked out that bar because I couldn't find my blind date, a friend of a friend who was allegedly just my type. Obviously not, because I keep my appointments."

Now I feel sorry for him. I wave a cube of lamb in front of his mouth. "Poor baby."

He laughs before biting the lamb cheekily from my fingers. I put a cube in my mouth and we sit, eyes locked as we chew silently.

I swallow. "If we dispense with the date talk, I'll let you enjoy my company for an hour." After all, what's an hour of a Vision Quest when there is tasty food, delicious wine, and eyes like these to gaze into? My phone bleats. "Excuse me." Damn it, Gene again.

"Just checking in. You were a little odd today. Where are you?"

"Supermarket. Ring you tomorrow. Have a good night." I hang up.

"This," HeroMan states, "isn't the supermarket." I go to respond. "Ah, ah, ah. He's a loud talker." He sits back suspiciously. "Who is he?"

"Boyfriend." I catch my Chorus of Husbands watching us keenly. "None of your business," I shout to them.

As one they raise their champagnes. "Hallelujah!"

I feel a gentle hand on mine. HeroMan looks at me curiously.

"Why don't we start again? Tell me your name. Mine's Sigmund. Yes, as in Freud. It means *victorious protector*. My friends call me Ziggy."

I stare blankly. "Sigmund?" I'm not sure whether he's having me on.

"Please, *Ziggy*. The only time I get called Sigmund is when someone's being stupid. I hate it, and you better get used to it."

There's a permanency about his talk. But wait, this isn't the Z I'm looking for. I dip another calamari ring into the sauce and whip it into my mouth, negating my capacity to speak.

"I know what you're doing." He grabs the last lamb cube. "A name is all I want." He pops the cube into his mouth, his eyes on mine.

I swallow, sip my wine. "What's your name mean again?"

"Victorious protector. How long's this boyfriend been around?"

I ignore his question. "Are you sure your name's not Presumptuous Sweet-Talker?" I begin pulling apart the other lamb skewer.

He grabs my hand. "Your name?"

I stare at him. He's bought food and wine and I won't even give him my name. I owe him that. *Idiot! You didn't ask him to buy anything.* "True." I realise I've spoken out loud. "Agnes," I lie. "It means *A woman cautious around men who think they can buy her time with delicious food and wine*."

He whips out his mobile and thumbs against it as if calling the police to report me. "Aha! Agnes," he smiles. "A woman who is chaste."

I pull his mobile towards me. "You looked it up?"

He smiles. "What sort of things are you chaste about, Agnes?"

"Men," I fire off, getting up and away before he can stop me. I take respite in the Ladies, lean on the sink at the far end, view my apprehension in the mirror. I expect to see Ziggy's followed me, but there's nobody in the reflection but me. My cheeks are flushed and rosy. There's a lie in my eyes, fun on my mouth and confusion at my brow.

"Shit! What are you doing?" I shake myself, hands grabbing the sides of the sink. "You didn't come out this afternoon to pick up a guy! You're All Powerful! On a Quest! Finding your Self! Stay on task! Even if he is gorgeous, hunky, sweet, and thinks he's in love with you."

I laugh, and my voice softens. "Love at first sight? Why don't you take that, see where it goes?" My face drops and I kneel down, place my head on my folded arms against the sink. "See where it goes, see where it goes," I murmur. "That's all I've ever done." I jump up again. "I want Action! Achievement! Stability! Independence! Direction!" I sigh, stiffly lean against the sink again, my forehead on the mirror.

A cubicle door opens. The woman is tall and middle-aged, black roots hovering at her blonde crown. She rushes to the sink closest to the door as if needing to flee, washes her hands nervously. "I'd take it, dear," she blurts. "Love at first sight can't be denied. Love's all you want to chase." She hurries out.

I check the other cubicles, then return to my solemn reflection. Great. Wisdom dished out in a toilet. A HeroMan in love with me at first sight. My knickers flashed to a bar full of men. It could be worse. At least I put my knickers on. Gene's words still infuriate me: "Shall I come about nine-thirty?" *You might like this guy better.* He's picked me up in a bar! *But he's seen you with your dress up to your waist and he's still interested.*

I'm on a Vision Quest. Ziggy is not in the equation. I wasn't looking for him, and I'm still looking for my Self. I push open the door. Perhaps my HeroMan will have left by now. I walk smack into Ziggy.

His face hovers happily above mine.

I link my arm in his and smile sweetly. "Where are you taking me tonight, Ziggy?"

# 6

It would be ironic for Ziggy to take me to a wedding, but that's what he's proposing. If you'll pardon the pun.

Yep, his Idea Of A Date is to take me to his cousin's wedding. That's why he was surprised the Husbands mentioned "wedding", and why I'm thinking Chaos Theory has a sense of humour.

Ziggy's friend apparently suggested he had the Completely Right Woman to accompany him to the wedding, hence the afternoon blind date, which turned into the interlude with me when the Completely Right Woman failed to appear. And so our first date is not to the movies or dinner or a football game, but to a wedding.

He still doesn't even know my real name.

I have some issues with my name. It's strong at full length but shortened it's not to my liking at all. It's Candice. You see what I mean. Too many ways to pronounce it: Cand-ice, Cand-ees, Cand-iss. The correct way, for me at least, is the last. In its long form it has a regal air, but as *Candy* there are too many jokes. Mind you, Sigmund doesn't seem much better, so here it's a level playing field, part of the Equal Reaction.

Still calling me Agnes, Ziggy asks if he can drop me home so I can get changed for the wedding. Unless I want him to buy me a new dress, in which case we still have time to go shopping.

"You're kidding me."

"Far from it. I've dropped a *Dress-Up* request on you only hours before implementation. It's only fair I offer to pay."

I'm certain a mix of emotions have transformed my face as I attempt to process this, because I see a suite of reciprocal expressions sweep across his face. "I've got a full wardrobe," I pout. "I'm sure to have something suitable." What I really want to say is either:

1. Do you presume I don't know how to dress myself?

Or

2. Yay, a new dress!

"Then I'll drive you home," he says. "You can leave your car at the pub, and I'll pick you up for the wedding."

"Why?"

He smiles. "It's not you, it's me. I want to make sure you don't decide against me once you're out of my hypnotic zone."

I'm not about to tell him where I live, or that it's so close we could walk our slightly tipsy legs there. And do slightly tipsy things together which involve intertwining those slightly tipsy legs, and more. Because been there, done that with Gene an hour ago.

"I'll meet you back here," I say. "What time's the wedding?"

He frowns. "Six-thirty. You're very untrusting, aren't you?"

I look askance. "I could say the same for you."

"Touché."

"Anyway," I humph, "given I've known you less than an hour, I'd say that was me being extremely intelligent."

"But look, I was a gentleman when you fell, I've supplied the finest of food and wine, I've invited you to a romantic event. By the way, what are you going to do about not being at the supermarket?"

I point my nose upwards. "I live in an era where I'm free to enjoy a platonic get-together with someone other than my boyfriend."

He sighs. "I don't want platonic."

I lean towards him. "It's all that's on offer."

He walks back to our table, picks up the wine cooler and takes it across to the Chorus of Husbands. They eke out the remaining wine amongst their glasses.

The one on the end raises his skerrick and says, "To weddings!"

Ziggy asks, "How do they know we're going to a wedding?"

"Don't worry about them." I giggle. My Quest has been fascinating so far. "I'll meet you back here, when?"

Ziggy pulls me towards him and I let him. A woman's got to maintain strict control of her situation at all times.

"Do you promise," he whispers, "to meet me back here? Don't break my heart now."

"Six?" If he goes to kiss me I'll let him do that, too. Remember I'm the one in control.

"Six." He releases me.

Disappointment washes over me. I feign the need to ablute, waiting in the toilet until I'm sure he's left. I check my feminist pink phone, yes, feminist pink, because nobody's telling me what colour phone I can have. There's a message from Gene: somehow, I've put my phone on silent. Definitely a Freudian Slip. Or a Sigmund / Freudian Slip maybe.

*I'm free tonight are you available?*

Odd. *Did you mean to send this to me?*

His response is immediate. *Sorry that was for Woody.*

One of the guys at his cricket club. Feeling guilty at my impending and undisclosed infringement of the Rules of Dating by way of my wedding attendance, I send him a smiley face. I decide against adding an X. Remember it's Z I'm after.

I begin chastising myself as I walk back to the flat. My Quest has so far been derailed by:

1. sex with my boyfriend

2. showing my (thankfully covered) nether regions to a bar full of men

3. a face-saving shot of tequila

4. being chummy with a Chorus of Husbands

5. lying to my boyfriend

6. accepting a date with a stranger

Methinks I'm not serious about this Quest.

I find myself at my front door, remembering nothing of the journey here. So like life. I stride towards the mirror, wondering who I'll see.

In every way I look the same as I did before I left. Hair the same, eyes the same, mouth the same, dress the same. I look closer. I look through the eye of my personality failure. I don't look at all introverted. All I've done since my Vision Quest began is to follow my intuition, listen to my emotions. Immerse myself in connecting with others. I can't remember following any rules at all.

Newton returns and my neurons automatically recite his first law: *An object at rest stays at rest and an object in motion stays in motion with the same speed and in the same direction unless acted upon by an unbalanced force.* I've been that object at rest, moving but not moving along the conveyor belt of life. Now I'm in motion, and I intend to stay in motion, my Quest rewarding me with a dress-up date with a handsome man. And indeed, the only unbalanced force that might object is having his own happy night out, therefore neither challenging my speed nor my direction.

I find my sexiest dress, a deep chocolate, one-shouldered, lace-over-satin, tight-to-the-knees beauty I picked up at the *Formal 4U* sale a month ago. I find my outrageously high black stilettos and lay the dress on my bed, the shoes on the floor, beaming with pleasure.

I think of Gene. I think of the Chorus of Husbands. I think of Ziggy. I think of Gene again.

Gene is a male nurse. You see it now, don't you? It's why he's so damn sweet. He's caring and kind and loved by his patients, and I'm cheating on him. Or maybe I'm not. It's a Vision Quest, remember, and I've held my ground with Ziggy, playing scientist instead of vamp.

I met Gene at my brother's place. Actually, he's my half-brother, and I've got two of them, both called Harry, which is how my mother and father met. What started as an innocent discussion about their Harrys at the high school Open Day concluded with a wild romp that night in a hotel-room which produced me nine months later. My mother's never been married but my father at that time was, and his wife was none too pleased with the result of Open Day night.

I digress.

Harry B broke his leg when he fell on an opponent after taking a shot in a basketball game (forty-year-olds should not play competitive sport). Harry K is a doctor, so B was going to ask him about his uncomfortably tight cast, until a team-mate said he "knew" a nurse.

Harry B was looking forward to a sexy female nurse turning up, and all the better if she was wearing a skimpy uniform with her boobs tipping out of an easy-access zip. But then, that's Harry B.

I was also visiting that day, which is how I met Gene. It was fate, Gene said. Gene's all about the Universal Force. As his real name is Godfrey you'd think he'd be an atheist, but he's constantly claiming coincidences are Spiritual Markers To Light Our Way. I'm beginning to think he might be right. And he might be wrong. For me, that is.

I don't know anything about Ziggy's paths, nor the Chorus of Husbands' paths. Perhaps they'll all be so insignificant that in ten years' time I'll have forgotten them. Or maybe in thirty years' time Ziggy and I will cry as we view our first grandchild.

Oh, God, I can't even fathom my Saturday night, let alone thirty years!

I switch out my break-neck stilettos for my shorter, gold, chunky-heeled sandals. They're my dancing shoes and they go nicely with the brown of my dress. I wash my hair, pluck my eyebrows, lay slovenly naked on my bed with a towel turban on my wet head. I think again about Who I Am. I didn't know I had this kind of subterfuge in me.

Gene's text message suddenly perturbs me. I grab my phone. *I'm free tonight are you available?* Why not *Hi Woody?* I scroll over his messages to me and each begins *Hi Candice.* Can he be hiding something? I scrunch my eyes shut, imagining Gene seeing someone else. My head starts to hurt from all the scrunching so I text him. *Are you seeing someone else?*

His reply comes quickly. *I do not understand?*

Of course he doesn't. It's me seeing someone else. You idiot, Candice. *Never mind have a good night.*

There's no reply. I get ready for my night out with a man who's not my boyfriend, guilt running a close second to excitement. I take another look in the mirror: my hair shimmers exquisitely, my make-up accentuates my features perfectly, my outfit looks fine enough for a fashion magazine. It's been a long time since I've looked this good.

Car this time. As I stride to the carport Laurie from the next flat wolf-whistles me from his doorway.

"My goodness, Candice, who's the man? Gene no longer around?"

I pause mid-step. "What makes you ask that?"

He grins. "In my experience a guy like Gene doesn't prompt a woman to look like you do right now."

I laugh. Laurie's close to seventy and has been married five times. His last wife dumped him just over a year ago and he's been living next to me for nine months. He's sharp, charming, intuitive. I'm guessing his experience is, unfortunately, on the money.

"Are we still gardening tomorrow afternoon?" he smiles hopefully.

"Of course. There's a few weeds. And tomatoes to pick."

"Wonderful! I could say *Enjoy your night* but dressed like that, I don't think there's any doubt."

I'm smiling as I drive the one minute to the pub. I'm lucky to have two nice guys in the flats, Laurie on one side and Rupert, a shy and quiet bachelor, on the other. Neither of them seemed to have much of a life so I convinced the landlord to let us change the stretch of grass growing along our side fence into a veggie patch, on the proviso I return it to lawn if he asks. On Sunday afternoons Laurie, Rupert and I spend an hour or three chatting and tending the garden.

I walk into the pub carefully through the bistro doors and glance around. Ziggy's nowhere to be seen. The clock says it's only five-fifty. *Too keen, Candice.* The waiter who served us earlier is at the bar, so I walk across and say hi. A woman with glossy red hair sits across from him at the bar. She looks me up and down like I'm a hobo.

"Hi to you, too," I say convivially and sit one away from her, glance at her wine to see if he's sold her on the pinot gris, too.

"Go away," she glowers.

I frown. "What? Why?"

"I'm waiting for someone. And you're dressed-" She looks me over again, "well, you're dressed like that."

"You're not shabby in the dress department either," I smile.

"I'm going to a wedding," she says haughtily.

My eyes feel like they're about to explode. "Really?"

"Yes." Redhead leans forward and says quietly, "It's a blind date. I was supposed to be here earlier but I got held up."

"Did they catch him?"

"Who?"

"Whoever held you up."

"Don't be ridiculous." Redhead leans away and presses her perfectly painted lips together. "I was getting my nails done and it took longer than expected."

"Ah. Were you meeting Ziggy?"

Her eyes are wide. "Uh, yes. Ziggy something. You know him?"

The waiter, who's been cleaning a glass all this time, steals closer.

"Ziggy? Yeah. Wedding's tonight. I'm going to the same one."

The waiter smiles.

"How do you know him?" Redhead asks suspiciously.

"Oh, the Zigster and I go way back." I ignore the waiter's stifled titter. "I wouldn't like to be you. Punctuality's a priority with Ziggy. The last woman, well, she was five minutes late and oh, the scene he pulled!"

Redhead frowns. It's quite cute. "But Christie said he's very sweet."

"Sure, if you're on time. But he's well known for his wicked temper where people are late. It's a bit of an obsession. And in front of all these people." I wave my hand around the room.

"I was having my nails done so I'd look my best," she falters, "for him. My friend said he was-"

"Ha! Forget Ziggy." I wave my hand again. "He's a flirt anyway. But the way you look, I'd try your luck elsewhere." Luckily the bistro is filling for dinner. "Lot of people here. Make for quite a scene."

Redhead stands quickly. "I didn't know." She harrumphs. "Just wait till I see Christie." She looks at me gratefully. "Tell him I said … well, nothing. Thanks for the advice." She rushes out the door.

"Impressive," says the waiter quietly. "And perfect timing."

Ziggy is behind me, his shoulders curving into mine, his arm around me, his warm breath in my ear. "You look fabulous," he whispers.

Ah, Newton's second law: *Acceleration is produced by a force acting on a mass.* Ziggy's presence, packaged now in a gorgeous black suit and lavender tie, seems to be hurtling my Quest towards a fateful conclusion, and after running the risk of losing him to Redhead I stake my claim, wrap my arms around him and kiss him deeply, feel the rising heat burst into flames.

"I'm ready to go," he whispers afterwards, and I know this, at least, to be True.

# 7

Someone has sandblasted the inside of my mouth. I move my head. Now someone's setting off rockets in my brain. I roll over and unglue my eyelids, gasp as I see next to me …

Nobody. I scan the room quickly. Ouch, that hurts.

I'm in my bedroom, in my bed, and I'm alone, ghostly whispers of last night running sickeningly through my head.

I peer under the covers. I'm naked.

Crap. I get up and pad gingerly out to the rest of the flat but no-one's there. Ouch! My hamstrings scream as I peek around the curtains. Double Ouch! I'm blinded by the sun's ferocity. I wait for the pain to recede and view the carport where the end of my car should be. It's not there. Questions pop in and out of my throbbing brain like bats in an attic. None of them are to do with a noble Vision Quest.

1. Where's Ziggy?

2. Where's my car?

3. Why am I naked?

4. How badly did I behave at the wedding?

5. How much do I remember?

6. What am I going to tell Gene?

7. Why are my legs so sore?

8. How can I tell if I've been plundered?

9. Where the crap to now?

I fill a glass with tepid water. *You've done it this time, Candice.* I wince. *An involuntary One Night Stand can only be made worse by the fact you told your incredibly sweet boyfriend you were having A Night At Home.*

My mobile squawks. Crap, it's Gene. *We have to talk.*

I crumple to the floor and lay on my back, my mind skimming across depravities that never seem to be adequately covered by the law, that can happen when you've brought home a complete stranger. Been completely out of it. Woken up naked. Double crap, I must clean under my couch, there are tissues and books and magazines and what's that rubbery thing at the back? Oh no! I roll over and reach out to it.  Phew. It's just a pink balloon, pathetically deflated and past its prime.

*Must not be like pink balloon!*

I rise, and see a piece of paper poking past my front door. I crawl unbecomingly to retrieve it, sit back and open it, hope it's from Ziggy.

Triple crap, it's from the boyfriend. *We have to talk, Gene.*

Bugger. He obviously came around after the club, didn't know where I was, left a note. Actually, I don't know where I was either. Who I was. What I was.

I sit on the toilet trying to decide if I've had sex or not, that is, since Gene. Shit, two men in 24 hours? I might not know who I am, but I certainly know what I am. I drag myself back to the kitchen dully and sip my water, trying hard to piece the night together.

I insisted we take my car as I wanted to be in control. In such a confined space the intimacy was extreme. Ziggy caressed my cheek then squeezed my hand, our eyes choking with desire. In that moment I was on full intuition and totally immersed in my emotions, but my intelligence was on holiday.

The church was fifteen minutes away. As we sat in the serenity of the chapel waiting for the ceremony to begin, I felt slightly ill because every statue - the Virgin Mary, Jesus, and some other kind, brave people I didn't recognise - were tsk-tsking me with their stony expressions. My eyesight wobbled. I thought I was going to pass out. Ziggy noticed and drew me close, putting his arm around me and nuzzling my hair. I peeked past him to the guests at the other end of our pew. They seemed to be a family of three or four generations. The mother smiled at me congenially. I quickly sat out of view.

The bride and groom appeared. They publicly announced their reckless promises of fidelity, loyalty and devotion and we sang happy hymns about Love. The ceremony was like others of this kind, reverential, calm, charming. Routine.

After that nothing was routine.

I remember being introduced around the room at the reception, the bride hugging me like I was a long-lost sister, the best man kissing me with way too much familiarity, Ziggy's eyes adoring every moment of me. Unfortunately, I also remember the champagne, at least at the beginning. After the speeches everything got fuzzy, until the night's echo evaporated completely.

A cleansing shower. That might help. I pass the hall mirror and spot a bruise on my neck. God, it's a beauty. He must've tried to bite my neck off. I examine the rest of me but there's no evidence of other bruises. I hope the shower can rinse away the pounding headache and colossal guilt.

The only thing that slips down the drain is my self-respect.

I'm towelling myself off roughly, attempting to scrub away my regret, when I notice my beautiful dress is hooked on a hanger on my wardrobe handle. I see my strapless bra sits folded on the dresser, but there's no trace of my shoes or knickers. I was neat if not sensible.

Regrettably, or not, I don't see any used condoms. I check in my drawer but the box is unruffled. I know what that means and none of it is good. Crap, I'll need to find out about a morning-after pill. I know nothing about this side of a woman's life, having always been scrupulous about condoms because of my own unplanned conception.

I sit on my bed dejectedly. It's not hard to figure it out. What was proposed as love soon became opportunity, resulting in Ziggy having unprotected sex with me.

I hope he returns my car.

*Oh crap.* I whimper. I don't know Ziggy's phone number, his last name, where he lives. I might have to report the car as stolen. How would I explain the background behind the theft to the police? I lay my head in my hands.

Bam bam! The front door reverberates with a loud rattle.

I pull the curtains to one side: Gene! Double, triple, quadruple crap.

He raps loudly again, urgently, insistently.

"Hang on!" I throw on underwear, t-shirt and jeans, wrap a scarf around my neck to hide my giant hickey, check quickly in the mirror.

Gene is crying when I open the door. Oh crap, he knows. And I know now, too. I'm not a Quest Rider, I'm A Bitch. A Cheat. A Liar.

"I'm sorry," we say together.

I pause, stunned, but Gene continues without making eye contact.

"Yes, I'm seeing someone else I'm so sorry I never meant it to happen but it did and now I'm in too deep with her and I can't lie to you anymore and I'm really, really sorry."

*Huh?* "Gene, calm down." *What?* "Tell me what happened." *Who?*

He hurries along again. "I met her a month ago and I tried not to let it get in the way because you're really great really special but honestly it was just meant to be and last night I went around to her place to tell her we couldn't do anything about this intense feeling of love that we have together but she said God put me in her path and I knew it was true and then we … we …"

I laugh. I laugh because there's nothing else I can do. I'm special, alright. "Do you want to come in?" I ask this only because I can't think of any other options.

"No. I mustn't. She told me last night after … She told me I was never to see you again. But I couldn't leave it like that. When you sent me that text last night, I wanted to, wanted to tell you but …"

He begins blubbering.

Time to take charge. I step out and place my hand on his elbow, pushing him towards the street. "It's okay, Gene. Follow your heart. Work out wherever it is you're supposed to be."

He's calm now. "Yesterday I felt guilty about how I was feeling about her, so I came to tell you, but instead we had sex."

I laugh again.

Gene frowns. "What's so funny, Candice?"

"Life."

"Uh, where's your car?"

Crap. "Lent it to Harry K." Fear grips me as I imagine Ziggy suddenly appearing in my car. I smile kindly. "Go on. Don't feel bad."

"I want to hug you goodbye, but I shouldn't."

I envisage my scarf pulling askew with alarm. "Then don't." I turn back towards the flat, my legs heavy. "Good-bye, Gene. Good luck."

I need to make sense of this tangle. Gene cheated on me, and I presume I've cheated on him. His was intentional, mine was not. One point against him. But I set up my infidelity to happen, dressing as I did for a date with a stranger. Score back to Zero. Gene doesn't know about my infidelity: he's honest, I wasn't. One point against me. But I don't know what happened last night, and certainly if there was sex it wasn't with me in full command of my faculties. Score Zero again.

Which is not the Z I was looking for.

I probe my lack of anger towards Gene. I've spent most of our relationship soothing him and I've done it again, even in a situation where he betrayed me. He even asked to move in yesterday when he came to tell me about his other woman. He's a nutcase for sure, but it was me that let him run riot in my life.

I'm too wiped out to give my anger its head. I look up towards the street but there's nobody there. I lock my door, take off the scarf, and go back to bed.

# 8

There's a glass of water next to my bed when I wake. With a jolt I realise
if Ziggy has my car, he also has my house keys. "Hello?" I yell worriedly.

Nobody answers.

I hobble around the flat as if I'm a hundred years old. I sob as I sit
on the toilet. I cry as I wash my hands. I wail as I sit on my couch,
wishing I'd never started my Vision Quest. Introversion never looked
so good.

I know this about myself: I'm not a wowser. I love to party, but I've
never overdone it like this, kept it to fun and not harm. And I was trying
to better my life yesterday, thinking deeply about my journey. I appear
to have gone, in spite of good intention, very much down my wrong Z.

An idea sparks. I grab paper and pen and sit at my table.

I write A: alcoholic. B: bewildered. C: crazy. D: disillusioned. I
change crazy to catastrophe and continue the list.

A: alcoholic

B: bewildered

C: catastrophe

D: disaster

E: entropy

F: frazzled

G: guzzler

H: horrified

I: insane

J: jaded

K: killjoy

L: lame

M: mortified

N: nobody

O: orgasmic

I start to giggle.

P: pretty

Q: quixotic

Where did that word come from? I don't even know what it means.
I grab my dictionary.

quixotic: *adjective. Not at all sensible. Unrealistically hopeful. Implausibly
romantic.* There's something running my life that's not me. I continue:

R: romantic

S: sexy

T: terribly, terribly sexy

U: unbelievably sexy

V: very sexy

W: wow! sexy

X: X-rated: way too sexy

Y: yippee, I'm so sexy!

Z: zero.

My mood disintegrates. I look back over the list, try again.

The A to Z of being Me

A: astute

B: beautiful

C: courageous

D: determined

E: enthusiastic

F: fastidious

G: gregarious

H: hilarious

I: ingenious

J: joyful

K: kind

L: loving

M: masterful

N: neighbourly

O: optimistic

P: persistent

Q: quiet and reflective

R: responsible (yes, even after last night I believe this)

S: sexy (all the way through)

T: thoughtful

U: underwear-wearing (giggle)

V: vivacious

W: warm

X: x-cellent at being me

Y: yummy

Z:

Nothing comes for Z. But isn't that what I'm looking for, not who I am? I don't need to be everything now. And Gene, well, he's on a Vision Quest too, hoping some special force will light the way. His current love was Meant To Be, just like we were. I feel sorry for her.

She'd better watch out. Coincidence is everywhere if you look for it, and Gene does with a keen eye.

I like my new A-Z. I throw my first attempt in the bin. It pops back out. Gene would say this was A Sign. I pick it up, ram it down so hard it'll never see the light of day again. My head punches me when I straighten up.

I need hot, greasy comfort food. I slip on my sandals, avidly avoid the judgmental gaze of the pub, head to *AJ's Snack Bar*, a groovy little Fish'n'chip shop on the main road. That gets me at least from A to J.

I sit under an umbrella with a bucket of chips and a can of lemonade, refurbishing my salt and sugar levels while the cars fly by. So many people rushing from A to Z. Maybe I can be in no hurry. Ziggy was a side road. I pledge to avoid them in the future.

I remember I don't have a car. Or a boyfriend. Maybe I need some help. A counsellor. Or a psychiatrist or psychologist. It's obvious from my current car-lessness that I've lost the means to find my own way.

I eat my last chip and sip my lemonade on the walk home. Mrs Snitch is cleaning her fake lawn with a mop and bucket, so I turn down the side-street that divides houses on the right. Another diversion. I laugh. It didn't take long before I've managed to go down a different path. I've only walked this street once when I moved in a few years ago. It's not posh at all, but the gardens are neat, old-fashioned, English-style, roses and silver birches and the occasional hibiscus and plumbago. Always a green well-cut lawn.

I pass one garden unlike the rest, its lawn replaced by boxed veggie gardens, fruit trees and a home-made scarecrow. I see four pairs of gum boots on an odd-looking rack at the front door: four adults' boots and four children's. I smile at the gardeners busting a rural journey through urban life. Rule breaking. I love it. Bring it on.

I reach home, boot up my laptop, throw the can in the recycling. I pull out my original A-Z from the bin: it might give me some clues to where I'm going. Or where I've been. Or something.

Ziggy's words, *Where've you been?* are indeed the question, but the answers aren't forthcoming. I seem to be getting further from the Truth. I realise I haven't brushed my teeth all day. Now that's a problem I can fix. I'm surprised at how much better I feel doing that one small thing. Perhaps it's the little things that mean the most.

My screen is ready to search. Counsellor? Psychologist? Psychiatrist? I choose the first. Nothing takes my fancy. I try psychologist: there's a directory. I decide to go straight to Z, because that's where I want to wind up. There's only one: *Ziggy Zbigniew.*

I go cold. I click on it and there's my Ziggy, well, yesterday's Ziggy, smiling at me, with the words *Finding your best life* beneath him.

Crap! I jump as my door rattles again. It's not Ziggy, surely. *Stop being quixotic.* There's no such thing as coincidence. I pull the door ajar.

"Good, you're awake. And feeling the worse for wear, I imagine."

That voice. I jag the curtain next to me aside and see the end of my car in the parking area. Confrontation time. I open the door wide. Ziggy's adoring face peers at me, a bunch of colourful flowers in hand.

"Agnes? Last night was not one of abstinence." He smiles like a kid staring at a present-laden Christmas tree.

 Well, that's bloody great news. Not. "Returning my car?"

"Do you remember what I told you last night?"

"That you like answering questions with a question?"

"Can I come in?"

*You probably already did.* But, my keys. "Come in." I step away from the door. He doesn't move. He's trying to read my expression.

"These are yours." He hands me the flowers.

I take them slowly.

"And these are also yours." He holds up my missing knickers.

I take them fast, jam them into my pocket.

Ziggy steps inside. "Your pretty shoes are still in the car."

For someone out of touch with their emotions I sure do have a lot of them: guilt, shame, desire, gratefulness, melancholy, anger, intrigue, confusion, happiness. Such an odd assortment.

I hand him back the flowers, shuffle through a cupboard for my one vase. I'm not a big one on cut flowers. They should still be growing in the ground, not decomposing in a vat of increasingly putrid water.

I fill the vase with water, place it on the table, face Ziggy for the flowers. It seems he's had his eyes on me the whole time. I put the flowers in the vase, turn back.

"Do you need a lift home?" My voice is pure exasperation.

His smile disintegrates. "My car's at the pub. You know that's walking distance. Why are we communicating only with questions?"

Little flashes of light play around my eyes. "I have no idea what happened last night."

He closes in, his warm eyes searching mine. "We had a marvellous time."

I back away, walk to the couch. "Yeah, well, great. Pity I don't remember any of it."

He sits down next to me.

I can't meet his eyes, so I close mine. "Do I need to apologise? Because I'm sorry if I embarrassed you. And do you need to apologise?"

"Are you kidding? You were a hit! My family's been sending me texts all morning."

I open one eye. "You need to explain."

"Wait, you think I took advantage of you?" A look of horror scrawls across his face. "Who do you think I am?"

"Ziggy, I don't even know who I am."

"I'm not a rapist," he says softly. "It's against the law for me to have sex with someone who's intoxicated. But if you're sober? Single?"

I feel his mouth at my neck. Jeez, is he hoping to make a partner for last night's triumph? I pull away. "Why are my legs sore?"

He rubs his hand along my arm. This does nothing to assuage the arousal that's rising against my will. "You danced the whole night. I've never been on a dance floor so much." He smiles. "You also danced with my father, several cousins, the groom and the best man," he says appreciatively. "Uncle Bert. Poppa. And the bride. You started a conga line that even Grandma Bates joined." He laughs cheerily as I cringe. "I'm not surprised you're sore. You could dance professionally."

I wince again, although dancing is obviously a much-preferred reason for sore legs than erotic acrobatics. Visions of my arms waving whilst my head twisted and my legs did a quick-step fill my brain.

"I'm sorry. Was it very bad?"

"Bad? You were the floorshow!" He laughs. "Incredible!"

"Why did you have my knickers?"

Again with the smile. "I got you into the car at the end of the night and went around to drive, then you showed me your knickers and threw them onto the back seat. Then you tried to sit on my lap and kiss me. I had to push you off. You kept trying to undo my fly all the way home." He laughs and shakes his head. "I have the self-control of a saint."

An email alert blinks my computer screen back to life, and he catches sight of his image. "You were looking me up!"

I don't know what to say. *Yes?* When I wasn't. *I need a therapist?* Which I do. I point to my neck. "Did you do this?"

He looks bashful, boyish. "Sorry. You dragged me out to your car while we were waiting for dessert. I copped flak from my mother and all my aunties for that."

None of this makes sense. "You're a psychologist called Sigmund?"

He shrugs. "My parents are both psychologists."

"And fans of Freud."

"Not necessarily. They're more Jung, Rogers."

I get it now. I was trying to work out The Meaning Of It All when I don't have any skills with which to implement such a search, and Ziggy has them in bucket-loads. Score big for the Zig. And instead of taking control of my life, it's helter-skeltered away from me quicker than you can say *Where's my knickers?* "Thanks for dropping back my car."

Even his scowl is attractive. "Nothing happened except a good time. What happened with your boyfriend? Do you remember what we agreed?"

Here I'm at a crossroad. I no longer have a boyfriend, which means I no longer have the cover of a boyfriend. And honestly? Ziggy's lovely, but he's full on, don't you think? My options are:

1. Tell him I'm single.

2. Tell him it's unprofessional for a psychologist to break up a relationship for his own gain.

3. Tell him my boyfriend is coming over any minute and he's a jealous behemoth.

4. Have Shut-Up Sex with him.

Shut-up Sex was what I had with Gene yesterday. Jeez, that needs analysis, but first I must confirm the goings-on of last night, because surely drunk girl, naked in bed, no-one else to act as witness …

I stand up to gain advantage, and use my best steely grimace. "The truth. At any time and in any place did we have sex?"

"You might've forgotten I wasn't drunk. But you're a cute drunk. A great dancer. You're my favourite party girl." He smiles adoringly. "I had a first-class time. I'm sorry you don't remember any of it."

I look away. "Why was I naked when I woke up?"

He stands up, and I have no choice but to look at him. I want to throw my arms around him, feel his tongue in my mouth.

"I helped you to bed and went to get you a glass of water. When I came back you were a magnificently naked and snoring starfish." He laughs as his eyes scan across me, remembering my unfettered body. "A very beautiful one. After admiring you, I hung up your pretty dress, folded your bra, rolled you onto your side, covered you with the quilt, stayed for an hour to make sure you were okay, locked up and left."

I blushed. "What did you do in that hour?"

He shrugs. "Watched TV, checked on you from time to time."

"And your car is still at the pub?" *Get your mind off those puppy dog eyes!*

"Yes. You were rather poor at giving directions, but you told me you walked to the pub yesterday, which helped." He smiles cheerily.

"Why didn't you go get your car instead of driving mine?"

"It gave me an excuse to return."

How the crap do I move this along to its climax? Ouch! That's not a word to be aiming for. My head is banging, and I must make sure the rest of me doesn't do the same.

Ziggy takes my face in his hands. He gets in real close and pushes his mouth onto mine. I shiver, open my mouth up to meet his, feel him move even closer, hard against me if you know what I mean, and I stand completely still except my arms seem to have wound their way around his back, our mouths searching for our mutual pleasure, my heart rate climbing and my knickers asking to be excused.

I want him bad. Very, very bad. As bad as he can give it to me. From the feel of things his loins are trying to talk him into picking me up, taking me into the bedroom, laying me on my bed.

Which is exactly what he does.

# 9

My impulse control sounds shot, doesn't it? But that's not me, any more than the results of the personality test. I'm just lost.

Ziggy lays me on the bed, kicks off his shoes, climbs on top of me and our mouths work their way around each other while our hipbones attempt to merge. Those funny little waves of desire that spasm in a woman's tummy when she's grooving on something blessedly naughty roll through me. I'm mighty glad I brushed my teeth. But Ziggy's not taking advantage of the situation by removing any interfering garments. Instead he kisses me, stops to look at me, then kisses me again.

He sits up, frowning. "You're a tease." He gets up and adjusts his clothing. "I'm going to get my car. Then I'm going home. I want to know the minute you're single."

I say nothing. He pulls my keys from his back pocket and tosses them onto the bed. There's plenty of emotions in those dark eyes: frustration, resentment, regret, disappointment, disillusionment. See, I'm not out of touch emotionally. But now I feel worse than a tramp. Now I feel like a heel. I follow him out mutely, kiss him again on my doorstep. He looks at me with sorrow, then walks past Laurie and Rupert, who are untangling the hose. They smile and *Hello* him.

Laurie gives me the thumbs up. "Coming out with us, Candice?" There's almost a giggle in his voice.

"Sure. Give me a few minutes."

He grins. "Take whatever time you need, sweet girl."

Ziggy vanishes from the driveway without a backward look.

I walk inside and sit on my sofa. It seems to be my favourite place for considering my Vision Quest and seeing exactly how far I've travelled away from it. There's something under my heel. It's my A-Zs. Great, that's the respect I'm paying my journey. But the second A-Z reassures me. The lack of a One Night Stand does, too.

To sum up, here I am, it's, let's see, twenty-six hours after I decided to reset my path and I've lost a boyfriend, gained a massive love-bite, found a psychologist who makes home visits, gotten unfeasibly drunk and been naked in front of a stranger. None of those were on my list.

But the Earth is a great healer. By the time I've drunk a full glass of water, put on my sneakers and found my gardening gloves, Rupert and Laurie have already ferreted out most of the weeds.

They look at my neck and smile.

"Gene's out of luck," smiles Rupert.

"Out of luck, be buggered," I say. "He's got someone else."

"Knew you were too good for him," says Laurie. "I like the look of this new man. Sophisticated. Self-assured. Knows where he's headed."

"Wish I could say the same for me," I frown.

"I'm not having much luck with these lettuces, Candice." Laurie sadly fondles a leaf.

I knobble my knees over. My legs groan in reply. "They need gentle fertilizing. And more water. They'll do alright. We need compost."

"Can we make our own?" asks Rupert eagerly.

"It'll take too long." Rupert's always one for DIY. When we began, I'd arrive home from work to find him digging out sections of grass, edging the area, mulching and fertilizing, planting our lemon tree in a giant pot. He seems to have blossomed, if you'll pardon the pun.

"Have we still got money in the kitty?" he asks. "I can put in more."

I laugh. "No, no! We've got plenty." The men insisted on giving me a hundred dollars each for our garden fund and then keep spending their own money whenever they buy something.

"Maybe we can go this afternoon?" asks Laurie.

"Sure." My headache is now an annoying whisper, my Vision Quest a distant memory. The Earth is a great healer.

"The new man's good-looking," Rupert nods to Laurie. "I heard a bit of noise last night. When I looked out my blinds very early this morning I saw a man leave. I couldn't tell if it was Gene."

"Oh no," replies Laurie. "It was this new guy. Leaving very late. I saw him, too. Must be pretty passionate, given her neck."

I didn't know my neighbours were such covert spies.

"She must be serious about this new one," says Rupert.

"I wouldn't be leaving at all," points out Laurie. "Be moving in straight away. She's a pretty girl. And lovely to boot."

"Maybe he just went home to get his things," smiles Rupert.

"She's too good for Gene." Laurie sits back. "She needs a real man. With plenty of sex appeal. Like this one."

I smile. "Uh, guys, I'm actually here, in case you've forgotten."

"What's this one's name?" Laurie asks me.

"Sigmund," I smile.

"Now that's a man's name." Laurie plucks out a tiny weed. "Masculine. Virile. Bet he's a crowd-pleaser in the sack."

"Time for shopping." I sit up, urge my legs to take my weight.

I load them into my car and think of Ziggy again. What did he say his name meant again? Something about protecting.

On the way to the store Laurie says from the back, "I've fallen on a bit of luck in the bed stakes myself."

"For the tomatoes?" I ask. "Do we need more stakes?"

"That's not what I meant," Laurie laughs. "The girl I lost my virginity to was at church. Last week."

"You lost your virginity last week at church?" I laugh.

"When I was fifteen."

My rear-vision mirror reveals Laurie reliving the pleasure of that time. I didn't even know Laurie went to church. "Was she the answer to your prayers?"

"What was she doing at your church?" asks Rupert beside me.

"Just moved into the neighbourhood," says Laurie. "And yes, I did actually pray for a woman. I'm sick of being alone. Don't know how you do it, Rupert. Anyway, I prayed and there was my Denise, as gorgeous as ever. I'm meeting her for tea tonight."

"Renewing old acquaintances?" I ask.

"Hoping to get her into bed." Laurie's tone is so casual I almost miss the turn-off. "She was mighty stuff when I was a teenager. Two years older than me and been around. A lot. Knew exactly what to do. Hoping she hasn't forgotten."

"What kind of a church *is* this, anyway?" I smile.

"One where you can pick up terrific chicks," replies Laurie. "You should come along, Rupert."

Rupert tells me, "I've never had sex with a woman."

"Don't know what you're missing," quips Laurie.

"Wait, you're a virgin?" I ask Rupert, glancing across.

"Never had sex with a woman," he repeats.

 A light goes on in my brain. "You're gay, Rupert?"

"No!"

"His hand's his best friend," explains Laurie. "Did you like those educational websites I showed you?" he asks Rupert.

I don't have to have a great imagination to know what he means.

"They're a place to start," Laurie continues, "but we've gotta get you some real action! You have to be alert for opportunities."

And that's a Vision Quest he can do all on his own.

"Just never had the opportunity," Rupert explains quietly.

"Had girlfriends?" I ask as I coast to the traffic lights.

"A few. Always wanted to wait for sex, never got to that point. I didn't like to push it."

I look at him. There's nothing wrong with Rupert. He's pleasant to look at, pleasant to be with, pleasant to talk with. God, pleasant? The lights change, I move forward.

Laurie says firmly, "You don't wait for sex, you set it up. Take them dancing. Wine and dine them. Buy them flowers. Tell them how beautiful they are."

Everything, of course, that Ziggy has done.

At the store, Laurie checks out seedlings whilst Rupert and I investigate the Garden Supplies section. He's loading the first of our compost sacks onto a trolley when Laurie calls me over.

"I've found a woman for Rupert."

"Laurie-"

He points. "There. Go break the ice. I'll send Rupert over."

A woman with dark hair and a friendly face innocently surveys the potting mixes. Laurie's five marriages now make sense.

"How old is Rupert?"

"Thirty-eight last week."

I reel. I thought he was at least fifty.

"Go on," Laurie insists. "Start up a conversation."

"You always seemed such a quiet man."

"Denise has shown me miracles can happen." He's wearing a look that can only mean trouble for his virginity-stealer.

The woman strolls towards the compost section, skimming the label of each pack, making her way down the aisle.

Rupert backs into her as he manoeuvres the trolley. "Sorry!"

I get closer, fascinated at the tableau revealing itself.

"You look like you know what you're doing," the woman declares. "What do you know about potting soil?"

Rupert's completely out of his depth. I hurry to help.

"You need something with plenty of organic matter." He points confidently. "That's the one we use."

Well, he's learnt something during our gardening sessions.

"Your wife likes to garden?" I hear a questioning tone in those words. Actually, more like a Quest-ioning tone.

Rupert spies me. "Here's my flatmate."

"Hello." The woman's glint evaporates. "You're his girlfriend?"

I smile beguilingly. "No. Rupert lives in the flat next door."

Laurie appears. "I live in the other flat. We're all single friends. Rupert's always teaching us about gardening. Isn't he, Candice?"

Rupert's look is pleading.

"May I, Rupert?" The chase is unconscionably thrilling. "Rupert always says to buy this one." I point to the same brand as Rupert and smile at the woman.

She looks from the sack to Rupert with admiration.

"Rupert," says Laurie, and Rupert abruptly remembers we're here, "I can take our trolley now you've loaded it. Why don't you spread your helpfulness around? I'm sure you'll be glad of it, won't you …?"

"Daisy." The woman beams at Rupert.

"We'll get you a trolley." Laurie winks surreptitiously to me before pulling Rupert away.

"Daisy's a lovely name for a gardener," I smile. "Rupert's a great guy. He can help you with your garden. Really knows what to do."

"Oh, I'm not-" she begins.

"Single? That's a shame."

"I am single. Just not looking for a man. Too much hard work."

"Pity. Because I've never seen him look at a woman like he's looking at you." I've never seen him look at any woman, but this isn't the moment to let the facts get in the way of opportunity.

Daisy smiles coyly at Rupert as he returns with Laurie and a trolley. "How many bags do you think I'll need for two big citrus pots?"

Rupert looks at me. I hold up three fingers on each hand, then push them through my hair. "Probably six at least," he tells Daisy. "I'll load them for you."

"How will you get them out at home?" asks Laurie.

"They are heavy," Daisy agrees.

"Candice drove, so take Rupert with you," says Laurie.

"If I'm not keeping you from anything?" Daisy smiles.

Rupert loads six sacks faster than I've ever seen him move before.

Laurie grabs my arm. "Let's go, Candice. See you, Rupert. Nice meeting you, Daisy, good luck with your gardening." He creeps closer to Daisy. "He's good with his hands. He can plant your pots as well."

We get out of there fast.

"You're a Woman Whisperer," I tell Laurie.

"Yep," he beams. "I gave Rupert a few tips while we were getting the trolley. He'll do alright."

"What do you think will happen?"

"Ah, Candice," Laurie grins, "I still believe it's a perfect world. Love is transformative. You have to watch for opportunities. After that, you're home free."

# 10

Rupert's missing for hours. Laurie and I scatter the compost while he tells me about his marriages. He's lived every moment of his life, with even his recent loneliness packaged as a space for learning.

He leaves to prepare for his date. I watch him haul himself through his door, worried the afternoon's kneeling and crouching might have ruined his capability to achieve his every desire tonight with the woman so memorable in her younger days.

The crouching and kneeling seems to have helped my legs recover. I chuckle as I wash up: what are the chances of a Sixty-niner getting lucky with Ms Seventy-plus?

Sixty-niner? Best I get my mind elsewhere. Out comes my laptop and I eagerly type up the wise words of my neighbour.

> 1. Love is transformative.

> 2. You can't know at the start how Love's going to end up and even if it doesn't work out you've had a wonderful time dipping into another person's life.

> 3. Always stay open to experience. Surprises can be found everywhere.

> 4. Never give up on connection. It's all that matters.

> 5. Treat your lover as you want them to treat you.

> 6. Be patient. Everyone is just trying to get their needs met.

I pause, wondering what the personality test would decide about Laurie. He's an extrovert, there's no doubt about that. I wonder if there's a test to determine a man's suitability as a husband. Maybe I should invent one.

Obviously, Wives 1 and 2 were able to marry Laurie without hesitation, but what about Wives 3, 4 and 5? How do you marry a man who's repeatedly been shown to be a failure at marriage?

I conjure up a test for Men Marrying Multiple Matches:

1. What was the birthday of your first wife?

2. What was the real hair colour of each of your wives?

3. Name the gift you gave on your first wedding anniversary for each wife.

4. Add up the total number of years married and divide by number of wives. Now add the age of your first ever kiss, divide it by the number of women you've had sex with, subtract the number of different addresses you've had and if the number's larger than zero, then you're …

You're what? What makes a good mate? Loyalty, negotiation skills, fidelity, and kindness are givens. Beyond that, how do you know?

How does my father, for example, know he'll stay with my mother? His first marriage lasted twelve years based on Doing The Right Thing, only to see it go awry on the very first day he met Mum. This relationship's now twenty-nine years old and I almost caught them at it when I dropped in unannounced a few weeks ago. Yes, *it*. Obviously there's still passion in the relationship. I wonder if they play *Let's pretend we're talking about our Harrys* like the day they met. That was a Quest but if it had any Vision I wouldn't be here talking about it.

There's a knock at the door. It's Laurie, checking he looks smart enough for Denise Who'd Been Around A Lot. Does that matter anymore when you're seventy?

"I won't expect you home for supper." He hasn't got a chance in hell with the post-menopausal Denise but I'll let her be the one to break his heart.

I'm in my pjs finishing up my lonesome dinner of fried veggie garden tomatoes on toast when I hear a strange noise. Is that Rupert's flat?

I bunch my ear up against his wall and hear a woman laughing. This startles me, as the flats on either side are usually as quiet as the moon. The laughter comes again, then moaning. Two different tones. It's him and it's her. I feel hot at the sound of it. Its solid resonance returns Ziggy to my mind.

Actually, I'm lying. Ziggy has hardly left my brain for more than a few minutes since his visit. What Rupert's seeming good luck does is heighten my need for Ziggy. The rigour of his relentlessness has reverberated regularly and I'm now ready to ring and request he reap what he reneged on. Except I don't have his number. I have no idea where he lives. I don't even know if he lives nearby. All I have is his workplace number, thanks to his website.

My laptop's run out of charge from being left on all day. I find my charger and reboot it.

Ziggy's work number has initial digits I don't recognize, so he probably doesn't live close. Or perhaps he works further away than he lives? But why did he choose my local pub?

How stupid. Investigative journalism at its best.

Did I tell you I was a journalist? You'd think I'd be more organised, more able to find the hard-hitting facts of my Quest, wouldn't you, with these qualifications? Unfortunately, my skills haven't generalized to every area of my life. I put *virile* into the on-line dictionary. *A male whose capacity for sex is strong.*

A satisfied and expressive squeal pierces the quiet. Bingo. Rupert's been taught well by Laurie's educational websites, because that was very obviously Daisy. Then there's thumping against the wall, on and on, with a man's voice muttering indistinguishable words. I've never been in the flat next door, but I'm guessing that's Rupert's bedroom on the other side of the wall and that's his bedhead having more physical activity than it's ever had. Dear sweet bashful Rupert going at it like a porno movie. Which, no doubt, Laurie has a library of.

I grab my laptop and charger, take refuge in the bedroom. I immediately hear Laurie next door. How sad! His date obviously hasn't worked out.

The same banging as that coming from Rupert's place starts to reverberate through Laurie's wall, accompanied by a man's and a woman's shouting. Really? *Really?* I walk back out to my lounge to hear moaning coming from Rupert's.

Crap. I'm saturated in surround-sound sex.

It occurs to me that to get back to my Quest, I don't need Men. I need the wisdom of Women. One sage in particular. I run to my car, text my best friend Kat. *You home?* There's no reply, but I'm not going back to witness Rupert's coming of age (actually, I think I spelt *coming* wrong for this particular situation) or Laurie's re-acquaintance with his virginity-stealer, so on I go to Kat's place, five minutes from mine. I text her again when I pull up outside her run-down arty share-house. This time I get *Be there in few minutes wanna meet me there?*

*Here already see you soon.* As I wait, I muse my A-Zs, the Z register, my learnings from Laurie. Nothing helps. I've spent thirty plus hours on my Quest, and the only way forward is surely with Kat.

Kat and I go back to the very first day, the very first hour, the very first minutes of high school. I caught her smoking a cigarette and downing a beer behind the shelter shed just before the start-of-year assembly. I'd gone there to hide out, frightened by the giants who held hands and snogged as the crowd swarmed past me when the bell went and my excited parents left. Was I going to be in a class with these adults? Feeling like a pre-schooler, I'd decided to hole up behind the shelter shed until everyone had gone, then I was going to flee.

There I found a waif-like creature sitting with her legs crossed and her bag at her side. She offered me a swig of her beer and a puff on her cigarette. Declining both, I decided to hang around nonetheless. She was surely breaking enough rules to give me cover.

"First day?" she asked.

I nodded mutely.

"Me, too. I know what class I'm in." She took a long drag on her cigarette. "Hacked into the school computer." She laughed at my wide eyes. "At the library. Fake details. What's your name?"

"Candice Kelly," I whispered.

She took her mobile out of her pocket and started thumbing the screen, the cigarette perched against her bottom lip. "We're in luck." She stubbed the cigarette out then pressed it under the shed wall. "Same as me. Mr Bob or something."

I took the mobile from her as she drained her beer. "Bob Ball. Room twenty-eight." I peeked around the shed: a flow of students was erupting from the hall. "Assembly's over."

When she got up she was tiny. Her uniform was remarkably short, hardly covering her rose-blown knickers. "I'm going to tell 'em it's a hand me down and Mum didn't get a chance to take the hem down. Too busy with my twelve siblings now Dad's left." She slung her backpack across her shoulders.

The thought someone in her family could be smaller than her left me wide-eyed. "Is that true?"

She put her arm up around my shoulders. "Course not. Hemmed it myself. But it might hold 'em for a day or two. Wanna chewie?" She grinned. "Covers a million sins. If you know what I mean."

Which I didn't.

The cigarettes and computer hacking had long gone but the drinking never had. The friendship has been as solid as concrete. We don't live in each other's pockets, but there's an indelible link between us.

Kat will zoom in on the truth of my current predicament. And that's absolutely the Z I need for now.

# 11

Kat waves breezily from the passenger seat of an unfamiliar junk heap. The hulking driver curls his vehicle carefully onto the front lawn, which looks like a used car yard. Her housemates are many and always randomly present or absent: Johnno, Trinity, Chrisso, Raffo, Mai-Lee, Mindy, Buff, Gigi, Leo, Ollie. At any one time some of them are in and some of them are out. Some of them sleep together and some sleep on the couches; and some of them are in arty isolation.

Kat hates her parents, moved out the weekend after we finished high school. She has the smallest room in this house, a minuscule room that used to be a walk-in closet, with only a skylight for sunshine. But she's happy here. It gives her seclusion and an extraordinarily cheap rent.

"Hey, Candice, what gives?" She's obviously high or drunk. "This is Thor." She thumbs at the man getting out of the driver's seat. "I'm a bit Thor my-thelf," she laughs.

Thor is massive. Posturing their way out of his black tank top are rock-cut muscles. He attempts to smile but his jaw is so chiselled it erupts as a grimace. His hair is black and wavy and his eyes are what I'd usually call aquamarine, although I don't know that's a colour you'd associate with eyes.

"Hello." I can't say the name Thor without feeling stupid. I turn to Kat, "I badly need a chick chat."

Kat spies the hickey and tells Thor, "Go home, baby, come back later. Maybe ten." She blows him a kiss.

Thor gets back in the car.

"Wow. Even I'm impressed," I say. "He fall out of the sky?"

She giggles. "I accidentally had sex with him, and he's been hanging around ever since."

"You what?"

She pushes open the front door. "He's a friend of Ollie's." She says this as if it's common knowledge. "He needed somewhere to bunk. Ollie sent him to Room 4, which is Mindy and Buff's room with the spare bed, but he came into my room instead. Where I was asleep." She giggles. "Naked. Spread out."

I'm reminded of my own starfish. "I get it."

"Guys." She says this to the fifty-odd men in the lounge room all seemingly with a beer in their hand. "Move." We can hardly get through to her room. "No, really," she smiles with indifference, "suddenly I wake with this massive guy on top of me. Completely gorgeous. I mean, what's a girl to do? So I went for it."

"Your life reads like a porno," I smile as we reach her room. I'm always amazed how small it is. Double bed, clothes rack, four-drawer filing cabinet and a thin, tall bookcase. And a mini bar fridge. Of course.

"Looks like you've had a little porno of your own, sweetie. Or a date with a vampire." She throws herself on her bed, kicks off her shoes. "Talking of teeth, I've had a bite from a manufacturer."

"Really?" Kat's been designing stuff since I met her. She sketches beautiful cutlery, elegant crockery and exquisite glassware. Unfortunately, no-one's ever been interested in her creations.

"Just a nibble. A buyer's interested in my salad servers. And taken my cake server and a few plates to his boss. Might be nothing. I'm sick of being poor, though."

I sit on the bed next to her, feeling surprised. She's always lived off her wits, a small stipend from the government and whatever male she's had hanging around. Jobs have been very few and very, very short. "Didn't think you even knew what money was."

"Thor works as a male model occasionally," she sighs wistfully. "Putting himself through uni."

"Is there any room for a brain above that jawline?"

"Oh, yes," she giggles again.

"Are you drunk?"

"Just on loving." She throws her arms out and grins.

Definitely drunk. "I'm in trouble, Kat."

"Men. Can't live without 'em. Can't live without 'em." She snorts.

"Oh, stop it. This is serious."

"Serious? You being serious? About men?" Her eyes are wide. "This is a problem! Obviously not Gene. What's this one's name?"

"Nobody."

"Oooooh!" she sings, "Candice has a new vampire! What happened to Gene?"

"Aren't you at all bothered by our ever-increasing age? Don't you want to know where you're headed?"

"Life unfolds one step at a time, like a lily-pad, to reveal an exquisite flower at the heart of it." She jumps up, opens the bar fridge, fishes out two small bottles, hands one to me. "Thor got a six pack of these from a friend for an unpaid job. A six-pack for his six-pack."

It's a sparkling red. "No thanks. *Never drinking again* is my mantra."

Kat rips the lid off hers and swigs.

Male clothing sits neatly folded in two of her shelves. "Don't tell me Thor stays in this room? How does he fit?'

She giggles. "We don't need much room when we're together." She takes another swig.

There's something weird about all this. "This isn't love, is it? Like real Love with a capital L?" They're a preposterous couple, she small and cute with her blonde hair up in two bunches and green eyes glinting, he huge and masculine, *virile.*

She nods vigorously. "I like the way he pumps his iron."

I hope it's not quixotic. Then again, I can't see Kat falling for someone regular. She's had weird boyfriends, one sang every word, one wanted to marry her on their first date. And I'm not talking just *proposed*, he actually wanted to find someone to marry them that night.

"Think down the track, Kat. How are you going to give birth to his children? They'll be gigantic."

"I manage gigantic pretty well." She giggles again.

I get close to her face, peer into her eyes. No sign of drugs. "Tell me you've been drinking or taking something."

"Honestly, it's different with Thor."

I laugh. "Is that his real name?"

"It's Thorin. He's studying exercise physiology. And I love him."

Between you and me, I'd probably go for it, too; Thor's a bit of a hunk. "That's one too many drinks talking, Kat."

Kat has already downed her bottle and is rifling out a cask of red from behind her clothes. "Don't discount alcohol as a love potion. Sometimes throwing caution to the wind is the only way to live."

And the only way I've ever seen Kat live.

She pulls a plastic cup from a stack, fills it with red, hands it towards me. "Frig, Can, have a drink, buddy, we've got a problem to solve."

I love Kat's nickname for me, and her motto every time I aced my grades. *Who can? Can can!* and she'd lift her dress high and kick her toes out, thereby attracting the eyes of any man in eyeshot. I shake my head. "I'm still hung-over," I say miserably. "Wait, you've got a problem?"

"Our problem is you, Can." She sips. "Have you chucked Gene or having both?"

I pace the three steps beside her bed and back again. "Yesterday I set out to get my life on track. Since then, it's read like a bad romance novel. Gene, it seems, is intent on finding The One. And I'm not it."

"Shit, Can, nobody thinks he's The One." She looks at me curiously. "So who is?"

"You make it sound like I know!" I plonk back down onto the bed. "Besides, my Quest is not about Love. It's about Life."

Kat smiles. "You idiot. Every woman wants love. That's why romance novels are a multibillion-dollar enterprise."

I pout. "Don't you think there comes a stage of life when you're over the whole romance thing?"

Kat erupts into laughter, then stares at my face. "Oh, sorry, I thought you were joking."

"Unfortunately not. I'm thinking of shelving the whole bullshit."

Kat puts her hand on my arm. "You're like a little lost lamb, sweetie. What's causing this, gal pal?"

"It's fucking love," I say angrily.

"Fucking? Or love?" She cackles.

I venture forward. "I had an opportunity to bang two guys in twenty-four hours, but I didn't." No thanks to me, as you and I know. "And Gene did."

Kat laughs. "He humped two men in twenty-four hours?"

"I mean sex with me and then sex with her," I pout. "The new one. And probably proud of it."

"He was sticking it in another chick? Man, that's down low if you don't get asked along to the party."

I laugh loudly, then frown. "How do men get away with it?"

Kat looks thoughtful. "Feminism's never going to make things equal, because we aren't equal. Men don't have the responsibility that comes with having a womb. If they get someone pregnant, it's just an emotional attachment to the baby. Or not. For women, it's physical as well. It's their body. And there's no control over the process. You have to go with it." She takes a sip, a gentle sip, so unlike Kat.

"What are you saying?"

A grin bursts across her face. "I'd like a baby!"

"What?"

"I want to have a baby with Thor. It feels right."

I blink. "Where would you put it?" I look around the little space. "What does he think? Are you pregnant already?" I remove the wine from her hand.

She grabs it back. "No, I'm not pregnant already. I'm just saying there are things I feel for Thor that surprise me. It happened straight away, that very first time I woke up and saw his face. He was so sorry about climbing on top of me, but he didn't get off. The look on his face was like he'd won a prize. He'd already stripped off for sleep. I kissed him, and …" She shudders. "Anyway, he's sweet and kind and thinks I'm adorable."

"That's because you are adorable. But he's sweet and kind? Not hunky and virile? Or opportunistic?"

She's not listening. "Gene was digging his shovel into someone else's turf? I'm glad in a way. Leaves your hole ready and waiting for the new guy." Her laughter crackles through the air.

"No new guy." *Tell the Truth, Candice.* "Actually, a guy tried to pick me up in a bar yesterday."

"And?"

"I woke up naked today."

Kat grins. "That's my girl."

"Nothing happened, he tells me."

"Listen, Can," she points her finger at me, "you've got a piss-ant life. Working for the man, living in that spinster flat, deadbeats for boyfriends. Of course you're wondering about life!"

No point arguing with any of that. "Do you think I'm an introvert?"

She snickers. "What? Absolutely not! Gene tell you that?"

"It showed up in a personality test."

"Fricking bulldust. No introvert gets a hickey that fricking big."

I'm shocked with her language and tell her so. "Since when did you start using *fricking?*"

She smiles. "Just getting myself into motherhood mode."

We hear a loud noise outside the door. Shouting. A thud.

"Frickin' men," Kat shakes her head. "Probably doin' dares again."

There's a knock at the door.

"It's me, baby, you decent?"

Kat is up and opening the door and throwing herself at the man there. The man with the abs. The man with the jawline.

"Hey, baby, I missed you. I need you. I couldn't stay away." There's a lustre to his voice that makes me shiver.

"Hey, baby," breathes Kat.

Thor picks her up and carries her to the bed, kissing her until he lays her down and they realise I'm on the other side.

"Oops! Sorry, Can," Kat smiles.

I rise. "It's okay. Nice to meet you. Again." I swallow. "Thor."

"Candice!" Kat shouts after me. "Remember, life never travels in a straight line." Kat buries herself in Thor's face and I exit, getting felt up constantly whilst squeezing my way out of the house.

It's dark. I didn't expect it. Then, there's been a *frickin'* lot of the unexpected today. I'm as horny as a stud bull thinking of Thor and Kat. Together. In that room. Not needing much space. I must find Ziggy.

No! Get back on track! I concentrate on my Vision Quest as I drive home. Then I go straight to bed and fall asleep, dreaming exotic erotic dreams of men I don't know.

"Please yourself," I say aloud as I wake sharply.

So I do. It helps me get back to sleep.

# 12

I spend Monday in our sun-filled warehouse office, writing a piece about the premise that computers have already taken over the world. That all of us, even the few who don't own one, are slaves to the computer: in the supermarket, at the train station, in our libraries. I think about myself, rattling away at my keyboard, knowing it's spot on.

We're all in today. Often somebody's out: interviewing, following a lead, checking out an interesting place or event. It seems the more of us here, the harder we work. Martin's preparing for an interview, Terri's madly finishing a piece she started on the weekend, Jamie our boss has his *Do Not Disturb: Already disturbed* sign on top of his computer (loves a good sign, has many), and for some reason, Clarissa keeps giggling quietly next to me.

"What's up?" I ask. "Whatever you're writing must be hilarious."

"Incredible weekend. Just don't ask me about it." She glances at Jamie to make sure he doesn't bound over, asking to be in on the gossip.

Clarissa's gorgeous. Shiny blonde hair that hangs perfectly at her chin, wide blue eyes and large full breasts. She's carrying a stack of weight, thanks to her penchant for chocolate and red wine. It doesn't worry her. Her startling looks, ebullient personality and encyclopaedic intellect pack quite a punch. I hope whatever happened on her weekend was less confusing than mine.

At four I'm first to leave, drained of my creative juices and desperate to get away from the pull of the computer I've been writing about.

Ten minutes later I'm home with no memory of the journey.

I hurry down the path. Ignore the bristling veggie patch. Fling myself in the door. Throw down my handbag. Boot up my laptop. Grab a drink of water. Find Ziggy's website. Ring his work number.

The receptionist's voice is brusque. I explain I want to contact Ziggy.

"Was it regarding an appointment?"

"I, uh-" I begin. "I went to a-" I pause again. "He and I … never mind. Could you please give me his mobile number?"

"I don't give his number to women who have a personal interest in the psychologist."

"I'm sure if you tell him it's-"

"Goodbye."

I sit for a moment, then ring again. "Hello, I'd like to make an appointment with the psychiatrist."

"It's you again. And he's a psychologist, not a psychiatrist."

She hangs up again. Time to call in the big guns. I go next door.

"Ah, sweet girl," says Laurie. "Isn't the world perfect? Didn't I tell you it was so?" His eyes are dreamy. "How's your new lover?"

"MIA."

He beckons me in. "What happened?" He listens attentively, then laughs. "I adore subterfuge in love. Makes the outcome all the sweeter."

I hand him the number. "Have you seen Rupert today?"

"Heard them leave for work this morning." He pokes the number into his phone. "That's mission accomplished." He whispers, as if the receptionist can hear, "It's ringing!"

I move in close.

"Zbigniew Consulting. How can I help you?"

"That's a very friendly voice on the line! Delightful! And just what I need, thank you so very much, my dear. Who am I speaking with?"

"Esther."

"Are you as beautiful as your name, Esther?"

She titters. "Obviously."

Laurie sows his seeds of persuasion. "Nice to know there are such friendly people in the world, when life can be so very, very disheartening. And for that reason I'd like to make an appointment with the," he checks my note, "psychologist, please." He nods at me.

"Yes, sir," the receptionist purrs. "Have you been here before?"

"No."

She tells him to arrive ten minutes early and then gives him an appointment in a month's time.

"Oh no," he purrs, "I'm afraid I need one before then, my precious girl. You understand."

I hear her stumble. "I'm sorry, that's when the first one is available."

"I'm sure there's a spot put aside for emergencies. You sound very competent, dear Esther. What can you do for me?"

"I can do forty-five minutes for you tomorrow, at nine-fifteen," she says pertly, like she's making a date. "I'll see you when you come out, because I only start at ten. What's your name, sir?"

He finishes up with, "You're a treasure. Thank you, Esther."

"It's a date," I say. "She can do you for forty-five minutes."

He laughs. "The scene is set for you, Candice." His phone rings again. "Hello!" He puts his hand over the mouthpiece. "Denise!"

I walk back to my Spinster Flat, the only one who thinks there's something other than romance to spend their life's pennies on. I kick off my shoes and flop on the couch. A nine-fifteen appointment on a Tuesday. My head fills immediately with visions of Ziggy and me in his office doing things I've seen on *educational websites* that boyfriends have shown me, hoping to get the same kind of action. My mind wanders across Laurie and Denise, Rupert and Daisy, Kat and Thor. I wonder if arousal is contagious. I wonder if I care.

I take a long look at my neck in the mirror. Thank goodness for the current fashion of wearing scarves. I wish I could remember Ziggy doing it. He's foggy in my mind and I can't recall him at all.

I step into the shower and close my eyes under the bliss of the spray. Ziggy's eyes, his voice, beckon me. I open my eyes and scrub.

*Concentrate, Candice.* I'm going to be late in to work tomorrow to make a nine-fifteen appointment. That means making up the time tonight.

I'm rigorous with my writing schedule and, besides, deadlines don't ever stop for appointments. I'm probably well ahead in my schedule, but I can't be faffed checking. I finish my shower quickly and dress, then look at my next topic. It's an interview at nine in the morning.

Crap. I ring Martin. He's busy with his own interview. I ring Clarissa. She's not well, going to the doctors at nine. I ring Terri. She's happy to take it over, especially seeing as the guy's a hunky actor. In response she gives me her project. *The New Toxic Sludge: Relationships.*

Great. I spend two hours researching dating, divorce and disease. It leaves me with anything but a thirst for romance. But it's Purpose not Romance I'm seeking, so I type up a short summary of my findings:

1. Relationships suck.

2. Dating sucks.

3. Divorce sucks.

4. Disease sucks the most of all.

Without warning the air comes alive with reverberating bed against wall and shouts of unshackled desire on both sides. That years of silence have been replaced by ferocious lust drives me to only one conclusion: I must consider the place of Romance (and its cousin, Sex) in my Quest. Which means Ziggy Zbigniew, the psychologist I'm visiting tomorrow. Who marked my neck with his passion. Who fell in love with me At First Sight. Who's seen me naked.

Could make for an interesting session. Don't know many other psychologist's sessions would start out on such a footing. Can't wait to see his face. And anything else he cares to show me.

# 13

Head banging. Heart banging. Trying to not think about banging whilst sitting in the waiting room of one Ziggy Zbigniew of *Zbigniew Consulting*.

I arrived at eight-fifty-five. The place was silent. I don't know what Ziggy's car looks like, so I don't know if his was one of the three in the car park. Receptionist not in till ten, I remember. All doors closed except the entry. Small sign at the desk says *Please take a seat*.

I must be the first appointment. My best investigative skills presume he opened up, went for a coffee. Or he's avoiding me.

No, wait, the appointment's booked under Laurie's name, Ziggy doesn't know it's me. Good thing it's a calm place, the carpet thick, the paintings displaying country idylls, the chairs in the waiting room deep and cosy, the beige décor trustworthy.

A door opens to my left. A tall burly man appears. "There you are!"

Crap! I'm booked in with a different psychologist!

The man rushes around towards me. As he moves out of the way Ziggy comes into view. His welcoming smile fades quickly.

"My name is Joe." The man sits and shakes my limp hand.

Ziggy frowns from the reception desk.

The man draws my attention. "We've been talking about you!"

I look at Ziggy in horror.

Joe continues. "He's marvellous, isn't he? Do you do your homework? Mine's to think realistically about my dream girl. And here you are! As real as can be! I'll give you my number." He stands up, gives Ziggy his credit card, grabs a pen from the desk, sits back down.

My eyes race from Joe to Ziggy to Joe to Ziggy. Ziggy's ignoring me as he manages Joe's account.

Joe writes *Joe* and a number on the inside of my hand. "Call me. I've got all the things girls like: good job, handsome, friendly."

Everything except personal space.

He continues on. "What's your name?"

"Candice," I confess without thinking. Ziggy looks at me sharply.

"Candy, sweet like candy," Joe grins.

I gulp.

Joe stands up and takes his card and receipt from Ziggy. "Thanks, mate. Feeling much better. Thanks for fitting me in. See you next week." He turns to me. "Hope to see you before then." He smiles and shakes his head as if remembering a great joke. "Candy."

His departure leaves an uncomfortable silence. I hope Ziggy can't hear my pounding heart as he ushers me silently into his room. He sits and waves his hand at the chair opposite.

"How can I help?" he says formally, like he hasn't recognized me.

"The desk bitch-"

"Please don't swear in session." His tone is polite, his expression not. "What's brought you here?"

Always the questions. "What time do you start? Joe was here early."

"I don't talk about other clients. But why you told him your name so quickly is a mystery."

"Ziggy-"

"Exactly what is your name? Candice? Laurie?" He leans forward. "Or Agnes?"

"Candice. Candice Kelly." I flinch. "Laurie's my neighbour. He made the appointment because the desk b-," I stumble, "-your receptionist refused to give me an appointment."

"He coerced Esther into giving you an emergency spot. I had to come in at eight to see Joe for an emergency emergency spot."

Surely most psychologist sessions haven't started like this.

"How can I help, Candice?"

His use of my name blasts me. "I have feelings for my psychologist."

His shoulders relax, the rest remains formal. "Usually this is transference, the therapist becoming a person the client can rely on. But it's too early to be the reason here."

Neither of us says anything for several moments.

He leans towards me. "You're paying for this session. You may as well make the most of it."

I blush. "I was on a Vision Quest when I met this," I swallow hard, "guy in a pub."

"Maybe he is your Vision Quest." The smile at his lips fades quickly. "He's not."

Ziggy looks deflated. "What is it you're looking for?"

I blink. "Meaning. Purpose. Explanation. Reason."

He leans towards me again. "What is it you're looking for?"

"Myself." I dip my head. Ziggy's disappeared, and I'm inside the cavernous hole I remember falling into when I got the results of my personality test. Who's this woman sitting in this office with this man who's seen me with all my defences, including attire, down? I clear my head. "Why did you leave on Sunday?"

"Do you mean the first time or the second?"

I frown. "Both."

His eyes are guarded. "Professional conduct requires we work on your issues. This is not a date."

I stay my eyes on his. "This guy I met got me drunk, gave me a hickey, kept my knickers."

He shoots back, "He kept you safe, refused your drunken advances, gave you a good time. A magnificent time."

"He took me on a date even though I had a boyfriend."

His eyes light up. "Had?"

"We're talking about Saturday night."

He sits back, displeased. "Let's look at your actions." He counts on his fingers. "You went willingly on the date in spite of the boyfriend. Dressed sexy to increase desire in this man. Danced close with him." He raises an eyebrow. "Took off your knickers, twice, and sat on his lap in the car without them on." He puts his hands behind his head. "I don't think you can question his restraint, or his morals."

I'm beetroot. "I took off my knickers twice?"

His eyes are steel. "The first time was when the love-bite occurred. I ran my hands along your leg, nothing went further because I pushed you off my lap and took you back inside after instructing you to put your knickers back on. When we returned to the car to drive home, you took them off again." He pauses. "This is a serious matter, Candice."

Serious, oh yeah. I stamp on my urge to recreate the night, remove my knickers, sit on his lap. I've never been Kat, able to pursue the rush of lust then get on with life like it was a good meal, but right now the lust is rampant.

"I did a personality test at work and it's thrown me."

He becomes animated. "Name of test?"

"Wilson something?"

"Wilson Monk Personality Inventory." Now he's smiling. "How did it come out?"

"Awful. Not like me at all."

"That test has a regular amount of validity, but no test's completely accurate, and sometimes, depending on your day, they can miss their mark. What disturbed you about it?" He pauses. "Hmmm. Interesting."

I glance at Ziggy's big desk. If only I was involved in an escapade I'd read, involving a man, a woman, a desk and a locked door instead of dissecting my errant personality. "Do you think I'm an extrovert?"

He cocks his head. "Not sure. With alcohol, yes. Before that I see more extrovert than introvert. We're all a mixture. Does it matter?"

"My behaviour: does it show you I'm rule-driven?"

He laughs. "You can't surmise that's what the creative-procedural axis of that test explains. It's about following your impulses or following your head. Is that what you were doing Saturday? Trying to prove you're a rule-breaker?"

I remain silent. Anything I say might be used against me.

"You were game-playing Saturday. That guy you met loved it. You were subdued on Sunday, and he was still drawn to you. Besides, I have it on good authority he comes out as procedural on that inventory. Following rules means everything's done fairly, nobody gets hurt." He sighs. "He left on Sunday because there were plenty of people to get hurt. You showed no inclination to chuck the boyfriend, and he didn't want to be the reason your boyfriend had his heart broken. Nor did he want to find himself in that terrible situation."

I blush again and rise. In trying to find my feet, I've trodden on Ziggy's. "I've had enough for this session, thank you."

Ziggy signals me back down. "I haven't set your homework."

I put my hand self-consciously over Joe's number.

"And don't ring Joe," Ziggy continues. "He doesn't need you to stuff him around."

I start speaking but he cuts me off.

"Here's your homework, Candice." He says my name like he's my teacher. "I'll see you again." There's no undertone. "Think about the personality the WiMPI described for you. What of it can you see in your parents, siblings, boyfriend, friends. I'm looking for where you're mirroring someone, where you're rebelling. Write it down and bring it next session." He stands, shakes my hand warmly.

I follow him out like he's the Pied Piper. There's a woman and child sitting in one corner of the waiting area, a man at the other corner and, a petite young thing at the reception desk. She pretends to sort papers, then looks up with her long eyelashes. Her face falls.

"That'll be two hundred and fifty-five dollars," Ziggy says.

*Friggin' how much?*

"I can put that through." Petite scrutinises me sharply.

"No need, I'll do this one. But she needs another appointment."

Petite checks her screen as I hand my credit card to Ziggy. "Wednesday fortnight at eleven," she pouts.

"Got anything this Friday?" Ziggy hands me back my card, proffers the machine for my PIN.

She squints at me, not the screen. "Booked all day."

"Book her in at the end." Ziggy shakes my hand. "I'll see you then. Make good choices until I see you Friday." He stares at me for a few moments, and I wonder whether he's about to tell me off.

He simply says, "See you then. Laurie."

# 14

Creeped out by the receptionist's bare-faced analysis of me as she gave me my appointment card, I figure it's time to re-visit Kat. Thank goodness she doesn't keep regular hours. She responds to my text with *We're having brekky at home see you soon.* I presume *we* includes Thor. I won't get any sense out of her if he's there waving his abs at her.

When I arrive, he's at the clothesline hanging out her washing without a shirt on, like something from a fantasy novel. Kat's on the phone, her diminutive body clad in a tight, white singlet and baby-pink knickers, her hair in short plaits. Nobody else is around.

She waves me into a seat. "When can you send it? Sure. I'll have my lawyers look at it."

I look at her questioningly.

"Yep. Sure. Sure. Sure. Okay. Excellent. Sure. Okay." She hangs up.

"Lawyers?"

She waves her hand. "Just messing with their heads. They're buying my salad servers. Maybe crockery designs. Things are moving."

"Everything's rolling your way." There's a touch of green about my response.

She smiles. "When you're in the flow, you gotta go."

"Why's the Thunder God hanging out your smalls?"

She laughs. "We were out there when the phone rang. You okay? You look a bit cheesy."

I pout. "Cheesy? Like how?"

"A bit squeaky. Rather flat. Stuck in a press until you're square."

Which is exactly how I feel. Squeaky. Flat. Square.

"You need to let go, Candice. I'll tell you what happened after Thor and I had sex that first time." My eyes follow hers out to the line. Thor is hanging out her tiny underwear with his giant's hands.

I turn back. "Okay."

She continues to watch Thor. "We fell asleep. When I woke up, he was watching me, soaking up every detail, trying to make sense of me, kind of." She turns back to me. "You know what I mean?"

"I have no idea what you're talking about."

Thor comes in, puts down the empty basket at Kat's feet. "Hi Candice," he growls. He looks at Kat. "Who was that, baby?"

"Money, baby. Sold some artwork."

I have no idea what all this *baby* shit is. I've never heard Kat speak like this. She's normally very anti-*baby,* says it's demeaning of women, that it's youth-icising them. Now she's using it herself.

But Thor's talking. "That's cool, baby, I'm proud of you. I'm going to my place then to the gym. Got a lecture at two. You coming over after or should I come back here?"

Kat looks wrong-footed. "You going home?"

There's no malice in Thor's words. He's got a lecture. He's coming back later. I watch the tension with interest.

"You got Candice here. Come to my place about five. Okay, baby?"

"Sure," says Kat, although she looks anything but.

Thor kisses her on the forehead and leaves. Kat looks perplexed.

I wait for her to speak, but she doesn't. "Sorry I broke up your playdate."

She purses her lips. "I thought he was staying for lunch, staying until he went to uni." She squints. "See, that's exactly what I didn't want to happen, ever. To get needy."

There's an anxiety to Kat I've never witnessed before. "It's alright. He's coming back. Or you're going over there."

"I'm so intuitive, usually." She's still buried deep.

I stand up. "We're going to lunch. He doesn't need you till five. That makes for a lovely long lunch."

"No work?"

"Did it last night." I smile. "I was on a roll."

"Let me get dressed." She totters up from the chair. "I need you today, Can. That was weird."

Fifteen minutes later we're seated at Buddy's, our favourite hang-out: seagulls hovering, waves crashing, the smell of hot seafood and cappuccino in the air. I pour us both a water as we wait for our meals. On the way here Kat explained the company has contracted her for her salad servers, but now they also want to use her designs on their range of crockery - plates, cups, saucers, mugs, bowls, platters, salad bowls. The deal will bring her in a living wage for the first time. They're paying her a hundred thousand as an advance. I wonder if she'll vacate her little room. But all she wants to talk about is Thor's abrupt departure.

"Perhaps he had work to do, Kat. Or perhaps he doesn't like me."

"Don't be ridiculous, all men like you." She grabs the wine glass out of the waitress's hands and takes a big gulp. "It's me."

"He left for a few hours!" I smile encouragingly. "He wants to see you later. Where is his place, anyway? How old is he?"

"Next street. Lives with his parents. Twenty-four."

"What does he think about the baby thing?"

She brightens immediately. "We think it would be a wild ride to get me pregnant. Can you imagine, Can? All that energy and craving and bodily fluid put to a good cause instead of winding up in a condom."

"Babies last a long time, Kat." This sounds like nonsense. "You have to get them through till they get to school, then school takes a long time. It's a responsibility you can't take back."

She flaps her hand. "We'd be fine!"

"Your ovaries are messing with you." I ignore her tinkly laugh. "You know from your parents how fucked-up a job two people can do."

Her face falls. "That's fucking absolutely true."

"How long's Thor been around, anyway?" I think back to the last time I saw Kat, and I reckon it was beginning of the month. Three-ish weeks ago, where the only contact was me texting *Whatcha up to Gene driving me nuts* and her replies along the lines of *The days are banging on!* No sign of Thor before that.

"Twenty days today." She throws her arms out expressively, almost knocking our steak sandwiches out of the waitress's hands. "Sorry," she giggles.

The waitress smiles congenially and puts the plates in front of us.

I've always bought for Kat. She never has enough money to pay for her basics, let alone extras. She was there for me so often at high school that I don't mind at all. She always makes sure she fills up when I shout and then doesn't eat for the rest of the day and sometimes, the next.

You're absolutely correct in what you're thinking: Kat's a disaster. She's worried me just as much as she's defended me. Now she's talking long-term investment with a man who looks like he's serious about his body and determined about his career. But serious and determined about Kat? Who knows. Nevertheless, it's time for priorities.

"I wanna talk about me," I mumble through my mouthful of sandwich. "I'm in trouble."

"Baby trouble?" she smiles.

"No. Quit with the baby stuff." I swallow. "And what's this crap about *baby this* and *baby that?*"

"I don't know." Her smile is radiant. "Everything I ever thought about myself gets in the way of my relationship with Thor. He *baby*-ed me and I *baby*-ed him back and it kinda became our *thing*." She takes a bite but she's still smiling.

"Back to me," I insist. "I'm seeing a psychologist."

Kat chokes. "You the fuck what?"

"You the *frig* what." I laugh. "It's this guy I met. He's a psychologist. I went to see him at his office-"

"Didja do it on his doctor's couch?" She laughs so hard the lettuce flies out of her mouth and lands perilously close to my plate.

"Nothing happened," I smile, guarding my plate.

She gulps, smiles back. "Is he the Hickey Master?"

"Yes." I can't help but laugh along with her. "Listen," I put my sandwich down because it's impossible to talk, think and eat, "he's lovely. Intelligent. Fair. Honest. Sweet. Protective. Handsome. Well-dressed. Capable-"

"Shit, alright, already. Frick, Candice, when's the wedding?"

"Last Saturday."

Her eyes bulge.

"His cousin's wedding. I was still seeing Gene. Officially. But Gene was poking this other woman, except I didn't know, so nothing happened but then I could've told him I was single the next day when I asked him why I woke up naked but I didn't because I don't want my whole frickin' life to be about who I'm with!"

Kat clicks her fingers and makes a drinking signal to the waitress, then holds up two fingers. She turns back and smiles. "My diagnosis is you're fucked up and need to see a psychologist."

We laugh. The waitress brings two more wines. My glass is still half full. Kat gulps it down and gives the two empty glasses to the waitress, takes a slug of her new one.

"Kat, if you're going to have a baby you can't drink so much. Or at all. And you're going to have to pass a human being out of your-"

"Wasn't Thor odd?" she interjects. "Didn't you notice a difference?"

"Stop being a space alien."

Kat sighs, turns her wine glass distractedly. "I think Thor and I got out of hand. That first night, the morning after, I had to get the pill. But we talked about what if we did nothing, saw what happened?"

"Does that mean you didn't-"

She shrugs unconcernedly. "It all happened in the moment. Like we woke up in the middle of a date, so there was no pre-date shit. I knew him already," she smiles, "of course, because of Ollie. I thought he was fucking hot but that was all, until I woke up with him on top of me so I kissed him and put my legs around his waist and then he stuck his-"

"I get it. Don't elaborate!"

"Okay." She giggles, lost in the moment. "Basically, we were both already kind of in the throes of it, and that was that." Kat blushes.

Kat blushing? "Jeez, Kat. Fuck. Shit. You're out of your mind. *Baby*."

Kat continues with her sandwich. "Love's a gamble," she says, her mouth full. "I rolled the dice and lost my head."

"Did you get the pill?"

She closes her eyes. "Yes. But afterwards there was this anti-climax, and that was when we started talking about a baby."

"After your first date. That wasn't a date at all."

She looks out to the horizon, as if the answer is sitting out there riding on the wild grey sea. "I never thought I'd say this," she whispers, "but love changes everything."

She's so unusually fragile. I put my sandwich down again, squeeze her hand. I remember Ziggy squeezing mine.

"If only it works." She smiles awkwardly. "When you've got nothing but yourself, there's nothing to lose. You can take yourself anywhere, pick up and go, be out of luck and still have reason to start again. But now, suddenly there's love and there's money. I don't know, Can, it seems too hard. Now I've got things to lose, it feels uncomfortable."

"But you and I have something."

She smiles and nods. "Candice Kelly, the world's best friend."

Her mobile rings. It's the company. I finish my sandwich as I watch her, wondering how I'll keep her safe in the world of big business. A hundred thou sounds like a lot of money for an unknown designer.

I don't talk about Ziggy again, just listen to Kat, watch the change in her. She's like a little creature in a kid's picture book, being led by instinct alone, navigating the world in her creaky worn and patched boat, being tossed about by the changing weather, looking for dry, safe land.

# 15

Kat's keen to send her designs through to the company. I drop her back to her place then drive to the office.

But she's on my mind, stuck so fast I can't distract myself, particularly because I'm the lone star in our section of the office. Terri and Martin are still at their interviews, Clarissa's called in sick, Jamie's at a meeting.

After fifteen minutes of dawdling I go to the toilet, look in the mirror. No difference to how I looked during my Saturday mirror time, before I went to the pub and met the inimitable Ziggy. There's my jet-black hair, hazel eyes, a nose, a mouth, a chin. Apart from hue, everyone in the office, in this city, in the world, has these features in some guise. I'm no more worthy of how I look than is anyone. I have no issue with people who take pride in being beautiful, or smart, or self-assured, but it's pure dumb luck.

I decide not to waste a trip to the bathroom. I sit at my bodily task reviewing the unrealistic standards we're besieged by. All heroines in books and movies have beauty, brains and hearts of gold. They have the wherewithal to get out of tricky situations, their values lead them out of the thicket in which they find themselves, they're there to show us The Message. And The Message is: if only we stay True, we can Rise Above It All. So long as you have beauty, brains and a heart of gold.

I steal another look at my reflection as I wash my hands, thinking again of Kat. She's stayed true to one thing: herself. She's broken rules where they've suited her, run an uncharted path of freedom and child-like innocence, lived in the moment. Confronted by stability, she doesn't know what to do with it. Rising Above It All has brought problems, not solutions. Since when were money and love bad things?

I return to my desk without answers, look at my next assignment. *The New Woman: Spirituality, swearing and sex.* Crap. In fact, oh God, triple crap and fuck.

I get the title. We women are no longer under the spell of What's Right And What's Wrong. We've knocked down most of our boundaries, stepped easily over fences that once seemed insurmountable. It's an Anything Goes type of world now. But with change comes confusion. What is it we want? What is it I want?

I begin typing, enjoying the rhythm of my words. When I switched to English lit at uni I was still hell-bent on changing the world, making people see things in ways they hadn't considered before. How I wound up working at a table-top magazine is anybody's guess. A woman's gotta work and even I, with my lofty ideals and high morals, had to start somewhere. It's probably time to move on, but I can't be faffed.

Terri comes in, looking decidedly ruffled and extremely pleased.

"Holy crap!" I exclaim. "What have you done to my interview?"

She snickers and sits at her desk next to mine. "God, he's gorgeous! The interview was quick, but he wasn't." She giggles like she's drunk.

"Terri!"

She waggles her chair excitedly from side to side. "Can't be stuck in a rut, can you? Gotta take a chance sometime."

I gulp. "Holy shit. Are you seeing him again?"

"Oh, yes, tonight."

It hits me with a smack. That was my interview, and I could be in her place instead of swapping it out for an article on toxic relationships. I've never been one for love on the run, but the way my brain has been functioning this week, maybe I might've been.

She continues blissfully. "He's been working out for *The Muscle Man.* Can you imagine?"

Oh yes, I can. All too well.

She slides her chair up next to mine, leans in to whisper, although there's nobody around, "I was there for *hours!*"

I've known Terri for three years and she's never done this in that time. What worked against her Better Judgment now?

"Is it physical or emotional?" I'm hanging on her words.

"What does that mean?" She sits away distastefully.

"Sex or love?"

"We'll see," she smirks. "He's taking me to Opening Night tomorrow night. That's gotta mean something?"

If Laurie is the Woman Whisperer, I must be the Sex Whisperer. Gene, Rupert, Daisy, Laurie, Kat, now Terri.

I should take a moment to tell you more about myself, in case you have the wrong impression. It's not that I'm a prude, but I think things get dangerous if you're not watching where you take your next sex step.

I haven't had that many lovers. Five to be exact. Okay, if we're being exact then a couple more than five, although those didn't count for anything except cringe-worthy memories. I've followed my relationships loyally while they've been a going concern but the break-ups, whether my choice or not, have delivered acute disappointment. One moment you're the best woman in the world and the next you're either a despised bitch or a snivelling wreck.

Love stinks. Better not to get hooked in the first place.

I'd been single for almost a year when I met Gene. I only decided to try again because Gene seemed so sweet and, you know, a male nurse is surely a safe bet. The score, before Gene, was two apiece: two I was the dumper, two I was the dumpee. I don't know what I'd call the Gene finale. He was certainly the infidel, but I ran a very close second. I don't think I was ever attached to Gene, not emotionally, nor intellectually, nor spiritually. And physically, yes, but with the rest of the criteria missing even this wasn't working as well as I'd hoped.

I'm cautious to whom I reveal my nakedness, so I look before I leap into bed. In one case this meant a month, in two others two months.

One was more, much more, really, and then I wish I hadn't, because my intuition was correct about that one. Gene was a month. Never have I done what I did with Ziggy, a temptress looking for trouble.

At four o'clock my period comes. My failed personality test and consequent Quest may just have been a blip on the hormonal radar.

My article research is informative but depressing. Women now swear regularly, mostly when they're angry, which is apparently often. None of us think it helps. Which surprises me, because when I'm with Kat, I love filling the air with expletives. I don't do this with anyone else, certainly not with a boyfriend, not even during coitus.

Sex is more difficult to pin down. Men, it seems, are straight up shooters, if you'll pardon the pun. They think about it frequently, want it often, get it whenever they can, and the quicker to the finish line the better. I don't think you'll ever see a men's magazine with the headline *How to achieve your best orgasm ever* or *She was just using me for sex.*

Women, well, it's complicated. Longer to peak, needing a plotline, culturally guided, emotionally inclined, physically inept, we're still learning how to meet our needs. Certainly, my life mirrors this, but in ways I'm not going to tell you because frankly, some things deserve to remain private.

Spirituality is the new religion. I'm born under Libra the Scales, and therefore I like to weigh up the arguments before making a decision, according to my horoscope. I think I'm just naturally vapid. But I've learned if someone asks about my beliefs, and I reply I'm a Libran, they just smile and say, *Ah, I see.*

Unable to find a fun ending for my article, I head home where I lay in bed with a heat-pack on my stomach and a book in my hand. Another heroine passing time until The End while we all learn a lesson.

At six it's pain relief and limp zucchini with partly-sprouting onion chopped for my tea, supported at least by the much-needed crunch of fresh carrots, capsicum and spinach from the garden. There's a link, I'm sure, between my alcohol consumption and my capacity to deal with my period. Saturday night managed to make up for the rest of the month in that respect.

I'm mid-way through consuming my stir-fry when the banging starts again at Rupert's flat. Banging is positively the right word. Who would've guessed Daisy would be such a goer? Or Rupert? I take my stir-fry into my room and start to eat in bed. No sooner is the last carrot stick in my mouth than Laurie's sexy-genarian romp starts up on the other side of the wall. Unbelievable. Are they syncing on purpose?

Cursing poor architecture and feeling better for the drug-assisted relief, I head out. I'm sick of running into sex lives, so Kat's is out as well. I head over to my parents' place.

It's six-thirty. Mum and Dad should've finished tea.

Harry K's car is in the driveway. He's the brother I share with Dad, so he's Harry Kelly. As you can tell, the only way we can tell the stepbrothers Harry apart is to say the first initial of their last names, like a classroom where there's more than one kid with the same name. Apparently, early on, Mum and Dad decided not to call them *my Harry* and *your Harry* as they felt it would be divisive and they wanted them to belong to one big happy (they hoped) family, so they're Harry B and Harry K. They're both tall but Harry B, like Mum and me, is lean, Harry K, like Dad, is brawny.

The one that's not here currently, Harry B, is the one that broke his leg and introduced me to Gene. I'm glad he's not here, although I love him dearly. He's been cracking jokes like *I wish I could find me a hot nurse, too,* and *At least he knows all about anatomy* and *Does he have a sexy nurse's uniform?* He'll be devastated to know he's lost the butt of his jokes.

Mum's name is Judith Baxter. She got pregnant at seventeen to a neighbour's visiting cousin. She and Harry B (who always got birthday presents from the neighbours but never from the cousin) lived with Gran and Pa before moving in with Dad when I was a mere bun in her seemingly hot oven.

Harry B and I are close in spite of our age difference. Mum told me she was celibate, filled with guilt about her teenage pregnancy, and making Harry B her number one priority, helping out at his primary school and working through her degree one or two topics at a time until, when she was twenty-nine and in search of a high school for Harry, she met my father, the gorgeous and gregarious Ashton Kelly, who'd been married for twelve years and was about to turn thirty. Mid-life crisis, anyone?

Mum and Dad have a few things in common. Dad married Harry K's mother Sylvie because he'd gotten her pregnant. After giving birth to a ten pounder, his still-teenage wife decided never to have another baby and to opt instead to return to school, get a degree and start climbing the executive ladder, leaving more and more of the child and home care to Dad. Dad tells me he always wanted another child, although I think that was the furthest thing from his mind when he rang the number my vivacious mother gave him *in case you want to share parenting experiences.*

Words can be powerful, my mother has always told me and, true to form, *sharing parenting experiences* came to fruition nine months later with my arrival. I presume they shared plenty of stories about similarities in their lives on Open Day before they wound up exultantly sharing a hotel bed, body fluids and genetic material that night.

You won't be surprised to hear I never take contraceptive advice from my parents.

# 16

The house is silent when I enter. "Mum? Dad? It's just me."

"In here," Harry K's gruff voice calls from the kitchen.

Harry K will always be slightly cross with Dad. Screwing my mother meant screwing his life.

Harry B and I grew up together; Harry K was only with us half the week until I was eight. Harry B always felt like my real brother. Harry K sometimes seemed like the kid who came for sleepovers.

Harry B likes to think he's funny. Harry K actually is.

"Hey, sis." Harry K tosses a grape into his mouth, leaning against the kitchen bench. "Haven't you left home yet? You look fantastic. If I didn't share half a crate of genes with you, I'd be chatting you up."

"And Joanna would have your balls in the toaster-oven."

He laughs. "That's a nice half a dress you're wearing, Candice."

"Piss off, K," I smile. "It covers everything it needs to."

He grins. "There are bits that don't count as indecent which all men know are the roads that lead to paradise. That moron Gene must be gone. Who's the new guy?"

I grimace. Why is it so obvious? "Where's Joanna?"

"With Simone and Rowella at a kid's party. Bloody stupid time, after school. Some special movie screening." He chucks another grape in his mouth. "She's coping with the spews again."

"No. Don't tell me." I blink as he grins. "Jeez, Harry, you've impregnated her again?"

"I love it when you get all medical." He laughs loudly. "The way she got the spews was, however, more fun than six years of medicine."

Harry K is a doctor, Harry B a lawyer. My professional journalism at a magazine you stick on your coffee table to fill in the minutes when you're waiting to do something else therefore hardly rates a mention.

Mum appears. "Now I have two of my favourite people visiting! When did you get here, Candice?"

"She was hoping to find the rest of her dress," sniggers Harry K.

Mum hugs me and holds me out to look at me. "You look fabulous. Not with Gene anymore?"

"What?"

"It's just he's not the sort of guy you'd wear a dress like that for."

"He's pathetic," grins Harry K. "Gives male nurses a bad name. Most of them are brilliant."

I ignore him. "Yes, Mum, although I have no idea what you mean, Gene is gone."

She smiles. "There's a new man on the scene, one who makes you want to wear a dress like that."

"Yeah. I took him home and shagged him," I lie. "On the first night I met him."

"Candice!"

"Monkey see, monkey do," laughs Harry K. "Runs in the genes, oh wicked stepmother of mine."

"Harry, that's enough."

Mum's now fifty-eight. The ravages of menopause have left her pert and lean, and her hair is black like mine but shorter, curling onto her collar, no greys anywhere. She has a light in her eyes I've always found comforting, a playfulness that draws us all to her. I think about the night she decided to break her vow of celibacy with a married man on the day she met him. So unlike her. She was a year older than I am now and had a twelve-year old son. "Mum, can I have a chat?"

She looks at me worriedly. "Serious?"

"Life."

"That is serious." She smiles.

My brother smirks. "If this is girl talk, I'm outta here."

I put my hands on my hips. "What are you, seventeen?"

"I'm not into *I said, he said.*"

A veil peels away, and I see a man who entered his teenage years raised by a cuckolded mother who took every opportunity to discredit the Whore, and the Seed that meant she couldn't ignore the traitorous deed of her husband. He's a little boy who could no longer trust his father to keep him safe. I wrap my arms around him. "I want you to stay. Please. I value your opinion."

He looks at me in surprise. "You do?"

"Yeah." I let him go. "You've hit forty. You've lived a lot more life than I have. You've got a wife, a family, a big house, an important job."

"Don't lay it on. I know my life is over."

"What?" Mum and I chime together.

"Sure. What's there left to do?" He flips a grape into the air as he talks. "With the new baby Joanna's going to be really busy. I just turn up to work, do my appointments, then go home. Nothing ever happens." He tosses the grape listlessly into his mouth.

He's just as lost as me. My Vision Quest melts like ice cream on a summer's day.

Mum's speaking. "Everything you ever wanted and it's not enough."

Harry K looks like he's about to start an argument. Then he softens. He's always like this, like he expects Mum's skin to tear open and a fire-breathing dragon to erupt, then realises she's human flesh and bones and that she loves him as much as she loves me and Harry B. "Jude-"

He's never called her Mum. He's the only one with three parents: Harry B and I just have two. Dad is my father, after all, and Harry B hasn't known another father. But Harry K's always been confused. He was a hit-and-run lover until the regal Joanna showed up and refused to take his bullshit. We weren't surprised when after only six months he asked her to marry him. And not at all surprised when she refused. It took eighteen months of Joanna getting him ship-shape before she agreed, and then the wedding was done the way she wanted. Which again, we weren't surprised at. We have a saying: *What Joanna wants, Joanna gets. What Harry wants, nobody gets.*

Mum hugs him. "You have every right to be unhappy. Don't you?"

He breaks away. "I didn't say I was unhappy."

"So, you're happy." She's challenging him, putting it out for him to doddle around.

Harry K shrugs. "There's nothing more to ask for."

Mum repeats, "So, you're happy."

He pulls off a handful of grapes and shoves them in his mouth.

Mum turns to me. "What did you want to talk about, sweetie?"

"Jeez, this is interesting enough!" I can't take my eyes off Harry K. "Did you want another baby, Harry?"

Harry K stuffs more grapes into his mouth.

"Are you happy, Harry?" my mother asks him again.

He swallows. "I love Joanna. And the girls. But we've got two easy kids. I think we should've left it there. Each time it's Russian roulette. I see enough parents at the surgery with kids who don't eat, don't sleep, don't learn, maybe we'll get one like that this time?" His voice is tinged with anxiety.

"Then you'll manage." Mum smiles kindly.

I see why he comes to visit her. I think he gets along better with her than with Sylvie. Everyone gets along with Mum.

I remember Ziggy's homework, and it's easy. Mum the extrovert. Dad the extrovert. The two Harrys, extroverted. Kat, off the scale. "Hey, do you guys reckon I'm an introvert?"

"Nurse Gene tell you that?" Harry K grabs me, wrestles me in the way he's done since I was old enough to walk. "He's the bloody introvert."

I laugh, enjoying the feel of Harry K around me. Yes. Gene. The Nice Guy who was really a Bad Guy.

Mum stands back against the bench, smiling at us both.

I break away from Harry K, so he only has me around my wrists. "Tell me what you think about rules. Should you follow them or not?"

"Rules? Rules? What's that got to do with anything?" He lets my wrists go, picks off another grape. "Are you making up one of those stupid magazine quizzes? *How to get the best from your sex-life,*" he says in a squeaky voice. "*Find out what a man's really thinking when he's sticking it in you.*" He returns his voice to regular. "I can tell you what he's thinking." He grins. "Nothing." He pops another grape in his mouth.

Mum and I laugh.

"Here's my thoughts," smiles Mum. "Everyone has rules. Those that break the rules have that as a rule. It's a rule about being contradictory."

I like this. It feels right. "Mum, that night you met Dad, why'd you break your rules?"

She looks uncomfortable. "Love is–"

"Transformative," I smile, and she nods happily.

"The end of all your fun," interjects Harry K. "What?" He looks from Mum to me. "And replaces it with another lot of fun," he scowls.

"Harry," I say softly, "Maybe the fun is wherever you are. At any time." But that's wrong: I agreed to a date with Gene because I was lonely. He was so humble and adoring that I couldn't say no. And then I'd so lost my Self that by the time he started reciting the *Meant To Be* routine, I didn't know how to escape. Then came the personality test.

Maybe I should ask Terri her profile, perhaps that's the key to her unprofessional shagging of MuscleMan. What about Martin, the office curmudgeon, what did he say about his personality test results? What of Clarissa, a sparkling extravert if I ever saw one? Or even Jamie, our boss? All of us answering test questions like *When you're at a party, which of the following is likely to be the first thing you do?* and *Which of the following outcomes would you most like to see for yourself?* Then being labelled by the test like we're goods on a shelf.

*Candice: Warning. May contain nuts.*

But surely we're too complex to be labelled as one product? Yes. YES. YES! Why categorise us into a small number of brands when we're all as unique as snowflakes? Why not see us as a giant supermarket of traits, all the apples with their own bruises, the bananas with uneven colouring, all the loaves of bread cut in their own particular way?

And why did I let Gene put his goods into my shopping trolley anyway? Who am I truly? Friendly or attention-seeking? Vivacious or needing approval? Extraverted or scared to be alone?

Is my price discounted because of my age, or more scarily, who I am? Mum's right: we're all rule-driven, all following our own compass, all making up a template of certainties to follow, all tripping up whenever we venture into foreign territories where the rules vary.

Suddenly Dad's arms are around me. I didn't hear him come in.

"My beautiful daughter, wearing half a dress," he smiles.

"See?" grins Harry K triumphantly.

"Gotta go!" I yell before racing to the door. Now I know the traps, and I have to get them out of my head.

# 17

## *Rules Underpinning a Life Extraordinary: Summary*

| | |
|---|---|
| Always be who you are. | Don't be who you're not. |
| Look for your Z. Find your Z. | Don't wind up where you're not meant to be. |
| Love is transformative. Love changes everything. | Don't settle for less than Love. |
| Watch for opportunity. Life is a strategy. | Don't miss the doorways that open. |
| The fun is wherever you are. | If it's not fun, get out immediately. |
| Words can be powerful. | Be careful of other meanings. |
| Take a chance. | But not the wrong ones. |

I'm so buoyed by my wisdom that I revise my A to Z list.

A: astute

B: bountiful

C: courageous

D: determined

E: enthusiastic

F: friendly

G: gregarious

H: hilarious

I: ingenious

J: joyful

K: kind

L: loving

M: masterful

N: neighbourly

O: optimistic

P: persistent

Q: quixotic

R: responsible

S: sensible

T: thoughtful

U: understanding

V: vivacious

W: warm

X: x-cellent

Y: yummy

Z: still unknown. And this is okay!

I'm happy with my Quest now. The personality test screwed me up. I was a nebulous limbo-rider, blind to the fact that my life was taking place without me.

As I stick on a load of washing I notice abruptly that everything's quiet. This feels so unexpectedly odd that I check my phone in case Laurie's called me. I have no idea why he'd do so as he never has before, but sure enough, there's a text from him. *Dinner at pub with Rupert. Want to join us? Our girlies are coming too so you'll have female company Laurie x*

Sure. Third wheel at a pub meal with two lust-fuelled couples. At the pub where Ziggy happened. Laurie sent it two hours ago so they're probably sloshed or they'd be back in their flats, pumping away. I text him back. *Have been at mums thanks for the offer.*

Immediately my phone beeps. *Sure? We're still here. Walking home sometime. We're a bit tiddled. How did it go with your fella?*

*He gave me a counselling session!*

*Sweet girl you can do better than that.*

Can I? I think back to Kat's chant: *Who can? Can can!*

Maybe I can, but not tonight. I've had too big a day. I pull myself into the bathroom and clean my teeth, stare at my face in the mirror. I look different tonight. Resolute. Determined. Indomitable.

My mood dips quickly as I sway across my morning meeting with Ziggy. What kind of footing are we on now I've made him my psychologist? Why did he make me his last appointment on Friday? Is six o'clock Date time, or just an emergency time and there'll be someone after me, like his client Joe this morning?

I get into bed and snuggle down tight. *Can can!* I need Kat's no-crap attitude and persistent faith in me. But she's probably with Thor.

Now I'm thinking about Kat and Thor and the odd beginning to their odd relationship. If Thor only lives in the next street, why didn't he go home to sleep instead of going to Kat's room? Why take off all your clothes and lie down on top of the naked person who's lying there? By accident? It seems so implausible that I want to call her. Sleep steals my motivation and it's several hours later that I wake up to a constant knocking.

I fumble to my phone: 1.37. The knocking gets louder.

"Can? … Ca-a-a-an? CAN!"

It's Kat. Sounding like never before. I run to the door. Open it.

She races in. Slams the door wide. "He lied!" she screams. "He lied!" she screams again as the original is still ricocheting off my walls.

I grab her arms to soothe her. "Thor?"

"He lied!"

"Kat, what did he lie about?" I lower my voice, she pauses, like a baby intrigued at something novel. I pull her towards the couch.

She winds herself up again. "He-" she shouts.

"Shhh." I start loudly, drop it to quiet. "Tell me."

"That night."

We see what's coming, don't we? Thor was going to screw her whilst she was asleep. Without her consent.

"He knew I was there that night." Her voice cracks. "He came in to talk to me, saw I was asleep, saw I was naked, came in anyway." She raises her voice again. "He was trespassing!"

"Shhh." Trespassing isn't the crime here. "Then what?"

"He stripped off and got onto the bed." A sob escapes her. "He said he didn't know what he was doing."

Doesn't look good, does it? I didn't expect the end so soon this time. Or for it to be such a catastrophe.

She whimpers like a kitten. "He knew what he was fucking doing. He was doing fucking." Her voice trails away. "Intending to, anyway."

She looks almost ashamed. I wait for her to continue.

"He told me I said, *Come here, baby*."

I can't help it. Laughter bursts out of me like a balloon popping.

She gasps. "I would never have said *baby!* I hate that word."

I wipe a tear of laughter from my eye: she does hate *baby*. But it's all I've heard lately. "Do you remember it?"

Her indignance grows. "Absolutely not! He asked if I was sure, I said *I've been waiting for you, baby*, he lay on me, which woke me up."

"I don't get it, Kat." I reserve the fact she's never been happier. "He was doing what he was invited to do."

"He says!"

I frown. "You think he's lying? About what you said?"

She hunches. "I don't know. I don't say *baby*."

"Were you dreaming?"

"Maybeeeeee." She sounds unsure.

"What happened when you woke up?"

She puts her chin in her hands, her elbows on her knees. "I guess I looked surprised. He said he was looking for somewhere to crash. I thought it was fate. So I kissed him, and it was like Wow, then I wrapped my legs around him, manoeuvred myself so he could push-"

"Yep. Okay." Crikey, I could do without the descriptive. "Kat, I don't think it's rape."

"Totally consensual," she says, in her old familiar way. "But tonight he confessed." She's quiet now, like it's old news. "He was on my bed hoping I'd wake up. He was going to ask about screwing me. But he couldn't believe his luck because I kinda asked him. He thought I was awake because I was talking. Had to come up with something quickly. So, he lied. Then everything clicked and we were both surprised at how we were feeling. His lie had kinda confused things."

"Does he want to finish it?"

"No. We talked about the baby tonight and both agreed we don't want to do that yet, that we got carried away. But Can," her voice is almost inaudible, "our love was based on a lie."

"Bullshit," I smile encouragingly. "Why'd he want to screw you? There's a house full of women. He could've asked anyone who was awake. Which was probably all of them, knowing that house."

She fiddles with her sleeve hesitantly. "He was standing in Ollie's door the day before, talking to him and Mai-Lee, they're together at the moment, and I was getting changed. I knew he was there but I stripped off anyway." She giggles. "Made sure I was good and naked. Took some time selecting shorts and a tee from my rack, put them on without underwear where he could see." She clasps her hands together, shoves her arms down between her knees. "I was sending him a signal, but he shouldn't have lied. If he'd said, *Oh goodie I wanted to fuck you and now it's going to be easy,* or *Were you sleep-talking or did you really just ask me to bang you?* I would've said yes and he could've given me a jolly good-"

"Jeez, Kat." It's not about anything but Kat feeling scared and looking for a way out. Of the best thing she's ever had. "How do you feel about him?"

Her lashes swiftly well with tears. "I want to be with him. But he lied." She pauses. "Lied."

"How does he feel about you?"

She smiles stupidly. "He wants me to move into his bedroom with him. His parents have agreed. They like me." Now her mouth is broad. "Nice to have parents who like me."

"You stupid ass. My parents love you."

"But I need more, Can, it's like I have to over-fill to make up for my shit parents."

"Love is transformative." It's becoming my mantra. "Don't make up shit that's not real. You were the one parading around naked. I know women can dress any way they want to without the rest of the world thinking they're asking for it, but Jeez, Kat, you were naked! Naked! No wonder he came to you expecting sex. He was on a Quest, Kat, a Quest you put him on."

"He was crying when I left." Tears well again. "Candice, I'm so lost."

"How did you get over here?"

"Ollie drove."

"Give me your phone."

She hands it to me obediently. Grins childishly.

I toss my eyes to the ceiling. "Jeez. I always thought you were different. Now you're just like the rest of the fawning womenfolk." I thumb through her contact list, can't find his name, flick back. Thor's listed as AAA Thor. I put her phone on speaker.

He answers quickly. "Baby, come back! I've been out looking for you. Where are you, baby, I'll come get you, please say you forgive me?"

Kat snatches the phone. "Oh, baby!" She starts sobbing.

"Oh, my darling Katyliciana."

I look at her phone in shock. It's the first time anyone's spoken her real name in my presence. A name I'm sure was made up by her drug-fucked parents. It's a daring move from Thor.

"I'm at Can's!" she blubbers.

Now I've heard everything. Two hard nuts playing soft as butter. I wander to the kettle, although caffeine's the last thing I need this time of night. Mind you, I've done stupider things with Kat. Like the many times she's called me at two a.m. to collect her for pizza and beer. Or when she made me date a guy's brother so she could get a date with the guy. Or when she joined a nudist colony and asked me to join her to see the sunrise with her new (and naked) friends.

I stand next to the kettle as it rumbles, watching Kat as she talks with Thor and waits for him to arrive. The meeting at the door is something that'd be quite at home in a cheap and trashy romance novel, except it's Tiny Trixie and Colossal Cuthbert. They shout frenzied *I'm so sorry* and *It was all my fault* and *Oh I love you more than I've ever loved anyone* over the top of each other.

Amidst the noise I calmly finish making my tea. Thor leads her out the door, their eyes firmly fixed on each other's, their voices still loud. They don't close the door. Nor do they say good-bye.

I walk to the door and look out. Thor's car is across from our driveway. Kat moves up and down on Thor's lap, her face locked on his. Oh, God. They're having make-up sex. In the roadway.

I shut the door quickly, sit down at my tea, hear noises next door. Moans. Banging. They've woken Rupert with their shouting. Thud, thud, thud. A woman's voice. A man's voice. This time from Laurie's flat. They've obviously woken, too. Laurie's wall keeps time with Rupert's. I shake my head, sip my tea, try to distract myself by booting up my laptop. I sip and look at my next job: *The importance of orgasm.*

Crap. I hang out my washing, searching for answers in the black sky above. Nothing comes.

I shut down my laptop, pour my tea down the sink. I can't even drive away this time because my way is blocked by the lust-ravaged Thor-mobile.

I sigh, pick up my earphones and go back to bed.

# 18

I'm being strangled! He's at my neck, hands straddling its girth.

He dissolves as I rouse. I feel my neck, and pull the earphone cord off.

I'm okay. Must remember sex can be dangerous. Especially other people's sex.

It's Wednesday.

I examine my neck in the bathroom mirror, the love-bite now a shadow. My periodic aches and pains (get it? period-ic? shit, now I'm explaining my jokes) have disappeared and I step into the shower with a weary hangover from Kat's mid-night dramas. I wonder whether they're still locked together across from the flats or if they got home.

To whose home?

Moving in with Thor sounds serious. And crazy. I get they're on this trajectory, but the relationship seems based around sex every time they meet and calling each other *baby*. I need to make sure she's not in over her pretty little head. But who else but a guy called Thor would suit her?

I'm out of the shower but she's still running havoc in my mind, until, with a tremor, I remember Harry K's mood last night. I sit with the towel around me and text, *Hey K you ok?*

Nothing comes back and I forget about him as I weave my way to work.

Nobody else seems to be in. The whiteboard tells me Martin's interviewing all day, Clarissa's again off sick, Terri has the day off. We all know how she's spending it, with Opening Night tonight. No doubt *opening* day today.

Jamie appears with a mug of something steaming. He drinks only herbal tea since his wife left him. I suspect he's trying to counterbalance the enormous amount of whisky he consumes whenever he gets stressed. Which is all the time. Today he looks happy.

"What gives, Smiley?" I ask.

"Is that any way to speak to your boss?" he laughs.

I smile. "Uh, okay, what's up with you, Tiger?"

He's beaming. "Don't you love life? Man, I had a brilliant weekend."

The way my life's going at present, this means only one thing. "Really? Romance?"

He does one of those massive belly-laughs he's renowned for with his massive belly. "The divorce, Candice. Remember? Because I sure as hell do." He grins. "She's going to pay. She Who Must Not Be Named."

"How come?" Surprise pulls me towards his desk.

He shrugs. "Boyfriend's rich." He sits down, puts his mug on the desk. It looks like coffee. "The arsehole's gone up in my estimation."

"Really? Romance?" I ask again.

He shrugs. "Seems only fair. I paid for the boob job he's enjoying."

"What is it with men and breasts? They're just mammary glands."

"Spoken like a woman."

He's very happy this morning. But then Jamie's often happy, an irreverent, amicable joker.

"Hers aren't even real boobs," I complain.

"Again, spoken like a woman. Haven't you ever heard about blow-up dolls? Us guys are keen on cheap thrills, anywhere we can get 'em." He takes a gulp from his mug. "Ah, coffee again. I'm going back to me, Candice. All that bullshit, dieting, abstaining from women, all I've done is get fatter and hornier." He grins. "From now on I'm looking after myself in an entirely different way. Happy ever after." He motions me to sit down: it's only then I realise I'm still standing. "You know that personality test we did?"

I nod and sit.

"Bloody personal development! Utter bollocks. Nothing like me. So, I took it again. A whole lot different. Truly me. Warts and all."

I stare at my boss, sipping his coffee, let loose by a new understanding of himself.

"The magazine's gotta change, too." He smiles, looks out the window beside his desk. "Times have changed. I'm taking all ideas. Let me know if you have any. Can't guarantee I'll use any of 'em, but I'll listen to what you say. What are you working on now?"

"Orgasm."

He roars with laughter. "Your own?"

"No."

"Then work on that instead of research." He points his finger. "And if you tell anyone I said that, I'll just deny it."

I smile. Jamie's been a wonderful boss, right through his heartache. "What do you want me to write now, then?"

"Anything you want. Pick a topic. Run it past me first. Okay?"

"Sure thing, boss-man."

"Just you and me in the office today, so don't disturb me. I'm working all day on me."

I return to my desk, floored by both the change in Jamie and his re-sit of the test. Can you do that? Maybe I should re-do it too. But maybe I don't need to. Maybe it was enough to make me clean up my life. My phone beeps. Kat texts me as we always do when we've left the other during torment. *Thanks still together @ his overnight gotta see you today got another call from buyer x*

I text back. *Sure when are you free?*

*Meet for lunch @ Buddy's 12?*

When I reach our treasured café, I'm surprised she's there with Thor. Although I shouldn't be surprised by anything associated with Kat, and even less that she's not alone. Thor seems as obsessed with Kat as Kat is with Thor. They stand as I arrive, she to hug me, he to be polite.

"Candice," Thor says.

I feel like shaking his hand, he's so formal. "Hello, Thor." I smile my brightest smile.

He smiles so sweetly I'm knocked sideways. For all his cut muscles and beefy jaw, I see what keeps Kat his constant companion. I hug him tightly. When I release him there's astonishment on his face.

"Let's eat," grins Kat.

We order. Thor and I get out our wallets.

"Mine," I say breezily.

"I'll shout," says Thor.

We face off, vying over Kat's neediness.

"Excuse me, you two, it's my shout," Kat says proudly. "I've sold my salad servers and now dinnerware and a cake server!" She giggles.

Thor and I look at her blankly.

"But Kat," I find my voice, "have you got the money yet?"

"Uh, no. Lend me a fifty, Can?"

Thor and I laugh. I get out a fifty and she hands it to the cashier.

"Honest." She sounds like a four-year-old. "I can pay you back."

We return to our seats. "Do you want me to send Harry B with you when you sign the contracts? He can pretend he's your lawyer."

She sits up straight. "Oh God. I signed the first one already."

"It's okay," I soothe, and immediately call B's office. We're not allowed to call him on his mobile weekdays between nine and six unless it's an emergency. Timothy, the receptionist, says he'll get him to call back. When I turn back Kat's sitting on Thor's lap, her arms around him. Thankfully they're not kissing. I cough loudly.

Kat slides back onto her seat.

"Who's Harry B again?" asks Thor.

"Her brother, one of the Harrys," explains Kat.

"Oh." Thor looks confused. "They're both called Harry?"

"One was Mum's, the other was Dad's." Time to get the conversation back on track. "Kat, you've sold more of your designs?"

"They're beautiful," says Thor. "Have you seen them?"

I've been watching Kat design things for years. Tables, chairs, sofas, alarm clocks, cars, bathrooms, skyscrapers, you name it, she's designed it. In high school she designed a whole house in modules you could take apart and put together again in different ways. "She's very creative, is our Kat." I check myself, disturbed I'm sharing her as if she's a possession. "You two sorted out your problems?"

"The relationship's simply settling," Thor's eyes are glassy. "It all began in such a peculiar fashion that we've had to wade together through the boundary-setting required of permanent relationships in order to conceptualise the path ahead of us."

"Huh?" That's as intellectual as I can get with the mumbo-jumbo that's just come out of the beefcake's mouth. I don't know if you get this picture: here's a man whose entire body ripples with power and who looks like he can laser-cut through glass with his eyes, and he's talking like someone from a daytime chat show.

"He means we're just getting to know each other," interprets Kat.

Our black coffees, mine and Kat's, arrive, as does Thor's milky tea. I stifle a laugh as my phone rings. It's Harry B. I tell him about Kat's contracts, he tells me to bring her over at seven. I explain this to Kat. Thor looks at me with a newfound appreciation. "You can come, too," I tell him.

His face lights up. I'm starting to like the guy.


I run past my place after Buddy's. I've dropped tartare sauce on my dress at the height of my nipple and look like a leaky lactating mother.

I always wear dresses, have I mentioned that? I have a few pairs of jeans and two pairs of black trousers I wear when it's really cold, but mostly I like dresses. Feminist that I am, I've always thought dresses suited me better. They hug my curves in the right place and show off my excellent legs. And now I'm an adult I no longer have to be careful of showing my undies on the monkey bars. Now it's just sports bars.

On the way back to my car I see a package poking out of my letterbox. I haven't bought anything online lately but there's my name and address in neat handwriting. There's only a post office box listed on the back, so I don't have any clue where it's from. I get into my car and tear off the packaging. My heart skips to see it's a book from Ziggy.

> *Hello Candice*
> *I'm sending you my copy of this book. It explains the personality tests in easy terms. You'll see some are more accurate than others.*
> *I'm hoping it might set your mind at ease. As this is my personal copy I'd like it back. If you don't find it useful you can return it on Friday.*
> *All the best*
> *Ziggy*

It's written on personal letterhead:

*Dr Sigmund Zbigniew BSc(Hons) MA(Couns) PhD(Psych).*

Doctor Sigmund Zbigniew? He's a *doctor*? What's a doctor doing sleazing onto a truculent Quest rider? His mobile number is listed under his name, so now I can contact him directly.

I turn the book over. *Testing Times: An Inventory of Inventories.* I expect to see it's written by Ziggy, but instead it's authored by Neil North. Which would be fine if I was looking for my N.

I feel feverish at this contact from Ziggy. He must've sent it soon after our appointment yesterday for it to arrive today. I carefully place it on the passenger seat and drive to work.

I tuck it under my arm like it's a puppy as I walk to my desk, and dip into it here and there, see a psychological test is usually called an *inventory, indicator* or *instrument.* I find most tests have very low validity and this seems to be acceptable. The internet tells me about face validity, content validity, criterion validity … Crikey! Ziggy's gone up in my estimation if he understands all this. I look again at the note. Instead of *All my love* it says *All the best.* All the best of what?

My thoughts are interrupted by a text from Harry K. *Sorry about last night just worried how Joanna will cope with 3.*

I laugh. Joanna does everything with a cool hand, even short labours where she got torn apart in the very part of the female body where a huge amount of nerve fibres reside. Given her short and shortening labours, Harry might be delivering this one himself at home.

This is Harry worrying how Harry will cope. He's terrific with Simone and Rowella but his words last night, that his life was *over*, haunt me. Do doctors feel they're stuck in dead-end jobs? How can that be, when they've rigorously gotten through so many years of med school?

I text him back. *Yeah Dr K. Later you'll wonder how you ever thought you could do without little Johnnie/Janie x*

Nothing comes back. I presume he's seeing another patient.

My head spins back to Ziggy: the way he was with me during the session, this book he's sent me, his note. God, his note. Nothing about *love*. But plenty of caring. I stand away from the book. I can't digest it right now. Nor can I get my head around writing an article. Jamie's no distraction as he's in an animated conversation with someone on the phone.

"That's right! Yeah, freedom. Thinking of going for a drink tonight to celebrate. You willing? Able? Sure. Your place? What time? Sounds perfect. Look forward to it. Me, too. Yeah. What should I bring?"

Eavesdropping feels uncomfortable so I wander to the other side of the building where the Creative Team sits. As if we writers aren't creative! These guys do our lush photographs, set out our articles, and are generally responsible for the visual layout of the magazine. As a print edition we need a certain something that makes people want to pick us up, to enjoy the immediacy of distraction and to immerse themselves in the beauty, humour and connection of our content. We survive on the loyalty of our readership to attract advertisers.

I spy Dale and Monty with their heads locked together working avidly away at a computer. When I get there, they're trawling a dating website. "You two looking for kinky shit?"

"Researching," states Monty. "Just looking at what makes one website stand out from the other."

"Sure." I drag up a chair. Dale and Monty are tall, blonde, blue-eyed hunks I couldn't take my eyes off when I first started here. I was bewildered when they didn't return my simple flirting. Thought they were being politically correct until one night I caught them holding hands. They're so alike I told them they're in love with themselves.

"See?" Dale expertly navigates his way around the site. Sensuous photographs appear of couples amid beautiful greenery and luxurious hotel rooms, or relaxing in front of the television, or in a spa. The man's arm around the woman's shoulder, the looks of love and desire in each couple's eyes emphasised in small insets below each photograph.

"Wow. I wanna get me some of that," I say.

"See?" says Monty. "You're in. Captivated. Like your brain is running a special program. It's hooked into the unmet desires of your life, what you think love should be like. Ever had that? Even in the early days of your romances?"

"No," I say, surprised. "That's what love's supposed to look like! But either it's early and you're on your best behaviour or you're past all that and the romance is over. What about you guys?"

"Same," says Monty. "Wanting sex with someone is very different to being able to explore the tedium of life together."

"When you're same-sex you see trouble coming a mile off. It's nice to leave it behind." Dale smiles at Monty.

"I have enough trouble navigating my own life, let alone thinking about the difficulties of same-sex. I slept with a gay man once." I'm instantly rewarded by surprised looks. "Friend of a friend. Parents away for weekend so I was hoping for some hanky-panky. Nothing doing. He was so euphoric about coming out that he got completely tanked, vomited three times then fell asleep. So I slept with him. No sex, of course. Most of the time I was awake, worrying he'd vomit in his sleep."

Monty puts his arm around me. "You're a gorgeous woman, Candice. I hope you find the right guy soon."

# 19

I meander melancholically back to my desk. The rest of the Creative Team look like they're busy with the next deadline. Jamie's desk is empty, computer off, *Out To Lunch Till Tomorrow* sign displayed.

I flick through Ziggy's book, wondering if the personality test was just a glitch. Grabbing my pad, I begin doodling. I'm directionless. I've no idea how to think up a topic, too much spoon-feeding at work, university, school. What is it I want to write about?

My Quest for The Answer flashes back to me. I write *Quest* and underneath it *Answer?* then *Looking for what I'm looking for*, and the words solidify. Men and women, aimless, hapless, fruitless, sailing through life as if it's going to go on forever, when plainly it isn't. Do we all want to make our mark on the world or are some of us happy just to be happy? Or happy to be unhappy? I try to meld my thoughts into some sort of coherent catchy prose. My thoughts don't co-operate.

I think about my brothers' highly respected careers. Jamie's words *the magazine has to change, listen to any ideas* flood me with relief. I enjoy working here and don't intend on leaving. I check my current work list: I'm up to date for this issue and have a couple in reserve, so I have time to choose. But where should I take my words?

I finger the cover of Ziggy's book. Dating websites ask the hopefuls to describe themselves, but how much can we say if we don't actually know? How much would I have known about myself before the personality test? And how much do we keep hidden because it's not pretty? Should daters do a personality test with their results posted on their profile? Could you trust it was really who the person was? These are questions I might ask Ziggy on Friday night. Whatever Friday night turns out to be.

A brilliant idea rips into my brain. I have to call Kat.

"Hang on," she says breathlessly.

I hear shouting, then Kat comes back on the line.

"Hey, Can!" she breathes.

"What was that?"

"Thor was just finishing up."

"Eeuw!" Kat's so transparent. "I've got a favour to ask."

"Fire away."

"You need to see Ziggy."

She says something indistinct to Thor. "Who the fuck is Ziggy?"

"This psychologist I met on the weekend."

"Ah, the Hickey Master. Wait, shit, are you saying I need to see a psychologist? Fuck right off, Can, I-"

"Not like that. I want to know what you think of him. I'll pay."

"Sounds dangerous. What if he starts analysing me?"

"Treat it as a mission. Be an investigative spy."

"I like that. Agent Kat!"

"You need to make an appointment for tomorrow, Agent Kat. I'm seeing him again Friday."

"Can I make shit up?"

"You can be whoever you want. Just tell me what you think of him."

Kat snorts. "This is like when you were keen on Parker at school."

"Jeez, don't bring that up."

I hear her explaining things to Thor. *She followed this guy we'd been at school with for a month. Kept asking me to find out if he liked her. Had a one-nighter with him, then hung around so she didn't have to say it was a one-night stand. Said they'd dated for three days.*

"Kat! Don't give my secrets away! Kat!" It's true Parker broke my pride, but I don't even count him amongst my boyfriends. It was aimless casual sex with a guy who didn't care a hoot about me. "Can you make an appointment? You'll need to make sure it's an emergency appointment. There's this receptionist gatekeeper-"

She snorts. "Goodie, I love a challenge."

"Excellent. Let me know when you're successful. Oh, and Kat, the appointment might be early in the morning."

"Okay. I'll get Thor to rouse me. If you know what I mean."

I do.

She rings back five minutes later. "What is that woman's problem?"

"The phone bitch?"

"She needs to see a fucking psychologist!" She laughs. "Sure she's not fucking him?"

It's lovely to hear my old Kat back, the *frigs* now faded. But she mirrors my anxieties: why is the receptionist so possessive? "You're just the person to find out."

"I've got a nine o'clock appointment. For one hour."

"Any problem getting that?"

"Nope."

Interesting. Longer appointment, less fuss.

"I told her to give me an emergency appointment or I'd call the association." She sniggers. "Whatever that is."

For a second I worry I'm creating drama around Ziggy's business, a situation that might be irretrievable. I brush it off nervously. "Well done, Agent Kat."

She giggles.

I love the sound of it. I guess Thor does too, because I hear him in the background. "Now what's the Thunder God doing?"

"Nuzzling my neck." I can hear the smile in her voice.

"Do you guys do anything apart from-"

"Hey," she interjects, "if it's on offer, why say no?"

Indeed. "Thanks for tomorrow."

"I'll report as soon as I get out."

"Don't be surprised how much it costs. I'll give you the cash when I pick you up tonight for Harry K's."

"When's that?"

"Seven. Be at yours at ten to."

Her laugh is now a tinkle. "See you then, Can."

I'm feeling nervous about this ruse, so I give up on work, go home. My mobile rings as I walk into the flat.

Harry K. "Thanks for the text. Sorry I'm such a grump."

I'm startled. Harry K's not normally the pathetic piece he is currently. "Everything alright with Joanna?"

He sighs. "I didn't react well to the baby news. She's been crappy with me ever since."

"Having morning sickness can't help her mood."

"Maybe."

"Was it an accident?" Surely a doctor and his wife know about contraception, or is there a flaw in our family genes?

"She said it was time for another one then suddenly another one was on its way. I don't actually know this'll be the last, either."

Joanna, used to running the world her way. "K, she's not in charge."

Harry K laughs. "Of course she's bloody well in charge! You duffer. It's been like this since we started dating. I liked it at first. She was the only woman I'd ever had any respect for."

I frown at his words. "She needs to have a husband she respects, too. Stand up to her. You're a grown man."

"I don't want to rock the boat. She's so efficient at everything. I just leave it all up to her. If I want a say, she'll expect me to dib in."

"You lazy bastard," I laugh. "You get what you deserve. Want a break tonight? I'm seeing B with Kat. And Kat's new boyfriend."

He guffaws. "This one lasted more than a day?"

"Actually, I'm thinking this one might stick. For a while at least. Anyway, she's got some sales of her kitchenware designs-"

"No shit? Little Kat earning some money instead of using yours?"

Is that what he thinks? "She has money. I like to buy for her."

"So long as you're not buying her friendship."

I pause. That one hurt.

"You could've bought a place by now if you'd saved more. Throwing your money away on rent, when you could've been at home."

"Like you were?"

"Yes, like I was."

Methinks Harry K has gone from one mother to the next. "I need my space, K. It was different when we were all together."

Which is true. Harry K was seventeen when his mother's boyfriend moved in, so we started to see a lot more of him. Sylvie remarried when he was twenty, and he decided living full-time with us was a lot better for his temper. He left home at thirty-two when he married Joanna.

Harry B left at thirty-four. At which time I was almost twenty-two. Being the only one at home was odd without the big bustling brothers around. Mum and Dad are lovely, but gradually the need to get out was too much. I think about my rent, how much of a hole it makes in my pay, and how much I could've put away by now.

"Candice? Sorry. What were you saying about Kat?"

I know Harry K hates to hurt people's feelings, especially Kat's, whom he respects deeply. "Harry B's looking over the contracts tonight. I can pick you up, too, if you want a break."

"Nah. With a bit of luck the kids will be exhausted by their party last night, which will leave Joanna free for my own selfish needs. No morning glory for us right now."

Jeez. When did the world get so obsessed with:

1. having sex,

2. talking about sex, and

3. filling me in about their sex?

His voice turns serious. "What you said about valuing my opinion?"

"Yeah?"

"You mean that?"

"Of course I did."

"Thanks."

I hear him smiling. "I love you, you silly bugger."

"Me, too." He pauses. "And hey, I love you, as well." He snorts, then hangs up.

I stick on a load of washing. My Spinster Flat is looking increasingly unloved. I flop onto my bed, feeling like a dot on a page. How much do we know about each other, all of us nibbling away at our own lives, carrying on in our own unexamined manner? All the self-assured ones like Joanna and Ziggy, all the irrepressible ones like Kat and Jamie, all the intellectuals like Harry B and Thor, all the lost lambs like Rupert and Harry K. And which category do I fit into?

Freezer fare for dinner, home-made soup from the veggie patch glut we had a while back. I pick some parsley as garnish and dig down to find a fair-sized Sebago under an overgrown potato plant.

Soon my soup is micro-waved, my toast popped, my potato mashed and salted. The garden's my Hero, I'm sure you see. After dinner I bung my pjs on, forgetting completely I'm picking up Kat in a half hour.

I start to compile a list for my Physical Union Self Satisfaction Indicator. First I'll start with the developmental stages of sex:

1. Ignorance: The bliss before you blossom.

2. Enlightenment: Finding out the incomprehensible truth. It goes where?

3. Inexperience: More incomprehensibility. You want to do what how?

4. Apex: Finding The One, if you're lucky.

5. Apathy: Hormones run out of steam. TV is a better option.

I laugh. I wonder if there is a Sex Inventory. Or would it be called a Sex Instrument? Imagine searching for that on the internet! There's a knock at the door. Probably Laurie. I open my blinds a little and see Gene standing there with a forced smile and a bunch of flowers.

Fuck. I stay quiet, hoping he'll think nobody's home.

"I saw the blinds move, Candice."

Fuckety fuck-fuck.

Now I'm watching myself. I see a woman worrying how to kindly rebuke a man who dumped her after he was unfaithful. Who had sex with her because he didn't know any other way to make it up to her that he'd fallen in love with someone else. Who texted her a message that he'd intended for his new love, then made it look like he was innocent. Who asked if he could move in while his heart was attached elsewhere.

I fling open the door. It protests with a groan.

Gene smiles contentedly. He waits for me to open the screen door.

I stay still, my sourness escalating.

"Candice?" He pathetically peers through the screen. "You have every right to be mad with me." He holds out the flowers, smiles ingratiatingly. "Sweetie? Let's talk. I can fix it."

I slam the door hard. Sweetie doesn't like to be called Sweetie.

He knocks again. "Candice! Let me make it up to you."

I can't speak. If I speak, he'll find a way to wheedle his way back into my life. He's always fed me those lines that are hypnotic to lost women: *You're the best, You complete me, You're my soul-mate, You're the other half of me.* He looked adoringly at me, was grateful for me, made me feel special. This startles me: was this an act? I remember how he was when he came to tell me he'd slept with the other woman, looking for my sympathy! I grab paper, write *FUCK OFF OR I'LL CALL THE POLICE* on it and slip it under the door.

After a moment, he knocks harder. "I love you! Open the door!" He pauses, shouts again. "I'm not leaving until you take me back!"

Time for action. My anger wants to punch him in the face, but I concoct a better plan. I hear his tender words of love and yearning over the running tap, and I see him smile triumphantly as I open the doors.

He's dazzled by a full bucket of water in his face.

"Oh, you poor dear," I laugh. "Did your iddy-biddy slutty-pants whore-bitch girlfriend throw you out?"

He's struggling to breathe. "She … I …"

"Go home, loser. There's nothing here for you. Never was."

His expression changes as he attempts to retrieve the situation. "I love you. I was just scared of you. You're so, so-"

"Ah, what every woman wants to hear. That she's so-so. Well, you're a stupid so-and-so." I twist the bucket childishly, feeling its lighter weight. Man, that felt good.

But I have no energy left. I turn at my door as he walks morosely up the driveway, the flowers a sodden mess dragging from his hand. The joy of action wears off, and I feel no glow of victory. *Victorious.* Wasn't that something to do with Ziggy's name? I don't remember.

I look at my watch, six-forty-five. Shit! I'd forgotten about Kat!

I run inside, chase on my clothes, grin as I walk past the puddle that looks, ironically, like Gene's face, and drive to Kat's.

# 20

Harry B welcomes us all with a hug, even Thor, who he's never met before. That's Harry B, always warm and happy.

"Which of you lucky babes does this hunk belong to?" he chuckles, his eyes grazing across Thor.

Thor is dressed in a grey short-sleeved shirt, tie, and navy pants. He's a man dressed to meet a lawyer. My brother, the lawyer, is dressed in past-the-knees skater shorts and a black t-shirt that says *Love Your Lawyer* on the front and *Just Don't Get Court* on the back.

"He's all mine." Kat smiles in a way she would've laughed at before Thor.

"Jeez, mate," says Harry B incredulously. "Taming the Big Kat. Are you extremely rich or enviably well hung?"

Kat and Thor laugh. I get the idea he's not far from the truth. And I don't think Thor's in the money from the look of his car.

I pull out a bottle of red from the rack next to the pantry.

"Want a straw with that?" Harry B asks. "What's up, little sis? This guy get you hot and horny, too? What's happened to the sexy nurse?"

"Lay off, B." Gene is the last person I want to talk about. I pour four glasses, walk across and hand one each to Kat and Thor.

Kat takes both. I return to mine on the bench and take a good gulp.

"Thor doesn't drink," Kat says casually.

I spray wine across the bench. "What the fuck?"

Kat giggles. "What the *frig,* Can."

I wipe my mouth. "You know she drinks, right?" I ask Thor.

"And swears." Kat has sculled half of one of the glasses already.

"You want debauchery done right, you go to Kat," Harry B grins.

"I wouldn't have her any other way." Thor puts his arm round her, squeezing her towards him.

I clean the bench, take the wines to the table and slide in next to B.

"Got the contracts, Kat?" asks Harry B.

She plops them on the table from a bag at her feet. She sculls the rest of the first glass of wine. "I've got a business name. *Pussy Kat.*"

Harry B guffaws loudly. "*Pussy* has so many connotations." He wipes a laughter tear from his eye. "Which one are you going for?"

"I'm reclaiming *Pussy,*" she points a finger against the table. "You guys have had a hold on it too long." She sculls half of the second glass.

"Too long's never long enough when you're talking pussy," Harry B smiles. "All day and all night isn't long enough to have a hold on pussy."

"My brother's a dirty-minded, foul-mouthed intellectual," I tell Thor. "Ever been around any of those before?"

Thor is speechless.

Harry B focuses on Kat's contracts. "Kat, you signed this one? Don't sign any more without asking me. For fuck's sake!"

"What's up?" I ask.

"She's getting two lousy per cent on her designs."

"That one's just the salad servers. But they want more. Plates, cake servers and stuff." Kat's looking at me with a *please interpret* expression.

"Nup," says Harry B. "They're hoping you don't know your rights. How much is a pair of salad servers, maybe twenty bucks?"

"Probably more, mine are—"

"You're going to make forty cents on each one. They double that price, you get eighty cents but they sell less. They sell one thousand, you get four hundred, they get almost twenty thousand. They make them overseas; production costs are small. They make your money."

"But they cashed me up with a hundred thou," whines Kat.

Harry B waggles his head. "Mmm. That's bait. They reckon that'll be enough to stop you looking further." He stares at her intently. "Once you sell two hundred and fifty thousand sets you start to make more money. That's a fuck of a lot of salad servers." He sits back, puts his hands behind his head, thinking. "When can you make an appointment to see them with me?"

"Will you represent her?" Thor finds his voice.

Harry B gathers the papers. "You bet. Leave it with me, Kitty-Kat. Make an appointment to attend with your lawyer, then ring and tell Timothy when you need me. He'll shift whatever I have at that time."

"Thank you," says Thor reverently.

"Yeah, thanks, you big legal son-of-a-bitch," laughs Kat.

"That's my mother you're talking about," I smile.

The doorbell rings. "That'll be my eight o'clock early." Harry B grins and hurries to the door.

A tall, slender blonde with high heels and a skin-tight dress the colour of her lipstick appears. She's carrying a shopping bag with a crusty loaf peeking out of the top. "Am I early, Harry?" she says sweetly, frowning at us at the table.

"No, it's fine. This is my sister Candice, her best friend Kat, and Kat's boyfriend, Thor. They were just about to leave," he tells us.

"And this is?" I keep my smile to myself.

"Andy," says Harry B. "Andrea."

The woman smiles radiantly. "Hello, Candice. Lovely to meet you. I've heard all about you."

"Now off you go, you lot," says Harry B. "Kat, I'll get back to you with the changes, you can look them over before we meet with the company. You got an email address yet?" She shakes her head. "Jeez. Where are the good old days when you had some technology spunk?"

"Didn't need it once I left school," Kat shrugs.

"Send it to my email." I corral her and Thor towards the door. "Enjoy the wine, B."

"Nice meeting you," Thor tells Andy affably. "See you next time."

Harry B winks as we exit.

As we walk to the car Thor asks, "You didn't chat with Andy? Was there something wrong?"

"There's no point getting attached to any of Harry B's girlfriends."

"She wishes she was his girlfriend," says Kat. "Probably midway through her tenancy in B's life, by the look of her."

"Harry B's commitment phobic." I climb into the driver's seat as Kat and Thor get into the back. "He keeps them until they get sick of the fling not going anywhere, then they leave, and he gets another one. Harry's smart, loaded, and extremely lazy." I start the car and tilt my rear vision mirror, catch a glimpse of Thor looking sadly at Kat.

"Love needs to know where it's headed."

I groan inwardly.

"He calls you Kitty-Kat?" Thor asks suspiciously.

"Don't get anything in your head about me and B."

I see Thor beam in the rear-view mirror. We don't talk any more about contracts or Harry B or love, instead I prep Kat on seeing Ziggy. "Don't tell him you're my friend."

"I'm a random client needing emergency rescue," she giggles.

That sounds dangerous.

"Tell him you've got a work issue," suggests Thor.

"What kind of work?" Kat asks me eagerly. "Can I make up something?"

"Stay away from work issues. Talk about the wardrobe you live in."

Thor says, "Talk about us moving in together. Ask if it's too soon or if we can go ahead." It's obvious which option Thor's rooting for.

"You know me," Kat cackles. "I've got a talent for making shit up."

"It's the creative spirit within you," Thor says rapturously.

"It's my fucking parents." Kat's voice is venomous. "I learnt from the best."

I wonder, as I wave them goodbye, why Kat wants to stay the night at her place if she's keen to move in with Thor. Perhaps she feels safe there given Harry B's revelations about the contracts. As I drive home,

I think how big Thor is in that little room. Kat is the fairy living in a mushroom house, Thor's the friendly giant. A giant who'd have trouble fitting into that mushroom house. But as Kat says, they don't take up mush-room together. I hope there's a fairy tale ending.

My phone beeps. Gene. *Please let me see you I think we can go forward from here you'll always be the one Gene x.* I laugh, and, as a joke, reply *Was this meant for me?* The incorrigible answer of *Sorry, no* makes my brain steam. I feel the bucket in my hand again and wished I'd finished by ramming it onto his head.

I turn into my driveway and stride into the flat where Ziggy's book lays analysing my anger. Unwavering now, I search the index for the WiMPI, find it's a relatively recent addition to the barrage of personality inventories. The main criticisms are its questions don't counter situational effects, and it places too much emphasis on traits which can change over time. I skim other pages, see there are much more reliable inventories. I wonder why the WiMPI was chosen. I find a chapter on *Choosing A Test.* It's cheap in relation to other tests. I've found my reason: the parent company that owns the magazine doesn't condone spending money if it's not required by law.

I hang out my washing from hours before, then get into my pjs again, feeling sad. I've been thrown off course by an idiotic, ill-informed inventory. But I haven't done any better myself, pushing my Self down tracks I shouldn't have followed. My thoughts flow back to my parents. How did they trust themselves when they were in the middle of the Open Day meeting, where all answers led to heartbreak, a large portion of which would be ladled out to themselves?

I fall asleep almost as soon as my head hits the pillow, but I wake often. At four, I realise I haven't seen Laurie or Rupert for two days. I feel alone and afraid without their man-guard on either side of me. I get up and spill my thoughts onto some paper.

# 21

At seven I see I've jotted down all manner of crap.

*Is Harry K in trouble? Mid-life crisis? Marriage ok? New baby okay?*

*Can Harry B save Kat from the mean company? Why was Andy bringing him food?*

*Is Thor incredibly well-hung? Is he the man for Kat?*

*Is that the end of Gene?*

*What was going through Mum's head as she broke her vow of celibacy? What was Dad thinking in the moment he started having extramarital sex with a stranger? Didn't either of them think about his wife? Didn't they think about pregnancy? Didn't they think about condoms and safe sex?*

*Is Daisy the woman for Rupert? Will Denise be Laurie's last wife? Can you tell any of this so early in a relationship?*

The worst one sits at the tippy-top.

*What will happen when Kat meets Ziggy?*

All reason has left me. I grab Ziggy's note that's still on top of the book, call the number listed. It comes up as *Ziggy*. No wonder I haven't seen his name in my contact list: it's at the end. When his voice pops past the ringtone, I know I've woken him up. "Ziggy, it's Candice."

"I know."

I frown. "Did you put your number in my phone?"

"Yes. Saturday night. Well, Sunday morning. You insisted."

Crap. I could've called him direct instead of making an appointment. But would I have done that when his demand was to call him as soon as I was single? And why didn't I realise he must've given me his contact details to be able to call him? Now I'm even more unsettled. "Thanks for sending the book."

"I hope it helps." His voice is friendly but there's no gushing of the warm affection I fought off on the weekend.

"Sorry I woke you up."

"That's okay. I have an early appointment, anyway."

Kat. Gulp.

"Don't be too fussed what personality you are, Candice. You're you, and that's all you need to be."

"I'll see you tomorrow?"

"See you then. When's your appointment?"

"Six."

I hear a smile in his voice. "Make it six-thirty. I always run over by the end of the day."

That's an extremely *evening* time to start our appointment. "Do you always work late?"

"I work as I need to."

Now I'm worried about Kat's appointment. "Ziggy, sometimes life is incomprehensible. I hope you understand that."

I hear bemusement in his silence. "It's what I deal with every day. See you tomorrow. Look forward to it." He hangs up quickly.

There's no relief in the call. No:

*How lovely to hear from you.*

*You're the best woman in the whole wide world.*

*I can't wait until you're in my arms.*

Dale and Monty are right. Romance is a programme, and mine has a glitch.

In the shower I wonder if the book is merely helpful assistance from psychologist to client. Or a reaching out to show he cares. A reminder that he exists. As if that's necessary.

I mooch my way to work. We have a full contingent today. Jamie calls a meeting and, as we thresh around ideas for change, I quietly observe the others. Terri looks like she's won the lottery. Jamie has the broadest grin I've ever seen him wear. Even Martin is pleased to see me. I see a lot of Harry K in Martin. I hope he's doing better than K. And, hmmm, Clarissa looks exceedingly well for someone who's been off sick, is overly animated in the meeting.

I follow her into the toilet afterwards. "Got something to 'fess, love pumpkin?"

She spins and grins. "It shows, huh?"

"Jeez, it's written all over your pretty face." I'm gobsmacked. "Really? Messin' with the boss-man?"

She beams shyly. "Last Friday we were the last to leave, after we did that stupid personality test day. He was grumpy because of the test, and I told him to lighten up." She giggles. "He said his lawyer was negotiating for his ex-wife to pay for the divorce and he didn't know the outcome. I said, *Is it very expensive?* And he said it was the principle of the thing, so I said, *Hey, let's go for a drink then, I'm not doing anything.*" She smiles brightly. "Turns out I was doing *everything.*"

"No wonder he's happy and distracted. Does anyone else know?"

"Are you kidding? Martin's always head-down, bum-up, and I have no idea what's going on for Terri. She's humming, smiling, happy. What gives?"

"Ah, ah, ah. I'm the keeper of secrets."

She smiles broadly. "Then keep mine."

I mime locking my lips. "Why were you off work?"

"Cystitis. Honeymooner's disease. In bed and on antibiotics. Don't want to get that ever again."

"Please," I flinch. "Sometime in the future I want to be able to take him seriously again. He's my boss!"

We return to our desks. Terri eyes me warily.

"I'm the keeper of secrets," I pronounce. She and Clarissa smile and glance away. I wheel over to Martin's desk. "What's your news?"

"What do you mean?" His Neanderthal brow knits.

"I just thought … never mind." I feel the hair on the back on my neck rise and I turn, knowing the call I've been waiting for is coming in even before the phone rings. I wheel back to my desk, huddle with my phone to my ear.

"Hey, Can." Kat's voice is sombre.

My stomach flips. "How'd it go?"

"Oh, sweetie, he's lovely! Gorgeous eyes. Looks right through to your soul." She pauses. "Wanna meet me for an early lunch?"

"Sure. Our regular?"

"Already here."

Something niggles me as I drive to Buddy's. Kat sounded subdued. But she said he was *lovely*. And Gene has scarred me: was there any chemistry between Kat and Ziggy? Not that Kat's ever done me wrong in the loyalty department. And she's more wrapped up in Thor than I've ever seen her with anyone.

She gives me a warm hug as I arrive. "Door bitch is in love with him, for sure. He's got no clue. I'd get rid of her asap."

I breathe out slowly. "How'd the session go?"

"He started by asking why I was there."

"Of course." My nerves ping again.

"I deflected, asked if his real name was Sigmund."

I can't remember if I told Kat that or not. "And?"

"He got me to call him Ziggy. Zbigniew's his name for real. Fuck, Can, don't change your name to Zbigniew. Candice Zbigniew. Shit!"

I swallow hard, my chest aching.

"Anyway, he asked again why I was there." She chuckles. "I know I was supposed to ask him about Thor, but I wanted to see what he was made of. So I said, *What if I don't want to answer that?*"

"Good answer, Agent Kat. Then what happened?"

"Didn't faze him. Just smiled at me in a kind, gentle way and said, *Okay, I'll start asking you some easy questions and you can answer whenever you feel comfortable. And we'll see where we go. Is that okay?*"

I smile in spite of myself. "Good answer, Dr Zbigniew."

"I started wise cracking. He said, *So, you're twenty-eight?* and I said, *I knew that already, what am I paying you for?* He asked if I lived at home and I told him about my parents." Kat abruptly tears up.

This takes me by surprise. Kat has always ignored the fact her estranged parents are drug-addled drunks who are regularly unemployed and destitute. She always came to high school without food or drink, often smelling of beer and cigarettes.

Our friendship was the making of both of us, I'm sure you see that now, the anxious me gently prodding her to give up smoking and sharing my lunch (Mum began packing double), the rebellious her teaching me how to stand up for myself. It's been a symbiotic relationship and there's never been any revelation we haven't been able to handle together. "What happened?"

She doesn't look at me. "I told him where I live and how I live, and about Thor. He asked how old I'd been when I'd left home, why I'd left home that early, so I told him everything." A quiet sob escapes her mouth. "He was so marvellous, Candice. It all came out, and I'm going back to see him Monday but you don't have to pay, I just want this fixed." She grabs a serviette and bawls loudly into it.

I'm mute. My Kat, *my Kat* is a mess. I've never seen her like this.

She wipes her nose and eyes, grabs another serviette, looks at me, her bottom lip quivering. "Well, don't just sit there-"

"Kat, I'm just … I don't know what to say."

She laughs softly. "You, the wordsmith, at a loss for words? Must be big stuff." Her face dissolves again.

I put my hand on her arm. "Let's go down to the beach."

We walk down the stairs and sit on a rock, our feet in the sand. She's full of energy now. *He asked me this* and *How did I feel about that* and *Where do I do that in my life?* "Oh, and here's the change."

"Keep it," I say as she digs into her pocket, my head trying to wrap itself around Ziggy's impact. I see a fifty dollar note on top of other notes. I flick at it, try to add it up. "What did he charge you?"

"Sixty. Said if I went to the doctor they'd cover me for his cost."

I frown. "He charged me over two hundred."

Kat's eyes are wide. "Two hundred! Fuck off!"

I grimace. How much is a visit to a psychologist usually? "What did he say about Thor?"

"Things are amazing with Thor," she sighs. "I told Ziggy he's one of the best things going for me. Apart from you, of course. And I didn't mention you by name. I haven't officially moved in with Thor, although he wants me to. Says he wants me out of that room. He's so protective," she smiles sweetly. "I'm staying there tonight. His parents are a lot like yours. Calm. Accepting. Welcoming."

When Kat first moved out of home Mum insisted she stay with us. Kat refused, as always making sure she relied on the only person she could trust absolutely. Over the years she's rented rooms in a number of houses, each time choosing a smaller and smaller and cheaper and cheaper room until she moved into her current hole five years ago. I didn't believe she could live in such a tiny place. I rented a two-bedroom flat in case she needed to move in and yes, I'm still looking after Kat but she's my Best Friend. She never agrees to move in, telling me she'd be *trouble*. My question now is obvious: is she running to A Better Future, or away from Poverty And Loneliness?

"Anyway," she continues, "Ziggy would like me to hold off making major life decisions before we talk more on Monday. I trust him, Can." She giggles happily. "Can can, too."

# 22

The afternoon passes in a blur. Back at the office I work on writing something new, something bold and brash, something daring.

Nothing comes. The screen is blank and remains so. My mind is floating on a haze of Ziggy. It's been only two days since I saw him, but it feels like two years. My hunger for him is now excruciating, and I don't mean in a sexual way. I miss the connection from Saturday afternoon. The connection we didn't seem to have on the phone this morning.

Terri tells me Jamie's approved a week's leave. MuscleMan has asked her to accompany him as he jets around the country. Her eyes are luminous with love, her mouth creeping into a smile at odd moments. This morning, when I asked if she wanted a coffee, she said *I'll follow you in* and unloaded how completely overwhelmed she was with the way she was feeling.

She's been single since she had a face-off with her boyfriend last year. He played the I-never-said-anything-about-marriage card. She aced him with the I'm-off-then card. He countered with the I've-discovered-I-can't-live-without-you card, only to be beaten by her Too-bad-I've-figured-out-how-good-I-feel-without-you card.

I wonder where her goal of being married fits into this current episode. The fact Jamie gave her a week's leave at a minute's notice demonstrates how generous he's feeling. Mostly thanks to Clarissa and the bank account of his ex-wife's new boyfriend.

Vision Quests abound.

Given the copious number of romances engulfing me, I return to my own Vision Quest at home to deconstruct my feelings for Ziggy. I'm getting quite good at this analysis thing.

| Episode | Effect | + / - |
| --- | --- | --- |
| Helped me up when I fell over at pub. | HeroMan status | + |
| Flattered me when he helped me up. | Made me feel good. | + |
| Bought food. | Looked after me. | + |
| Said "She's mine". Called me "girl". | Owning me. Youth-icising me. | - - |
| Persistent in blind-date adversity. | A nice trait. | + |
| Took me on a date. Looked after me when I was drunk. | Looking after me (again). | ++ |
| Didn't take advantage of me. | Expected. But still, a nice trait. | + |
| Refused to let me cheat on boyfriend. | See above. | + |
| Had a counselling session. Stuck by the rules. | More evidence he's honest and plays fair. | ++ |
| Charged me over $200 for session. | WTF? | ? |
| Kat approves of him. | Very, very important. | +++ |
| He supported Kat. | See above. | +++ |
| He's seeing me Friday. | ? | ???? |

I bring in my washing, fold it and put it away. All the while my mind wallows in Jamie and Thor and the Harrys and MuscleMan, pushing my curiosity about men to the furthest of limits until it all contracts down in a Big Crunch to a singularity: tomorrow's appointment with Ziggy.

The Vision Quest is entering a new phase. I admit I'm nervous. All week I've been hooked into Ziggy's campaign on Saturday and

Sunday to woo me, but now he's seen the meddling, panicked, manic, drunken woman with no idea about herself. How could a man with his credentials be attracted to such an abhorrent set of personality traits?

I make myself a strong coffee and pour it into an old mug of Kat's. She had a couple of years of pottery to perfect her designs in the real world. It was one of the only times she's stuck at anything since high school. She made a set of mugs on which you can fit a regularly-used throw-away lid (like from cream or yoghurt), therefore giving them a second use and making sure if you broke one lid, you could readily replace it. I get a lid out of my stash and bung it on, take the car down to the beach.

Buddy's is ahead of me, the scene of so much laughter and so many tears, mostly mine. It's closed for the night, so I saunter down to the soft sand below. I sit on a rock in the twilight as the fading blue of the day battles the slate of night. I feel palpably alone, and not in a good way. My stomach's swirling, my head's blanketed in doubt. Everything's changing and I can't see the end. *Courage, Candice.* Who can? Apparently Can can. I have to take that hope with me into an uncertain future.

Two flies begin having sex on my knee. Even insects have their romance shit working, the boy fly rubbing his grubby little hands together as he watches the unsuspecting female, then saying *oh, yeah, baby, that feels so good,* as the girl says *Are you done yet?* I shoo them off and concentrate on Ziggy as I sip my coffee.

Common sense tells me I'm in for a very big fall tomorrow. I haven't had such a connection since, hmmm, when? I wheel my analysis back across the panorama of my boyfriends:

> 1. *Jake Holly.* Sports jock. Together five months. Last year of high school. First sex. But I heard he'd scored points with Verity Hogan after a tennis round-robin. Rumour was it was Love-all. He didn't deny it but was surprisingly heartbroken when I finished it. Called me several times

daily, said it was harmless flirting (except for the times they got naked), offered to marry me (we were seventeen), begged me to give him a second go (when he'd already had a second go by screwing Verity). They married later but it broke up after a year.

1.2. *Parker Price*, Pretentious Prick. Year after high school finished. From our class. Six-pack brought out the bad girl in me. Lasted three days. Yes it did, regardless of what Kat thinks. I employed Kat's assistance in remedying the call of my infatuated loins after a chance encounter with the bather-clad Parker at the beach. Smelling easy meat, he invited me for lunch because his parents had left on a cruise. Pretty satisfying lunch might have turned into a pretty satisfying relationship if it wasn't for the *I'm not looking for a girlfriend* every ten minutes and the absence of any attention in between sexual escapades. He'd shag me and then watch television or read a book or even call a friend until he realised I was still there. I stayed overnight, hoping my continued presence would ignite the same torrid flame in his heart that I felt in mine. I don't list him as a boyfriend because, hey, three days. Saw him on a television commercial about a year later then he slipped from view.

1.3. *Costa Post*. Gay. Vomit Night. Enough said.

2. *Jaron Wyatt*. Two and a half years from when I was twenty. Meek, shy, sweet, intellectual. I thought of dropping him often because he never wanted to go out. Then he got diagnosed with agoraphobia. I loyally stayed with him to get him through. His doctor's advice was to get rid of me. I bawled for a week.

3. *Ben Klemsky*. I was a week shy of twenty-five. Lasted one year, twelve days, three hours. Everything going well, then nothing. No other woman. No reasons given. No gossip.

Just *I don't love you anymore*. Kat took me out drinking. Hangover suitable replacement for rejection pain.

4. *Bryce Brody*. Started a few weeks after my relationship with Ben imploded. Kat and I were playing a wicked game of wrong-handed tennis on account of the fact we'd found two all-white tennis dresses at a second-hand store. They seemed to be mother and daughter dresses, which was perfect for us except Kat's was a little long and mine was a little short. Bryce, playing on the next court, was intrigued by our antics and the repeated glimpse of my sparkling white knickers. Relationship lasted eight weird months. Goaded on by the tennis dress-up, he told me I'd look great as this and that superhero. I got sick of being a plaything, so I ended it. He walked outside my driveway each day for a week dressed as William Shakespeare, with *Candice* painted across his codpiece.

4.1. *Homer Johnson*. I was closing in on twenty-seven. Lasted just shy of a month, so I don't include him in my boyfriends tally either. I'm just mentioning him because he was the jerk who made me decide to give up on the whole man thing until Gene came along. Homer had a chip on his shoulder. Was writing The Next Great Novel. Almost put me off journalism. Also played tennis (Another tennis guy. Don't see a pattern, just bad luck). Was going to be The Next Best Tennis Player. I was simply an addendum to his life. I got out of that one fast.

I look up from my thoughts. Dusk has transformed into evening. I stand up and pour the remnants of my coffee onto the sand, feeling better for the fresh air and worse for the review of my romantic bruises.

My Vision Quest has done little except add to my confusion. Does there exists any mechanism for the attainment of a true Purpose?

My feelings of bewilderment deepen.

# 23

I walk heavily up the stairs cradling Kat's mug, remembering the existential texts I studied in high school and university. The pointlessness of purpose, humans as automatons run by mental templates, religion as an anaesthetic. It's obvious most of my Quest since Saturday has been about Ziggy's feelings for me rather than the guidance he's supplied, in spite of my protests regarding romance. I've fallen back into the same trap as always, looking for someone to solve my Life with Love. It's a game in my mind, now, the hollow echo of existentiality versus the full bloom of courtship. And the winner is …

Romance, the drug of the female population.

Is romance a means to an end or the end itself? Why do romance novels always prompt us to expect love to be a difficult journey, one where we have to learn a lesson before we're worthy of another person's heart? Because we've all read books, haven't we, where we know the two protagonists are going to fall in love and sort out their differences, but we go along for the ride anyway. The final *And they lived happy ever after* page is our reward for traveling alongside them.

Crap. This is what I've been thinking as I've fallen in love each time. It wasn't until Homer that I surveyed the critical damage. The Chorus of Husbands from the pub that very first day of my Vision Quest were right about wedding planning. I'd been going out with Jake for a fortnight when I started checking out my signature as *Candice Holly*. Each time, I was over the moon. Candice Wyatt, Candice Klemsky,

Candice Brody. Even, I'm sorry to say, Candice Price. Each time I began a relationship I was certain I could never feel as I felt for Jake/Jaron/Ben/Bryce/Parker/Homer. How can I possibly believe, after so much failure, that any man could be It?

And then there was Gene. Certainly not It. Which brings me back to Ziggy, a guy unlike any other I've dated. Can I say we dated? One spontaneous lunch, one drunken visit to his cousin's wedding, one psychologist session. Methinks *dating* is a misnomer.

I think of Kat's first lovemaking with Thor. In the middle of a non-date. Yet they seem happy together. My parents first date was also a non-date, just a chance meeting at school drop-off. And what would Terri call her impromptu shagging of MuscleMan? Hardly a date. Yet the connections have all continued.

MuscleMan had a small part playing a nice guy in his first movie, and I wonder if this set Terri up to think he is that nice guy. How can you believe an actor is telling you the truth? The answer comes quickly: it's the intensity of their gaze that makes you think you have the real them before you. I had that with Ziggy. And here I am, back to Ziggy again.

Maybe it's not my life that's going off-track, maybe it's me.

I roll over to my parents' house. This time they're alone, playing an old record and sharing a champagne on the back verandah. Mum pours me a glass and Dad fetches me a chair, both smiling at me lovingly.

"I know you've told me the story a million times about how you both knew you had something special right from the start but tell me the whole story. The whole, whole story. Was it love at first sight?"

Mum laughs. "I thought he was simply friendly."

"And handsome," smiles Dad.

Mum laughs. "Yes, handsome." She cups his cheek in her hand. "So very, very handsome."

Although this story reeks of betrayal and infidelity, I love the intimacy of its retelling, the inevitability of me.

Mum continues. "It was only when I was walking back to my car and heard him call my name that I knew we were on a crash course for trouble." She laughs. "We talked for ages at our cars-"

"Wasn't it an Open Day? Where were the Harrys?"

"Transition Day. We had to pick them up at the end of the day."

"We had our own transition day," Dad grins from behind his champagne glass.

"I thought you were looking for a school," I say.

"The Harrys had already won their scholarships."

Mum grins at Dad. "We spent the day together, one moment following another. A long chat at our cars after dropping off the boys, deciding to go for coffee, taking one car there, getting back into the car afterwards and kissing." Mum smiles shyly, sips her champagne.

I feel unusually uncomfortable about the discourtesy of their amour. "How does that work, deciding to kiss a guy who's married? After having nobody for all those years?"

Dad speaks for her. "We kept finding innocent things to do with each other. We went bowling-"

"Three games," Mum interjects. "We had one, then didn't know what to do so we had another game. And then another. By then our hands were sore and we had to find something else."

"The local Art Gallery was next." Dad relives the thrill of that day. "We held hands. I kissed her in a quiet corner."

This is more than they've revealed before. "A little public for the start of an affair, Dad?"

"I said that," Mum reminds him. "*We should stop. We're in public.* And you said, *But if we were doing this in private we'd be in trouble.*"

"We had to figure out what would happen when we picked up the boys," Dad continues. "Neither of us was talking a future."

"We decided to avoid each other." Mum smiles at Dad. "Not talk to each other. But I gave you my number anyway."

I smile. "In case he wanted to share parenting experiences with you."

Dad shrugs, swirls his champagne in the glass. "When she gave me her number, I knew I'd call. I knew straight away." He takes a long gulp.

"But what did you tell Sylvie? Did you lie?"

Dad shrugs again but his mood has dipped. "I took Harry K and his friend Dougie to Transition Day because Dougie's parents worked full-time. The boys decided to sleep at Dougie's. When I got back from dropping them off, Sylvie was immersed in her work. I said I was going out; she didn't even look up. It was time to move on."

"And you were turning thirty."

Dad sighs. "Yes, there was that, and Harry was going to high school and he didn't need me as much. But honestly, it was simply that I couldn't escape the pull of your mother. I sat at the beach for a few minutes, thinking about what I was about to do, then I made the call."

"And we met for a drink," continues Mum.

"And that was it," adds Dad.

They're gazing into each other's eyes. I sip my champagne quietly.

Mum begins again. "We were rambling about school and the Harrys and we both knew it was never going to be just a drink."

"We got to the hotel room so we could both take turns saying *We shouldn't be here like this*," Dad laughs, "and eventually we couldn't bear it any longer. I got home early in the morning. Sylvie said she'd forgive me. A couple of weeks went by where I knew very well that she hadn't."

I frown. "Then you found out I was on the way."

Mum looks bashful. "I didn't know what to do. All I could think of was your father. And now I was carrying his child. I couldn't believe my luck! Getting pregnant both times I'd had sex!"

I blush for her. I blush for me, too, the product of a night of adulterous fornication.

Dad laughs. "She didn't tell me about you until after I'd left Sylvie."

"If I hadn't been conceived you would've still left?" I ask eagerly.

"Yes. But the Harrys were in the same class. It was going to be a mess. We couldn't hide the fact, when the school year started, that we were having a baby together." He grins, raises his almost empty glass to me. "You made it easier, in some ways. Although not for Harry K."

Here's the thing: I've never felt like anything but a bonus prize. Harry K has always been glad to have a little sister. It was Dad he was cross at. K apparently called my mother a whore the first time he stayed with her. Didn't know what it meant, just heard it from Sylvie and thought it was what you called a stepmother.

"Why didn't you ever get married?" I ask.

"We were too busy," Dad says.

I'm intrigued by Mum's smile. "What?"

"My sixtieth is coming up," says Dad. "We're making it official before then."

"You're getting married? When were you going to tell me?"

"We're telling you now," Mum smiles.

Oh crap, I've interrupted their planning session. That's why they were sitting out the back playing the old music. The reason we're drinking champagne. Why they're more than happy to re-live the past.

"That's the problem with kids," I remark. "They think their parents are doing nothing but waiting around for them to visit." I hold up my glass. "To love." They clink their glasses with mine. "I hope you're going to ask me to be bridesmaid. And best man."

"Sorry to disappoint you," smiles Mum. "You can't be both. I recommend you be bridesmaid."

"I guess we're a team, the Harrys and me, so I'll let them join the fun." My face falls. "You wouldn't make Harry K your best man and Harry B your groomsman, would you, Dad?"

"Don't be ridiculous. They'll be the Best Men," he laughs.

"And I want two bridesmaids," says Mum. "You and Kat."

I burst into tears. Mum does, too. Dad follows. What a lot of sentiment. Who said I wasn't in touch with my emotions?

# 24

I arrive home excited about my parent's upcoming nuptials, what kid isn't? But the single glass of champagne has unsettled my stomach, and I haven't eaten since I saw Kat. Except then we didn't eat, just went down to the beach. So breakfast was it. What was that? Toast and honey and a cup of tea. Not much nutrition in my day.

The fridge reveals cheese. Ham. Well, I'm an experienced cook. And an ex-food critic for the magazine. A toasted sandwich it is. I pop out to the garden and pick some cherry tomatoes and a few leaves of basil. Thank goodness for the garden, my safety net in the chaos of my life.

The bread is just crusts. It's nine now, too late for the shops but maybe Rupert or Laurie are still up.

No answer at either place.

I sit down with a jolt on Laurie's doorstep. They're not home, again. I know where they are. And I know Laurie will move in with Denise and Rupert will move in with Daisy and I'll be here alone. *Alone.* The word echoes in my head. I pick up a nearby stone and throw it into the veggie patch. What if the new tenants don't like gardening? I didn't only set up the veggie patch to help Laurie and Rupert. I also needed a sense of community. Kat, for all her haphazard life, has a feeling she belongs. Her lunatic household has been a family, of sorts, for her.

My eyes catch an envelope poking out of Laurie's letterbox at the top of the driveway. I haven't checked my letterbox since the package yesterday. I stroll to it, looking up to the rising gibbous moon. I'm good with words, always have been. They're my comfort when the Road is unfamiliar, my solace when I'm confronting a Dead End. I round the letterboxes to find Ernie sitting on Mrs Feeble's fence.

"Hello, Candice," his voice tolls quietly.

I walk towards him a little. "Everything okay, Ernie?"

"Mum's not doing well." He exhales slowly.

"Serious?"

He laughs. "I told her I was getting married." He shrugs. "She likes my girlfriend. But Mum's very religious. She thinks it's a sin for me to remarry. Even though my ex has remarried."

"Even in this day and age?"

"Hard to beat. Mum's eighty-nine, thinks about heaven a lot. Doesn't want to screw things up this late in the piece."

I wonder how old Ernie is but I'm too polite to ask.

"I'm forty-eight," he smiles. "Her youngest. Only one in this state. I'm staying tonight. Don't want her to wake and go over it in her head."

I hug Ernie spontaneously, something I've never contemplated doing before. "Congratulations. I hope your Mum comes around."

Ernie smiles brightly. "She'll be right. It's only a registry wedding, so she'll get there. My brothers are coming over, they can help."

"That's wonderful. I wish you all the best." The silence thickens. I step away a little. "I came out to check my letterbox."

"You've all got mail." He nods to the fence.

There's a letter sticking out of all three letterboxes. I pull mine out and say goodbye, glance up at the moon again to settle myself, rip the envelope distractedly. It's a Notice of Sale. The landlord is selling the flats. He is, apparently by law, required to advise us of the fact that the flats have been put on the market, there will be an open inspection, an expectation that the flats will be tidy and the garden neat, bla, bla, bla. I walk inside in a trance. The letters in Laurie and Rupert's letterboxes are no doubt the same. I open my laptop and look up the sale.

*Gardener's Delight! This set of three neat flats boasts a large fertile vegetable garden that can be used by the tenants, which means rents can be higher than usual. These will be much sought-after flats. Like bees to honey the new owner will attract tenants who like to grow their own food. The savings in their grocery bills will be recouped by the new owner in rent.*

I'm cold through. No wonder the landlord allowed us to create the veggie patch: he thought it would make him a better sale. And where will I be, the only tenant left, with new tenants with their own ideas, maybe pesticides, weedicides, opinions of their own?

My rent will rise when my lease falls due early next month, obviously a strategic ploy by the owner. Or maybe we'll all be kicked out. I plug the crusts into the toaster, pull out the ham and tomato and stick them in a pan. My mind warbles through anger, duplicity, abandonment, bitterness, grief. I serve up the crusts angrily, add the ham irritably, chuck on the cheese grumpily, plonk on the tomato desultorily, eat my miserable meal gloomily. Put my pjs on half-heartedly. It's nearly ten and still no sign of life at either flat. I text Laurie, he's with Denise.

I don't have Rupert's number so I text him back.

*He's with Daisy. You ok?*

*Yeah. Fine.* I don't want to ruin his night with the news. But perhaps it'll help him make a case for moving in with Denise. It's not like they'll want to take their time.

This is the flat I moved into when I left home at twenty-five, when I'd been going out with Ben for a couple of months. It was hard leaving Mum and Dad, but we all managed. Rupert had been here for almost five years then. I didn't see much of him until Laurie moved in. Laurie wasn't in good shape when he arrived. His two sons from his fifth marriage took his ex-wife's side and refused to have anything to do with him for a few months. It was hard to watch him persisting in the face of their nastiness, then suddenly everything turned around when they discovered their mother had started up with Laurie's best friend as soon as she kicked him out.

Rupert and Laurie have become my friends. I'll be sorry for their departure from my life.

I open the fridge, looking for rescue. I pour a lemonade. It's lost its bubbles. I toss it angrily down the sink. I'm breathing in emotions instead of oxygen. Incensed, outraged, deceived, hoodwinked, defrauded, swindled, tricked, duped, scammed, deluded, alone, lonely, forlorn, deserted, dejected, crestfallen. Distressed. Sorrowful.

I brush my teeth. No mirror tonight. I lay in bed, tossing like a fish flipped from the frying pan into the fire. There are no tears. I don't want to cry. I hear the familiar *pling* of an email on my laptop. I must've forgotten to shut it down. I wander out, check on it.

Harry B. Kat's contracts. It's after eleven. Only Harry B would be up and working at this time of night. I laugh at the title, *All Kat and more!*

> *Hi Candice*
> *Here's Kat's contracts. We're meeting at 2 so please get this to her in the morning. Also see attachment for you.*
> *Love HB*

There are two attachments. I don't open *Kat's Contracts*. I jump in surprise as the other, called *You are Invited*, opens up. It's a wedding invitation. I keep staring at it, expecting it to be my parents', but the names are quite different.

> *Harry Baxter and Andrea Wilmington request the pleasure of Candice and partner at their wedding.*

There are details of where and when, and it's only a month away. I burst into tears. I'm floating in a sea of love on a surfboard that's been nibbled by too many sharks: Jaron and Bryce and Gene and Jake and Ben and Homer and Parker. I cry and I wail, I weep and I blubber, I whimper, I yowl, I snivel.

I sit, eventually, with a strong coffee. I'm never going to sleep tonight. I ring Harry B. He's still awake, of course.

"This is the way you announce such a thing, B?"

"Sorry." He laughs.

"I don't even know what to say. How? Why?"

"Dad was right." His voice is full of light. "You do know when you find someone you can bear living with for the rest of your life."

"Oh, Harry, *bear living with*?"

He laughs again. "You know what I mean. Stop romanticising it. Look at Harry K. Grumpier than ever since he became a father."

"Joanna's pregnant again. Have you heard?"

"She's a bloody baby factory. Got his nuts in a vice-like grip. I presume it was her choice?"

"He doesn't seem to have had much say in it. But Harry, you?"

His smile is evident. "Andy's very sweet. Kind. Loving. Calm. Listens to me. Laughs at my jokes, which is more than you do."

"How long have you been seeing her?"

"Almost a year."

"You never said."

"You never asked."

"I never expected."

"She's met Mum and Dad."

"Oh." I'm decidedly out of the loop. "She looks young?"

"Twenty-five."

Wow. Three years younger than me. "Fifteen years is a big difference, B."

"No-one's spoiled her. That's a big bonus."

I ponder his words. "What can we say about you?"

"Battle-weary. And captured by the enemy."

"A fine-looking enemy."

"And a fabulous cook. Feel-good food. We have a fun time. She's sensible with me. I couldn't let her go."

"Did she mean you to? Crap, it's not a shotgun, is it?"

"Just a giant cannon that belongs to me," Harry B chuckles.

"Eeeuw!"

He laughs again. "As soon as the wedding's done she wants to start, though. I'm ready. Feeling all grown up."

"Is this about turning forty?"

"Not at all. Andy's different. Worth the wait." He laughs. "More grown up than me, in some ways."

"And now you're not waiting at all."

"Why wait, Candice?"

"I see," I say, although I don't.

"By the way, we're having a dinner in two weeks for both families to come together before the wedding."

We talk for a few more minutes, then he tells me she's woken and wants him in bed. I didn't even realise she was there. I don't know what to do after he's hung up, thinking of my big brother in bed doing the do with sweet Andy the fun cook who's more grown-up than him and whom nobody has spoiled. I presume he means emotionally. I can't see a twenty-five-year-old that looks like her being a virgin.

Sex is everywhere. Except at the eye of the storm, where I live.

# 25

Kat's contract icon stares at me from the screen: that's nothing to do with love, right? I print it off and text her *I have your contract. Can I drop past in the morning?* As I press *send* I realise it's twelve-thirty.

My phone rings immediately. "What the crap, Can? You're never up this late unless you've got a man there. Which you obviously don't, or you wouldn't be sending me texts about the contract. What gives?"

I start to cry.

"Crap! Come over, Can. Whatever it is we can fix it."

"What are you doing awake, anyway?" I ask softly.

She giggles. "We were making out. Thor's had assignments all day."

I sob.

"Candice! Get in that car right now. Or you want us to come over?"

"Already in my car. See you in five."

The streets are silent. There are no cars, nobody walking, no shops open. As I approach the train-line the lights flash and the boom-gate lowers itself confidently, presuming my compliance. I want to drive through it, show it who's boss, but of course I sit obediently, wait for the moment to pass. The train rushes along, full of its own importance. There's a single person in its single carriage, sitting like a still frieze in its brightly lit interior, hurtling along its channel towards a known destination. If only I were so lucky.

Kat and Thor wait on the low brick fence outside her house.

Kat loops her arm into mine as I stretch out of the car, and we walk into the house and through to her room, Thor following us compliantly.

She pushes me onto the bed, flops down beside me, Thor snuggling up behind her. "Spill."

I sigh, my eyes on the ceiling. "Does it ever seem the world's turning without you?"

"Jeez. All the time until I met you, Can."

I smile. Thor leans with his chin on Kat's shoulder, his eyes curious.

"Okay," I continue. "I'm feeling like the only one stalled at the gate. Since last Saturday, here's the tally of people in a relationship: Gene, you two, Laurie, Rupert, Terri, Jamie and Clarissa."

"Jamie? No. Wait, with Clarissa?"

"Jamie and Clarissa, yes! Ernie whose Mum lives next to the flats, Mum and Dad are getting married—"

"What? Getting married? Really?"

"Yes." I pause. "Harry B."

"Harry B's marrying them? Can he do that? As a lawyer?"

"No, he's getting married."

Kat sits up, knocking Thor off the bed. "No shit!" She looks down at me. "That blonde?"

"No shit." I close my eyes. "Joanna's pregnant again. Jamie's getting happily divorced. For better or worse, for richer or poorer, everyone's tying the loop in their lives."

"What about your psychologist man?" asks Thor, having pulled himself back onto the bed. He sits up against the bedhead.

Since when was he allowed to ask about my Love Roller Coaster? "Got any wine, Kat?"

Kat flips over Thor, stands up, drags out a cask of wine, pours a glass, gives it to me.

"Not having one?"

"Resting my liver." She smiles at Thor.

"Fuck." I drink half the glass in one gulp.

Kat puts her head in Thor's lap. He plays with her ponytails.

"Remember Sunday," I say, "I was talking about where we're heading in life?" I down the rest of the wine and give the cup back to Thor to put on the fridge.

"This crap again," groans Kat. "You gotta just run with life, Can. No point trying to fight it."

"That's very intelligent, Kat," smiles Thor.

"Ziggy told me that."

I stop breathing. "What else did he say?"

"Most of it was listening. Even just saying my shit helped."

I've been deposed as confidante. "Different to us talking?"

She pauses. "Things I haven't told you, Can. Embarrassing things."

I frown. "I know about your parents. Drink and drugs."

"It's the details I haven't told you."

I'm scared now for what she's about to reveal. She doesn't talk and I don't talk and Thor is silent.

"They used to threaten the police would take me away and lock me up if I ever told anyone how things were. They told me it was my fault they were like they were. Blamed me whenever things went wrong. They used to laugh at me all the time like I was stupid. They even lied about my age, told me I was three years older than I really was and that I was really stupid to be in a class with kids who were three years younger than me. When I asked why my date of birth was three years out of whack at school, they told me that was when they registered me because they were so embarrassed at how stupid I was."

"Kat," I whisper, "you didn't believe that?"

Kat's inside herself. "Mum told me she'd never have another baby because they might be as stupid as me. She wished she'd never had me. They'd leave me alone at nights and get smashed or high. I used to think they might get killed and never come home. I didn't know if I'd be happy or sad about it. I didn't even know alcohol was bad. I used to drink it with my meals, meals I'd cobbled together if they were wasted."

"Kat-" My throat closes over.

"The kids at school told me I smelled, so I washed my clothes when I had a bath. Which I organised myself."

"How old were you then?" I feel destroyed.

She shrugs. "Young. My grade two teacher figured it out and asked to speak to them. They were sober that day, the bastards. But she knew. She bought me a water bottle, filled it every day. Organised for the school canteen to make me a meat salad sandwich every day, with a chocolate milk, which I guess she paid for. She slipped two extra sandwiches to me on Friday afternoons. And a piece of fruit for recess. She did this even after grade two, when I wasn't in her class anymore. I'd pick it up at the front office so other kids wouldn't know."

Thor and I remain mute.

"She pulled me aside at the end of primary school and gave me $100 in $5 notes. She asked what I wanted her to tell high school. I told her to write a note and I'd take it to high school, but I never gave it to anyone." She screws up her face. "Too embarrassed."

"Surely that's reportable these days?" My voice is high and squeaky.

Kat's eyes blink ever so slowly. "By then I knew how to look after myself."

"And you met Candice." Thor's voice sounds like he's narrating a documentary.

I burst into tears. How could I know her defiance was defence? "Kat, that's, that's unfair. That's, that's-"

"The way things were." She sits up straight. "It was only when I asked for the dole and explained about my birth certificate that they said it couldn't be true." She sighs. "Honestly, I think that's why I haven't been able to stick at a job. At a course. Having you at high school made me want to go every day. You were the one thing worth being there for. Same with Ms Walter in Grade Two. Just need someone to believe in me. Ziggy thinks I need to believe in myself. That's a whole lot harder. That's why I'm going back to see him again."

Thor's crying. I've stopped crying, because I know now. Thor sees in Kat what I do, that unconquerable stubborn spirit in pixie form, the absurd courage and determination of the little girl Kat still is. They'll be fine together. She'll get her design career and he'll do his exercise whatever-it-is and they'll be fine together.

"I've got your contracts," I murmur. "Harry B said you've got a hearing tomorrow at two."

She sits up excitedly as if the past never happened. "Show me! I wanna see what the Wise Guy's done." She giggles, tells Thor, "I always call him the Wise Guy because he is."

"So it seems," he kisses the top of her head, smiles half-heartedly.

We pore over the contracts, smiling and cooing over Harry B's effrontery. The contract names a company he's registered as *Pussy Kat Designs*, with Katyliciana Hinch as CEO. A note says she should dress in a suit, keep her mouth shut and let him do all the talking.

"Let's go out in the morning and buy you a suit, I say. "My shout."

"We'll all go," says Thor. "But I'll buy the suit, thank you Candice."

I smile. "Yes, that's best." I watch another tear fall down his cheek.

Kat flicks out her lamp and snuggles down in the middle of the bed. "Let's stick together. All for one and one for all and all that shit."

I lay down on my side of the bed, see Thor flatten against his side in the faint moonlight seeping in from the skylight. Kat flips the quilt over us all. Nothing seems to matter except the three of us.

"Aren't you seeing Ziggy soon, Candice?" asks Thor.

"Yes," I say softly. And suddenly there's four of us.

"Bad things happen to good people," says Kat. "The point is to always believe you can get yourself through," says Kat. "That's Ziggy's message. Believe in yourself, just keep going, and you'll see changes."

"Is it an appointment or a date with Ziggy?" Thor asks me.

"To be honest, I have no idea." I yawn, and it's the last thing I remember before morning.

# 26

Kat's phone echoes around the sterile walls of the waiting room. It's a text from Harry B: *There in 5.*

"I hope we don't have to go in without him," Kat whispers, her eyes owl-like with fear.

The receptionist appears as if summoned. "You can go in now."

"My lawyer's been delayed." Kat's voice is as snooty as the receptionist's. "You'll have to wait a few minutes."

The receptionist leaves without reply. Thor and I smile approvingly.

We hear Harry B with his lawyer's voice on. "Harry Baxter representing Pussy Kat Designs." He bustles into the waiting room, larger than life. "Sorry, Kitty-Kat. Got held up."

"We're fine," says Thor.

Kat punches Harry B on the arm. "Getting married at last, you big lump! About bloody time!"

Harry B rubs his arm, grinning. "Nice suit."

No matter that Thor and I are wearing suits, too. Kat and Harry B have always been like this. When Kat came around after school, Harry B always included himself in our girl-talk, even though he was twenty-five and finishing law. I asked her years later if there was anything between them, but she laughed and said *He's my brother* even though he isn't. And when I asked Harry B the same question, he told me *Not Kat. It'd be wrong.* They have a mutual respect for each other's bravado.

And now in any case pint-sized Kat looks cocky in her navy suit, white shirt and short heels, her blonde hair conservatively up in a bun, her make-up expertly applied by me. I've taken the day off work, needing to stay close to Kat after the revelations of last night. Jamie doesn't care so long as the work is done.

Which, of course, it always is. Here's my personality type: loyal, determined, dependable. Reliable, responsible. Trustworthy. Brave, indomitable. I know now. The WiMPI can go fuck itself.

"By the way, here's your reading for the wedding." Harry B gives me a piece of paper.

I glance at it, look up and smile.

"Okay, you two buzz off," he tells Thor and me.

"But-" begins Thor.

"We need to stay on track, not be hampered by you two bozos. There's a snack bar a few doors down. We'll meet you there."

"But-" Thor tries again.

Kat kisses him, thumbs her lipstick from his mouth, turns to me. "My lippy still on?"

"Yep." I smile. "Go get 'em. Baby."

"Rules, Kat," says Harry B. "Mouth shut unless I ask, then only yes or no. Now let's go." They leave together.

Thor watches in astonishment. He sits down.

I pull him up. "Have faith. Harry B does this for a living. Let's find that snack bar."

We walk out silently past the receptionist. I link my arm in his and press the lift button.

"How much will your brother charge?" Thor asks nervously.

"Harry won't charge. Kat's family." I unhook myself as the lift arrives. He is, after all, an impeccably dressed Adonis.

At the snack bar he orders a peppermint tea. I order tea instead of coffee and we sit down, him looking slightly awkward, me grateful for the chance to see what makes him tick.

"Tell me about yourself," I ask. "What's your family like?"

He smiles. "Regular. My parents still like spending time with each other and my older sister is my best friend."

I smile in surprise. "That's very sweet. But Thor, how does a guy who looks like you get such a loving nature?"

He looks affronted. "Looks have no link to who you are inside."

"I just mean, well, God, Thor, you're like-"

"Healthy."

"More than that." I tilt my head. "Why the muscle-bound motif?"

He frowns.

"When did you start lifting?"

"Nineteen."

Our teas arrive. I put two sugars in mine. He shakes his head when I offer him the dispenser.

"Do you compete?" I stir my tea.

"The first two years." He sips. "Too much of a bad thing. Drugs, heckling, everyone's competitive, trying to knock you down so you don't look confident, however well you've prepared your body."

Is that how they see it? Preparing their body, like it's a dish on one of those competitive cooking shows? I stir my tea again distractedly. "You're still cut."

"But not so much. I've reduced my training."

"Jeez, what were you like before?"

He takes out his wallet. "I don't show this to many people. It's who I was, not who I am."

I peer at the photo: his body's out of proportion. Massive upper body, tiny waist, biceps like they're cut from cement, only the veins showing they're flesh and blood. I look up at his taut body covered in its black suit, charcoal shirt, navy tie. His face has softened. I've judged him unfairly, considered his manner against the cut of his muscles, not the depth of his kindness and intelligence. "How did you come back from that without going saggy?"

"You have to cut your calories. Maintain strength training. My uni course helps me with all that."

"Is that why you're studying exercise psychology?"

He smiles at my error. "Physiology. No. Just interested in the human body. It's why I got interested in weightlifting in the first place." He looks at his tea. "You do a little gym, find you have a knack for weight work, do a little more, get encouragement, it becomes a drug in itself."

"Where does Kat fit into this?"

He pauses, sips his tea. "She had a disregard for her body. After our first night, we both started to change. I learn emotional strength from Kat. She learns physical strength from me. We went for a long hike that first day. Afterwards she slept for two hours while I went to a lecture." He smiles. "Kat doesn't like to be seen as weak. She insisted we go for another hike the next day." Now he laughs out loud. "Same thing. Slept for two hours. Since then we've been walking less, going faster. Yesterday we even ran a little. She's decided not to stop drinking but to see how long before she has a drink. I told her to have a drink each Saturday, see if she still needs it. I don't want her to rebound or binge."

I sit, frozen. I knew she was living life on the edge, supported her where possible, but we've run the slipshod life together.

"The best thing you've ever done was to pay for her to see Ziggy."

I stare at him. "For my own selfish reasons."

"It doesn't matter. I sense a new spark inside her. She's held that responsibility inside her all the years, those people that raised her-"

"Or didn't. Thank goodness for her grade two teacher."

He beams. "And you and your family. And now Harry, uh-"

"B."

"Harry B's looking after her."

A new picture flashes into my mind. Kat beached on dry land, her boat safely at shore, pixie hands clasped in victory above her head.

"And you, Thor. What a blessing you are."

He grins his perfect smile. "It fits together like a jigsaw, Candice. Do you see that?"

I laugh abruptly. "Yes. I hope you're right about my life, too."

"Can I see the words for the reading?"

I hand them over.

> *"What is love?" she asked.*
> *"I'll tell you what it's not," he replied. "It's not heartache, it's not yearning for someone you cannot have, it's not pain and suffering and tears and tragedy and hurt and shouting and rejection and fear and shaking and desperation and devastation and damage and betrayal."*
> *"Then what is love?" she repeated.*
> *"Everything good," he smiled.*

"I like it," Thor tells me.

There's a tap on my shoulder. I turn to see Ben Klemsky, the guy who dropped me without a reason, standing shyly behind me.

"Oh?" I utter. "Uh …"

"It's me, Ben."

I blink. "I know."

He looks at Thor. He looks back at me. "Can we talk? In private?"

Thor rises and Ben cowers slightly. Part of me is very, very pleased.

"I'll be in the men's room," Thor says, like it requires membership.

Ben swings into his vacated seat. "I was right."

"What about?" I feel like punching him across the table. Not good enough? My wounds from being dumped are still raw, still make no sense, still rankle.

He stares at me. The colour drains from his face. "I dumped you because you were too good for me."

# 27

The pieces slot together inside my brain with a satisfying click.

But melancholy washes over Ben's face. "You were everything. Vivacious. Funny. Smart. Pretty. Full of life. I could see the end." He shrugs resignedly. "I just pulled the plug first."

"You said you didn't love me anymore."

"All lies." His smile is crooked. "I've never stopped."

I frown.

"I felt double the pain. I'd hurt you and I'd hurt myself." He checks the toilet door before returning his morose eyes to me. "My wife and I have decided to separate."

I look at his finger. The wedding ring is still firmly attached.

"My wife, ex-wife, insisted we see a counsellor, but we couldn't save the marriage. It was only when she left that I realised it's always been you." He looks down at his lap. "I've booked an appointment next week on my own. I need to exorcise you."

I ask the question I already have an answer for. "Who you seeing?"

His face lights up. "You seeing a therapist, too?"

"No, just know a few."

"You won't know him." He looks sheepish.

"Try me." I smile thinly.

"Dr Ziggy Zbigniew."

It seems wise to continue with muteness.

Thor presses through the door and looks at me quizzically.

I eagerly beckon him to save me from this madness.

"Wow," says Ben. "He sure is massive." He turns and says quickly, "If you were free, I'd ask for another chance. I've changed, you know."

I think about revealing that, instead of the hulking Thor, my love interest is actually his therapist, but it feels wrong. I introduce Ben as *an old boyfriend of mine.*

Thor is perfect. He shakes his hand firmly. "You're lucky to have had her at all. She's remarkably unique."

I hug Thor tightly, partly for show but mostly because he's become my friend. I turn to Ben and shake his hand dismissively. I want no part of him in my future. "Good luck with your life."

His face is ice. "Sure."

We watch him go.

Thor asks, "What was that?"

"He broke up with me because he thought I was too good for him." I laugh at Thor's expression. "He wanted another chance, after breaking my heart for nothing, and get this, he's seeing Ziggy!"

Thor laughs. It's deep and rumbling. "It's a sign."

"Sign be damned, it's hilarious!" I fill him in on my history with Ben.

But he's too distracted to listen for long. "How long do you think Kat and Harry will be? Are they arguing, the company, I mean?"

"They'll be wanting to make it as expensive for Kat as possible, so she'll give in to their offer. They won't know she's getting B for free." I stretch out my limbs. "This could take over an hour, Thor."

He stares at me in horror. "I thought I'd be in there with her. What if the company decides against the deal?"

"Harry's a master negotiator. And he'll be representing her like he would me. Kat was always over our place during high school. I understand why now. Harry B has always been protective of Kat, as if he sensed something I didn't."

"How much did you know about her home life?"

"She'd come over after school and show up on weekends. Would never stay for a sleep-over, although I had no idea why. She gave up smoking that first year of high school on my encouragement."

Thor looks like he might faint.

"Shit. You didn't know she smoked?"

Thor sighs. "She breaks my heart. How early did she start?"

"She never said. Luckily, she couldn't afford many. She'd sneak them out of her parent's packets without them knowing. Only bought a few herself." I don't tell him the rest of her money, stolen from her stoned parents, was spent on beer.

Thor looks like he's about to swear.

I link his hand into mine. "She's not there anymore, Thor."

"She doesn't see her parents ever."

It's obviously difficult for him to comprehend this. "The day after our last exam she asked if I could borrow Mum's car, gave me her address. It sounded urgent. I couldn't believe how run down the house was. Paint peeling and wood rotting. Garden overgrown. Nobody else home. She had her stuff under her mattress on the floor, got them out when I arrived, her school backpack, a dozen plastic shopping bags, several of which held her school sketch books. She told me she was moving out. She left her parents a note. That's when I realised how bad it was, but I couldn't bear it, I was so young, I didn't know how to cope with it, but she had no choice, she was living it."

"I understand," Thor sympathises.

"She had a small room the first time, so I thought it'd be okay. Ziggy's wrong about standing on her own. She's done it all her life. Mum told me when I got home that day she would've been happy to foster Kat, but she never asked because she could see Kat was able to stand up for herself. Instead, she looked after her as best she could and sent her home again. But none of us are as strong as we are when we stand together, and that's where you and I, and our families, come in."

He knocks his chair over and stands unexpectedly. Kat arrives beaming at the door, Harry B smiling above her head.

"Fuck, I'm glad he's on my side," giggles Kat, pointing over her shoulder at Harry B. Thor lifts her and hugs her tightly. "Jeez, baby, it's okay." Her voice is strangled, and Thor lets her go.

"Well?" I ask as we sit down.

"You tell 'em, Wise Guy," Kat smiles.

"They must like her stuff very much. First contract nullified. New contract a pleasing ten percent. Review in a year, depending on sales, to see if an increase is warranted. No decreases. They get exclusive rights to her designs for five years. After that all bets are off the table and Kat can go to another company or re-sign if they want her."

"I'm worried about publicity," Kat interjects. "Mum and Dad might appear, wanting payola." She rubs her fingers together.

"Maybe we should change your name," smiles Thor. "To mine."

"Good heavens!" I say. "Slow it down, you two!"

"I agree," says Harry B seriously. "There's a lot you have to learn about yourself before you decide to rope anyone else into your issues."

Before I can clarify this, Kat offers to take us out to dinner.

"No can do, Kitty-Kat, I've got to get back to the office," says Harry.

"Friday afternoon and you're still busy?" asks Kat.

He laughs. "It's when I do most of my written work. By the way, here's your invitations." He hands out two crisp pale mauve envelopes, one to Kat and one to me. "I know Kat's got someone to accompany her, but what about you, Candice?"

I ignore him. "Kat, I can't come to dinner. You know that."

Kat smiles. "Of course! She's working on that *plus one* tonight, Wise Guy."

Harry B smiles broadly. "Make sure he's worth it."

# 28

Thor drove us around today, so I sit in the back, wondering how much Kat-sex the Thor-mobile has seen. The back is scrupulously clean, as is the front. The two of them are gabbling away about what Kat should do with the money when it comes, when it will come, what sort of changes she'll make to her lifestyle, how much tax she'll have to pay. I listen distractedly, my thoughts on tonight's liaison with Ziggy.

Loneliness dribbles into me as I get into my Spinster car still at Kat's, and they drive off to Thor's. But with so much Love in the air, I'm optimistic about my meeting tonight. Ziggy was kind at the appointment, helpful in sending me the book, friendly when I called. *There's no danger here,* I reassure myself.

*Bang, bang!*

I jump in fright at the hammering against my car window. It's Buff, one of Kat's many housemates. And no, he's not called Buff because he's hunky, it's short for Buffoon. Buff is renowned for his readiness to take on stupid dares, crazy antics and brainless challenges. And, whilst he's not fit, he's long and lean like a rock singer.

"My main girl, Cannndisssssss," he grins.

I wind down my window. "Jeez, Buff, that was too much."

He raises an eyebrow. "You coming in?"

I squint at him. "Are you tanked?"

He throws his head back and laughs. "I don't think Kat's home."

"She just left with Thor."

"All snug and cosy with that one. He's Ollie's mate."

"I know." I really should be going, but I don't know how to unhook from this senseless conversation.

"Not home much now. Guess she'll be moving out soon. Sad to see her go." Buff looks genuinely miserable.

I wonder if Kat's told anyone about her windfall. "Why do you think she's moving out?"

"Ollie told me. Thor's proposed."

I laugh. "You idiot. He hasn't done anything of the sort."

He frowns. "Hasn't she told you?"

My stomach tosses itself like a salad.

Buff opens my door. "Come ask Ollie then. He'll tell ya."

I don't move. "No need."

He crouches down next to me. "Come in for a drink, Candy."

I shudder. "Don't call me that."

"But you're so sweet," he laughs.

He might be high, but this is plain chat-up. "Is Buff your real name?"

He laughs. "Course not."

The pause is ridiculously long. Finally, I ask, "Well?"

"Well, what?"

Now I know he's delusional. "What's your real name?"

He laughs. "It's Gene."

"You're kidding me."

"No. Why?"

*Fuck.*

"Candice?"

"I'm going out tonight."

He purses his lips and stands away. "Who's the lucky dick?"

I frown. "Are you trying to ask me something?"

He smiles shyly. "Wanna have a drink sometime? Stuff like that?"

I laugh. "Stuff like that? Does that mean what I think?"

He closes my door carefully. "You know where I live, Candice."

I can't think of anything to say. I feel guilty as I drive off. A wave is poor compensation for a date, but it's the best I can do.

At home I run a bath, tired after the slapstick-iness of the Buff/Ben/Gene episodes, but Laurie knocks as I'm about to strip off.

"Have you got a letter?" He scrunches the landlord's advice angrily.

"Yep. I'm cross as."

"What are you doing about it? This is nonsense! Outrageous!"

I'm surprised by his rage. "How's Denise?"

He spits out his answer. "Thinks we're too old to start anything. She should've thought about that before she bedded me."

I can't help it: I laugh. "Laurie, come in, sit down, calm down."

We sit and I prise the letter from his hand.

"Firstly, Denise will come around. You've just come on too strongly. Being a woman is tough; in ways you'll never know."

He's insistent. "At my age, there's no time to waste." This isn't the super-confident Laurie I'm used to. He shakes his head. "She was supposed to be a means to an end," he mumbles. "Way back then."

Insight rocks me. "You mean, she was supposed to just take your virginity?" I pause, pondering. "And she took more?"

He smiles grimly. "All these years I regretted not asking her out afterwards. We were at a party, and I didn't know her at all. We got to talking and then went for a walk. We stayed up all night. I had no idea she was going to let me have sex with her. I was fifteen!" His eyes are alight with the vigour of that youthful encounter. "I didn't know what to do with her afterwards. I was too crazy after such an unimaginable experience." He frowns. "You don't fall in love with the first woman you root." He sniggers shyly. "Sorry."

"No need to temper your words for me."

He smiles gratefully. "All these years I've tried to recreate that incredible night. I put it down to novelty. *You'll never get that feeling again,* I told myself." His eyes are downcast. "But it's her. She's the best connection I've ever had. I don't want to waste any more time."

"Have you told her this?"

"I've said it with flowers. Treated her well. Cooked her dinner."

"Then let her get used to it. Don't push to make it permanent. Just hang in there, do what you've been doing, until you're as comfortable as her dressing gown."

Laurie laughs, then frowns. "Now the flats are being sold. What should we do? Turn the garden back to grass?"

"We've got a while to decide. Give it a few days. We should find out what Rupert's thinking."

"I'll give him a call," he says eagerly. "Are you free tonight?"

"I've got a date. Or an appointment. Or something."

"Ah, the psychologist!" He grins. "Glad that's working out."

I raise my eyes to the ceiling. "I wouldn't be that confident."

"Get on with it, then!" He rushes to the door. "Thanks for your advice, Candice. Good luck tonight. I'll let you know when Rupert's free. I'm not expecting to see you on Sunday afternoon!" He laughs. "Maybe Monday night?"

I smile as he leaves. I can well imagine how suffocating his enthusiasm is for Denise. But the vagary of Laurie's love-life has unsettled me. I decide to choose my eveningwear before my bath.

Classic black is the colour for such a night: elegant but stylish. Out comes my favourite little black dress. Court shoes for power not peril. My sheerest black pantyhose. Something more: a red scarf at my neck to cover my cleavage yet sound the siren.

I strip off, avoiding all mirrors. I'll finish with a shower to wash my hair but, as I ease myself into the hot water, I'm grateful for the opportunity to reflect on a long week of romances and revelations, confusion and curiosities, and past and present disappointments.

A mere week ago I was pacing my flat, head awash with the results of the personality test. Something is scampering around in my head but I can't decipher it. I sit up, trawl my memory across the day before the test, a regular Thursday workday followed by a movie with Gene. I wore my old lilac knee-length shorts and a cream floral t-shirt with my pink sandals. Not a dress or even dressy. So unlike me. Where, I wonder, was Candice Kelly on that Thursday night, and at that Friday test?

My memory flashes like lightning. Gene had visited me in his nurse's uniform a few weeks before, and I realised all I was seeing was the outer crust of an attractive man with a good heart inside. I needed to cease using looks alone to decide on a partner. I began to dumb-down my attire and, it seems, my personality, in order to be more *authentic*.

Will the real Candice Kelly please stand up?

Now I'm that little creature on the boat, sailing towards an unknown destination. Where will I wash up? Only tonight will tell. And then it will only be the beginning.

I hope.

# 29

Ziggy is dressed as on Tuesday. I've gone to a lot of trouble to look my best for tonight: disappointment and overblown hopes flood through my veins. I right myself, try to sound confident.

"Your door bitch—uh, receptionist has gone home?"

"She leaves at two-thirty on Fridays to pick up my nieces."

"Oh." I imagine the tragedy that must have befallen his family, quickly veer onto myself as a stepmother/aunt. "You have custody?"

"She's their mother!" he laughs. "My sister."

"I thought she was … never mind." I smile disarmingly. "Here I am for my *appointment*."

Ziggy cocks his head. "About that. You have to make a choice."

Silliness masks my anxiety. "Ooh, a choose-your-own-adventure."

"If you want to see me as a psychologist, I can't see you socially." His expression is stoic. "If you're here for a session let's begin, you're booked in and I'm ready to go. If you're here to spend time with me, *and* you've lost the boyfriend, I've got a table booked at Le Café across the road." His eyes scan my face. "If you also need a psychologist, I'll refer you to a colleague." He smiles. "I can help you with the personality test results if that's all you want. As a friend if nothing else."

I put on my cheesiest grin. "There's no boyfriend, and the café sounds lovely." I'm rewarded by a dazzling smile. "I have to apologise, though. I left your book home. Perhaps we might pick it up later?"

He walks to the lights and turns everything off. For a moment it's completely dark, then a dim light turns on in the foyer. I feel his hand in mine, as he bends his head to me. His tongue swirls around in my mouth, the intimacy of the contact flooding me with craving. If he starts anything, here in the dark, I'm in. But he stops, moves away.

I admonish myself for my lack of moral backbone. There's not enough light to see his face, but as he pulls me towards the alarm and punches a number in, I glimpse the hint of a smile. He keeps my hand in his as we wait at the road.

"You bring many clients here?" I giggle like a schoolgirl.

The road clears and we cross. "I've been here once for lunch with Esther," he says, then adds, "My sister, Esther."

"Oh yes, of course, Esther."

Le Café is not really a café at all. It's cautiously lit with dim lights and candles. An odd place to bring a sister for lunch. We follow a waiter to a darkened corner.

Ziggy immediately orders a half-dozen Oysters Kilpatrick. "And a serve of herb bread. We'll look the wine list over."

As the waiter leaves, I lean in. "You're not going to order for me, are you?"

His eyes are wide. "I'm starving. I've had a big week of emergency appointments, and no lunch today. You can order mains for us if you want. If you don't like sharing, just order your own."

I wonder if he's made the *emergency appointments* quip on purpose. Of course, I'm being paranoid.

"I presume Kat put in a good report?" he asks nonchalantly.

"Oh." I stare at him. "She said she didn't tell you I was her friend."

He shrugs. "She didn't. You told me about her at the wedding."

"Oh." Bugger. All that subterfuge for nothing.

He smiles. "She kept telling me she had this wonderful friend, called *Ca, Ca, Carol.* She talks about you like you're her guardian angel. I got a strong feeling she was genuine in her praise of you."

I smile. "Our connection is-"

"Authentic."

I feel bashful. "Yes."

He smiles. "I can't say what else we talked about, although I know you know it all. But if we talk about her, I'll have to refer her to someone else, which I don't think she'd like."

"No. Keep it to yourself. I'll get it from Kat."

The waiter returns with a bottle of water, two glasses and herb bread.

Ziggy rips it apart and puts half each on our side plates, starts to eat his as I pour water. He gives the waiter our wine menus, swallows. "What champagne do you have?"

The waiter rattles off a few. Ziggy chooses one. The waiter leaves.

"We're going to drink slowly tonight. Carefully, responsibly."

I busy myself in my bread. When I look up, he's watching me. "Are you going to charge me for this session?"

He frowns. "This is no session."

He adds nothing, so I fill the space. "What's a regular appointment?"

"What I charged you is my scheduled fee. I didn't want to charge Kat at all. I would've made the fee payable later, but she said she had the cash. I presumed it was your money."

"You give free consultations?"

"No."

The oysters arrive. "You know champagne's just as good," I smile.

"As what?" He puts an oyster on each of our side plates.

"You know, oysters."

He blinks. "We don't need oysters. Or champagne." His eyes scan mine. "Hmm. Maybe you do need to see a psychologist."

I slurp my oyster recklessly. "What wrong with me? Give me your diagnosis and see if it fits with mine."

"Hurt by love." It arrives with immediacy and certainty.

I can't deny his words. It's impossible to keep the faith when love's proven itself to be a fickle fiend. Attraction does not equal love, a point fervently expressed by the Harrys regularly during my teenage years.

*Easy cum, Easy go* was Harry K's favourite line. Harry B's was *Make sure the best of his love winds up in the end of a securely tied condom.*

Joanna secured Harry K's need for certainty. Now Andy's cool, calm, graceful yet domestic persona, very different to Joanna's fierce rules, mean Harry B's done too. I'm glad. I don't want him to be alone.

I don't want to be alone, either. I didn't want to go through what Mum and Dad did, wasting their twenties until they found each other. But here I am, having wasted my twenties, sitting across from a man who appears to be kind, settled, intelligent. Loving. Respectful. I reach over and cup his cheek. "So very handsome," I whisper, my mother's words resonating in my ear. I return my hand bashfully to my lap. "And if your diagnosis is right, what do you prescribe?"

He smiles and puts another oyster on my plate. "I don't prescribe. I'm a psychologist, not a psychiatrist. I don't right wrongs with medication, although there's obviously a need for that sometimes. In my job I consider behaviour: where it comes from, what it's trying to achieve, whether that's a good thing or whether it's trying to answer a need that may no longer be active, whether it's counterproductive or dangerous, what is the thinking behind it, and how to make it fit the outcome the person desires."

"Jeez, Ziggy!"

He swallows his oyster dispassionately. "Come on, you're one behind." He gestures to my plate.

"Sorry I made you go hungry." I pick it up and swallow.

He shares the last two among our plates. "For lunch or for you?"

I swoon a little as the waiter brings the champagne and a menu.

"Will you order mains?" Ziggy smiles.

The waiter gives me the menu. I skim it as he pops the bottle and pours. I order beef bourguignon, pot-au-feu and a mesclun mixed salad.

"Impressive." Ziggy holds his glass up as the waiter leaves.

I clink my glass on his, take a sip. "That's wonderful. Good choice."

Ziggy's eyes sparkle. "You know about French food?"

"I spent six months as food writer for the magazine when we lost our usual writer. Jamie, that's my boss-"

"You told me."

I shake my head. "You know everything."

He smiles.

"Jamie wanted to make sure he got the best, and eventually employed a freelance. In the meantime, he put me on kitchen duty." I grin. "Luckily, someone else was in the kitchen."

He grins back. "I was lucky the food was good at the pub then."

I feel suddenly brave. "I've been hungry all week myself."

He smiles slowly. "So, we've wasted the week."

"My week wasn't wasted."

His gaze is intense. It's like he's waiting for me to ask him something. "When you came around on Sunday, were you expecting sex? Once I was in control of my consent?"

"I was expecting you'd have dropped your boyfriend, given that's what we agreed Saturday night," he says emphatically. "When you were drunk you said you were only going out with him because he was pretty. And pretty good in the sack."

I cringe. "The whole night is foggy."

"I promised I'd be at least an equal value replacement." He smiles. "Before you got drunk, we'd had a wonderful time, and I meant it to continue. So did you."

"Did you mean you really were in love with me at first sight?"

He pauses. "At no time have I said I was in love with you."

I stare at him blankly. *What?*

# 30

Ziggy's face is full of humour. Quite the opposite of mine.

"I asked if you believed in love at first sight," he says. "I was asking your opinion. I'd been there to meet a blind date, and you turned up instead. Certainly, you captured my imagination by showing me your pretty knickers when you fell in the sports bar." He chuckles. "Actually, it was rather primal. A little like those baboons at the zoo who show their hindquarters to coerce their mate into sex." His laughter grows.

I'm not amused. "You were trying to get me into bed?"

He stops laughing. "The primal point of showing your rear in the animal world is to mate. It was only natural to wonder what you looked like underneath those pretty knickers. I found out a few hours later, and the only disappointment was not being able to do anything about it."

My face flushes. "You've behaved since then, haven't chased me for sex. Are you waiting for me to fall in love with you so we can pretend, as consenting adults, that sex is the next step?"

"On the contrary. If you think," Ziggy smiles, "that if you offered me sex I wouldn't take it until I was sure you were," he holds up his fingers to quote, "In Love With Me," he puts them down and smiles, "then you're idealistic and naïve. I have principles, but you're a beautiful woman and I'm as full of lust, possibly more so, as the next bloke."

"But on Saturday night I was naked and-"

"Drunk. But don't think I didn't want to."

"When I came to see you Tuesday you treated me like a client."

He frowns. "You made an appointment as a client in a different name. My fall-back position on the spur of the moment was to treat you as a client. Mixing business with pleasure is against the rules."

Our food comes. We stare at each other as the waiters put a dinner plate each in front of us, clear away the entrées, place food between us.

I haven't touched my champagne since my first sip. Ziggy's glass is empty. I keep my face neutral and take a couple of long gulps, avoiding his eyes, because it's his eyes that unnerve me. He's constantly connecting with me, watching me, wooing me, waiting for me.

He serves the food onto our plates. "You obviously like beef."

"The pot-au-feu comes with veggies." I keep my gaze strictly on his hands. "And then there's the salad."

"No, I mean both are beef dishes. I presume."

My shoulders sag. What do I say? I was nervous and went for the easy picks? He thinks I'm a French food goddess, and I'm not giving that up. "I wasn't thinking." I pause, and he pauses, too. I look up, find his eyes upon me. "The way you keep staring at me is quite unsettling."

"Just drinking you in."

This, of course, makes me even more uncomfortable. And should I tell him he's counselling my ex-boyfriend? Has Ben mentioned me by name? If I bring it up, will it put any chance of going further with Ziggy in a perilous position? I shake it off. "Tell me about personality tests."

"Personality tests are a difficult animal." He puts down the servers, fixes his gaze on mine. "You must be able to define personality in the first place, which is impossible. You might be outgoing with your friends, shy with strangers." He finishes his champagne.

"Situational effects."

"Well done. Does behaviour depend on your value system, in which case perhaps the tests are checking your values rather than your personality. Is personality learned or genetic? How much of our personality is chosen by us? Can a different personality be learned, like being more optimistic? It's a difficult subject area."

I try to sound well informed. "And the WiMPI doesn't do its job."

He smiles and refills our glasses. "I wouldn't say that. But there are probably more accurate inventories."

"You asked me to check on my family and friends."

He pauses. "What did you come up with?"

"No-one thought I was an introvert. My boss said his came out wrong as well. He took the test again."

"Interesting. Did it change?"

"He said it had. But then his ex-wife decided to pay for their divorce and he started a relationship with one of my colleagues, so he would've been very different after those things happened."

He frowns. "The test should identify your general personality, not how you're affected by specific events, although that sort of flux can illuminate a different set of characteristics."

"We all do have a general personality, though, don't we?" I say. "Kat is bubbly, I'm more serious. My brothers are alike but very different. Harry B is happy and friendly, Harry K is cynical and funny. But I guess that's to do with their experiences as much as their genes."

He looks at me oddly. "Harry what and who?"

"Oh," I laugh. "Something I didn't tell you!" I lean back, enjoying a little mystery at last. "I have two half-brothers, both called Harry."

"You talked about your brother Harry. I didn't realise there were two. It was a little confusing, now it probably makes sense."

I gabble on. "I'm the only child of my mother and father. Harry K is Harry Kelly, he's Dad's son with his ex-wife, Sylvie. Harry B is Harry Baxter, Mum's son. She was a single mum. Harry K is married with two kids and one on the way, Harry B is about to get married."

"I see."

"They're both adorable, but unique in their own way." I know from his expression that I'm prattling. "That's a stupid thing to say, isn't it? Of course, being unique means you'd have your own way."

"I understand what you meant," he smiles kindly. "Everyone knows we have different personalities: some of us are quiet, some are loud, some are stay-at-homes and some like to party."

"But we're a mix, aren't we?"

"Yes. But even that differs for each individual."

There follows a long silence. Talking about work has quietened him. I change the topic several times, tell him about Laurie and Rupert, that my parents are getting married, about Harry B and his unexpected wedding. He listens intently but doesn't ask for more information about any of them. Perhaps he thinks I'm trying to get his services for free. But his eyes still seek mine, and I feel drawn to him. I want to go around to his side of the table, sit on his lap, put my tongue in his mouth.

When he begins discussing the food, I know for sure he doesn't want to talk about psychology. We talk about the texture, the taste, the flavours, and he asks me about my time as food writer, leads me onto my inspiration for articles. Our conversation takes an uncertain curve as dessert is served, swerving crazily onto the place of work and its consequent economic stability in the lives of women.

I hear myself saying officiously, "If you've ever heard of Jane Austen, she seems to preach love as a redemptive force. The women get rescued by love. Which they require, of course, given the misogynistic inheritance and employment rules at the time. But here we are in the golden age of feminism and we still don't know how to do it. So much of our fashion, literature and media revolves around how to look your best and what to do with a boyfriend if you get one, instead of career and financial acuity. The focus on love doesn't make sense when you look at the other things we've got going for us."

He goes indubitably quiet. "I didn't take you for an Austen girl."

"We're all Austen *women*, whether we've read her or not," I continue without checking for his reaction. "Her heroines are always trying to figure out their place in the world, a world which doesn't support them in the way they want. Perhaps not much has changed."

Ziggy grimaces. "Sense and Sensibility is a political novel."

I frown, trying to understand whether I've been shooting out my opinions to a man who did a thesis on Austen. "Political?"

"Sure. Elinor can't inherit or earn her living. We see an exceptional human being who has no failing except being born a woman. And what happens to the family is what's threatened for the Bennett girls in Pride and Prejudice. They get kicked out of their home on the death of the father. Austen had several main themes: the powerlessness and strength of women runs through her novels."

This shuts me up entirely on the theme of Austen.

Now our talk is aimless, as if we've finished all our topics and are merely passing time until the inevitable question of *What will happen at the end of dinner?*

I'm sure you're as nervous about this as I am. Yes, you want us together at the end of the night, wrapped around each other, the vibe exhilarating, love shining in our eyes, my Vision Quest complete, a happy ever after in the offing. But aren't I more than a lover, a partner, a conquest? Isn't my role as a woman living in a time of equal rights, environmental awareness, political correctness, with a secure well-paying job, worth more than a simple sex-scene, however thrilling?

Ziggy pays the bill entirely and takes my hand as he walks me back across the road. Okay, just so you know, I'm all for bringing on the sex-scene. I hope thrilling is an understatement.

At my car, he stares at me with something that looks a lot like regret. My stomach bubbles oddly with excitement and panic.

He smiles. "I've had a lovely night, Candice. Thanks for coming out with me." He's close now, his arm around my waist, and there's a warmth when his lips meet mine that resounds with the same longing of Sunday morning. I move in, lose myself in his arms, because it's always this way with Ziggy, like he's fully present with me, and not merely thinking of the next step.

Then he breaks away and looks embarrassed, like he's about to reveal he's got an extra set of nipples or a third bum-cheek.

"What's going on?" I ask quietly.

"Sorry," he smiles wanly. "Just thinking about your kiss." He's back on for another go, and my worries slide away easily under the heat of him. I'm about to ask if he'd like to retrieve his book from my flat when he breaks away again and puts his hand on my car door handle.

"I'll make sure you're in safely," he tells me.

I unlock my car and nervously get in, expecting him to say *I'll see you back at your place,* or *Shall I follow you?* or *Why don't we go back to my place this time?*

There's no uncertainty in his voice. "Safe trip home, Candice," he says, and closes the door.

I blink away my tears and drive off.

What the flaming stinking donkey crap just happened?

# 31

Racks of clothing surround my aisle in the brightly lit department store. My way is blocked by a tower of boxes yet to be unpacked. I return to the opening, spin left past the lipsticks and eye shadows until I find a new dead end, this time a perfume counter in the middle of the aisle.

Hmm. I follow my steps back again and peer down the numerous aisles ahead, see blocked avenues down all but one, take a turn amongst the shoes until two aisles diverge in front of me. They both look clear. I follow one and am obstructed by a wall of boots. *It's a maze*, I mumble as I wake, reeking of failure, disappointment, bewilderment.

Nothing else to do but get up and pee.

On my arrival home last night I poured myself several consecutive glasses of wine, played the most lonesome tracks in my music collection, sang along to most of them very poorly, and finally crawled into bed well after three. Fortunately, Rupert and Laurie were tucked away in their lover's nests, away from my caterwauling.

Unfortunately, self-medication only worked until this morning, where the full blast of scorn has joined the throbbing of my head, and I must deal with the betrayal of my wayward personality yet again. I avoid my reflection as I wash my hands, then sit at the dining table, waiting numbly for my laptop to boot up so I can trace back over the night to locate where things turned regretfully rotten. The honest truth does not lift my spirits. Not that I know the honest truth. My laptop sits waiting patiently now. I create a table, fill it with my analysis.

| My digressions | Thoughts |
| --- | --- |
| A discussion about feminism is not the sort of discussion to have with a prospective boyfriend. | Unfortunate but true. I blame the champagne (once again). |
| Discussing the personality test may have prompted him to pinpoint a personality flaw in me. | So many to choose from. |
| In trying to look intelligent, I may have held us back from talk of relationship. | Perhaps, like Jane in Pride and Prejudice, I seemed *indifferent*. |
| I decided against cleavage. | Plain wrong. |
| Was I too respectful of my food? | He appreciated a girl who had *no regard for manners* last Saturday. |
| Was it my previous drunkenness? | A big contender. |
| Perhaps I wasn't the woman he thought I was last weekend? | Further information led to disappointment. |

I sit back, dissatisfied. It still doesn't make sense. I had the impression he was enjoying himself. I remember him laughing, smiling, watching me. Then there was the kissing, both in the dark at his work and in the dark of the car park. Perhaps the dark hid some detestable feature about me? But the dinner was long when it could've been much shorter. He didn't try anything, although he did mention sex, referring to the incident in the bar, the first in a long line of knicker-sightings.

Perhaps he expected me to ask him for sex? He said he was just as lustful, even more so, as the next guy. I don't want the next guy. I want Ziggy. It adds up to one thing: I was too difficult. Rejection stings like the crack of a whip. And with Ziggy, it's the worst I've experienced.

There was no *Call you later*, no *See you again*, no *You know I love you.* In fact, he refuted the belief that we'd stumbled across Love At First Sight.

Crap. I know What I'm Looking For. My parents' experience of being so immediately sure of each other has left me yearning for Ziggy to be my sure thing. I believed it to be true, took evasive action so I couldn't get hurt, yet I have been anyway. My wretched insolvency now adds up to the Zs I wasn't looking for. Zip. Zero. Zilch.

Bitterly, it's not the same for men. They get turned on by rejection, suddenly seeing themselves as the woman sees them and mending their ways, therefore pleasing the woman enough to make them fall in love with them. But rejection, in any woman's accounting, is bad news, because we have no right of reply without seeming desperate.

*Thank you for your recent date. Your feedback is important to us. Please fill in this survey so we can improve our outcomes.*

I dither about the flat, breakfasting, showering, putting a fresh pair of pyjamas on. It's defeatist, I know, but I need a day in bed, even if it's on my own. I toss my laptop onto my mattress and open the curtains and windows wide. The light and fresh air give me an immediate boost.

I check my phone for a text from Ziggy. Nothing. Something quickly appears. It's Kat. It's 7.30. Kat's not an early riser: has she been up all night?

*We're @ Buddy's for brekky after a power walk wanna meet us here? You and anyone else who might be with you LOL x*

I reply, *Spending the day in bed.*

She rifles back, *Give your luv to Ziggy for me.*

I don't respond. I imagine Kat sitting on Thor's lap while they wait for their breakfast. I imagine breakfast will not be the sort she and I usually order after a date-night which requires debriefing with your best friend, but a healthy one of free-range eggs and multi-grained toast and juice. I imagine them looking into each other's eyes adoringly, holding hands romantically, eating off each other's plates sweetly. *Stop, Candice.*

My phone beeps again. Ziggy?

Laurie. *Rupert free Monday. Want to go to pub for meal & discuss?*

May as well get the bad news over with. *Free tomorrow for gardening?*
*Leave it for this weekend and enjoy yourself.*
*Okay. 6pm Monday?*
*Great I'll book for 3. Why gardening tomorrow? Go ok last night?*
What's the honest answer? *Truth is I have no idea.*
*Sorry to hear. Rupert and I think trash the garden. Then see if the flats sell!*
This lowers my mood even more. *Let's talk Monday. No rash decisions.*

I put down my feminist pink phone and listen carefully to the nothing around me. I'm all alone in my flat. All alone in the entire building. I lay down, my eyes staring at nothing out the window, feeling the breeze against my face. My head clears. With nothing to lose and nobody to please, I feel astonishingly and suddenly free. I get, now, what Kat said, that without any fixed reference point ahead of you, you can be anything, do anything, and nobody cares but you.

Anything. A voice whispers a word in my head. *Podcast.*

I sit up quickly. Really? Why haven't I considered this option before? Podcasting, blogging, social media microblogging. Social media is currently done ad hoc at the magazine because we've always seen ourselves as a mostly analogue alternative to the online circus, but there's opportunity there. I check out the magazine's website and scurry across ideas, throwing them onto a blank document on my laptop. My energy surges. I search the net for resources, backgrounds, templates. I buy an eBook on Podcasting and another on Blogging and I keep typing. My experiences run onto the page like syrup from a jar.

I'm out to connect with women everywhere. Why is it, for example, that women have to "hook" themselves a husband, even though that means looking after said husband, but men, who seem to need someone to look after them, don't want to get "caught"? The themes scramble across an entire page. What are our needs? Our labels? Our wishes? Our heartaches? Our disappointments? Our realities?

It's too much. How can one woman cover all of this? *Breathe.*

Our lives vary so dramatically: old/young, black/white, educated/uneducated, free/oppressed, poor/rich, straight/gay. Add in trans and the diversity is enormous. All I can do is aim for a realistic but positive inflection.

Soon I'm exhausted. I bung on the kettle and search for peppermint tea. Thor has given me a hankering for its refreshing, calming taste. I find a battered box containing two teabags lurking at the back of the pantry. As I put the box away, an almost-empty bag of party-poppers falls onto my head. Last New Year's Eve I was in a party mood despite being single (or maybe because of it) and talked Laurie and Rupert into having a bash. We borrowed my parent's barbecue and set up a bar at the back end of our driveway where's there's a big concrete slab. I set Rupert to hanging fairy lights everywhere while Laurie hung balloons, and I set up my lounge room and cleaned my bathroom and kitchen.

The guests came in and out all night, including Kat and her housemates, my parents, Nan and Pop for a couple of hours, Harry K and Joanna and the girls, Joanna's parents and younger sisters and their boyfriends, many of my colleagues, Laurie's sons and their families, a few of Laurie's friends, and four guys from Rupert's work. It was a glorious romp during which the barbecue got fired up, the music had everyone at least tapping their toes, and I didn't have to walk far to sleep off my indulgent night.

The next morning my lounge floor was littered with the sleepy heads of Kat's crew. Someone walked around to the service station to get eggs and bread, I hauled the leftover sausages out of my fridge and sent Kat to wake up Laurie and Rupert, and the barbecue was fired up again for brunch. Nobody left before early evening. Harry B wasn't here, obviously partying privately with Andy. Jamie and Clarissa were dancing close at one stage, but nothing seemed to happen after that. Nevertheless, it seems to have been smouldering all this time.

The kettle boils. As I pour the water into my mug, spoon in the required sugar and jiggle my teabag, an idea pops into my head. I grab the party-poppers and return to my laptop. I let each one go above my notes, shouting, *Hooray! Well done! You go girl! That's the spirit! Good job!*

I collapse on the bed and laugh, feeling freer than ever. I glance across my writing. It's good. It flows. I've set sail at last. If this were a commercial, my smile would have little stars twinkling at the corners.

The veggie patch catches my happy eyes as I return to the kettle. My weekends have pivoted around it in the absence of a boyfriend and even when Gene teetered into my life. It's been a part of my evolution. I don't want it trashed. And isn't it good that someone else will feel excited about growing their own food, regardless of whether it's in line with my own environmental practices?

I take my mug to the sofa. There's a feeling of wellbeing about my person, more than normal after a wrecked date. I'm up, not down. Sensible, not sad. Filled, not deflated. Pleased with my morning's work, not lost on a sea of ill-considered yearning. I've learned a thing or two about being where I need to be. A dog appears outside the window. I rise to shoo it away before it defecates in the garden. Another dog appears and mounts it from behind. Jeez, what is it with my life? "Fuck off!" I yell from the door. They scamper away quickly with the deed incomplete, which I know because they begin again at the edge of the driveway. "Fuck on," I whisper, and slink inside.

I don't get it. What's the meaning of all this coupling around me and why do I even care about a relationship and where the fuck is feminism in all the romance in books and movies anyway? It comes to me then: my personality type centres around my feminist leanings. Can I call the podcast *The Feminist?* Too general. The veggie patch catches my eye. *Confessions of a Feminist Environmentalist.* Too many *ists. Confessions of a Feminist EarthMother?* I'm getting a fuller picture of myself now. It's a lovely feeling. You can't stick me in a box with a label because I'm many things. The party-poppers remind me of Ziggy's words: *You're my favourite party girl.* Inspiration flashes like lightning because here's who I am: *The Feminist EarthMother PartyGirl.* It fits. It's perfect. It's me.

I stand and cheer loudly. Z or no Z, my new life has begun.

# 32

My phone startles me. I gasp to find it's dark outside.

Kat's voice sounds far away. "Can you walk?" she chuckles.

"What do you mean?" I lay back on the bed, jet-lagged and alien.

"Had fun in bed today?"

I've completely forgotten this morning's response to Kat. She's left me alone, thinking I've spent the day with Ziggy, and I've been so enthralled by my new direction that I've ceased being traumatised. Now rejection comes roaring back at me, and I recoil in distaste. "Ziggy packed me into my car at the restaurant last night and sent me home."

"What? But this morning you said-"

"Sorry. I needed space. It's true I've been in bed most of the day. But Kat, I've had the most extraordinary time. I'm writing for a podcast! It's just what I needed, I've spoken with Jamie, he's going to use it as a spin-off from the magazine with me possibly interviewing women and don't you see it's a change of direction without there being any loss, I love my job and the people I work with and-"

"Can! Fuck. Can! Shut the fuck up and go back, what about Ziggy?"

I pause, trying to sum up what can in no way be made sense of. "We had a fabulous night." I sigh. "He's a remarkable guy, Kat."

"I know that. So what the fuck-"

"Nope, no fuck. No fuck at all!" I droop. "He didn't say anything negative, or positive, just nothing happened at the end of the night. No asking for a second date, no suggestion we go home together, nothing." I laugh. "But I can't regret today. It's been fantastic!"

"You've gone all bipolar on me, Can," says Kat with concern. "One second up, one down. You need a psychologist."

I laugh. "Don't you see, if I was with Ziggy today, I wouldn't have had this brilliant idea! It might have passed me by, maybe lost forever. When I asked Jamie for a week off to get it established, he told me *I'm not losing you, take whatever time you need.* Ultimate support. I can't be sad about last night because I've had today."

"You can't marry your words, Can."

I frown. "I admit I was down this morning, but this cheered me up. Ziggy's no longer on my radar."

"No," she says decisively. "I don't accept it. We're coming over, we're bringing the minestrone Thor and I cooked, and we're going to problem-solve this."

I hear traces of despair in my voice as I joke, "I've stepped into an alternative universe where you've been replaced by a health nut and my One True Love has vanished into thin air." I pause, forcing myself to smile. "I'm not unhappy. Actually, I'm doing well."

"I can hear it in your voice, wait, what the fucking fuck did you say? Did you really say *One True Love*? What, just what, just-"

"Come over, bring that hunk of yours to my Spinster Flat. You and I are riding the wave of the inevitable, Kat. Tell him we'll celebrate with juice in champagne glasses." I hang up before she can say any more, return to my writing. After a few sentences, I throw myself back onto the bed, laughing happily. Best friends are fill-in partners, soothing the hurts and revving up your emotional life, keeping your heart happy and being your Significant Other. Who needs a man to spoil the fun?

Ten minutes later I hear them bustling up the path in the same way they blustered down it on the night Thor's original intentions were revealed. And, well, Kat's original intentions. Which were basically the same, although they didn't know it. Thor heaves in a large pot of soup with a cooler bag over his arm and Kat shoves a bag in the door.

"That's our overnight gear." She hugs me. "You don't need to be alone on this Saturday night. I'm getting out the sofa bed."

"People will start thinking we're having a threesome," I smile. "Anyway, I'm not lonely."

"Everyone else is paired but you," she pouts.

I laugh. "Great, now I do feel like a spinster! By the way, the Spinster Flat's being sold."

"No shit?"

I nod. "Yep. All rugs being swept out from under me. It's a woman's liberation." I laugh. "I'm free as a bird."

Thor is looking through my cupboards. We hear a *pop* and I turn to see him opening a bottle of champagne.

"Really, Thor?" I ask. "Alcohol?"

He pours three glasses. "Champagne is for celebration and friendship. It has its place in life. Just not every day. And never cheap."

Kat is at the stove, warming soup and finding bowls. Thor pulls the lid off a platter containing crackers, brie, pickled octopus and kalamata olives. I sit at the table enjoying their comfort. Thor places the glasses around the table and sits down across from me.

"Candice," he booms, "What is it you've been doing today?"

Kat sits down and holds her glass up. We clink together and sip.

"First things first." Kat takes the brie Thor's cut for her, lumps it onto a cracker. "What's this crap about last night?"

I disentangle a tentacle. "He doesn't want me." I pop the octopus in my mouth. They watch despondently as I swallow. "I'm through chasing fantasies. The real point is I'm on a journey. I knew it last weekend, then the whole week's been teaching me stuff."

"Stuff?" Kat piles brie onto a cracker, feeds it to Thor.

"Everything. The whole week's been about romance. I've never seen anything like it. There must be a reason for it happening, and the only reason I can think of is that in pausing on my path I've stepped into a parallel universe. Face it, you in a relationship and getting paid for your designs? My parents getting married? Almost-seventy-years-old Laurie having a girlfriend? Virgin Rupert-"

"Rupert's a virgin?" She swallows her champagne. "No shit!"

"Not anymore." I throw down a bolt of champagne, rip the pip out of an olive. "There's no reality like an alternative reality." I chuck the olive into my mouth.

Thor states, "To calculate the chances of all these romances happening you'd have to consider the chance of each one happening."

"And the one I thought would happen, which was Ziggy." I pick up another chunk of octopus. "I'd decided to look for my Z. Where I was was at A. And I was headed for Z." I chew the octopus like it's rubber.

"You can't get much more Z than Ziggy Zbigniew," Kat smiles, as if she's found the solution to my problems.

"That threw me off the scent," I say decisively. "It was a joke by the Universe. *You want Z, here's one we prepared earlier.*"

"You look really calm," says Thor, "for someone who's been blighted by the blistering ruination of love."

I pause with my glass half-way to my mouth. "Shit, Thor, all these poetic words, how did you get so expressive?"

He smiles proudly. "I did two years of an Arts degree majoring in English literature before transferring to exercise physiology."

I stop breathing for a moment. "I've landed here from another planet. I don't get you humans. Don't get you at all." I slug down the last of my champagne.

Thor chuckles and gets up to turn off the soup while Kat and I stare wordlessly at each other. "Soup nearly ready." He returns to the table.

"So are you, Can." Kat offers me cracker and brie. "Ready for someone good."

I take it from her. "Buff came on to me after you left Friday. Now there's the right bloke for me."

Kat laughs but I can see she's been in on the act.

"Don't judge Buff," Thor says decisively. "His and Mindy's parents are very rich."

"Rich? What?" I forgot Mindy was his sister. "Why do a grown-up brother and sister share a room? Don't you find that weird?"

"Their parents screwed them up good and proper," says Kat. "Opposite ways to me, but the result was the same. They shared a fucked-up childhood, and sharing a room gives them comfort."

"He just got a promotion at work," adds Thor.

Kat laughs at the surprise on my face. "He got a job ages ago. Clean for a year. Not even drinking." She takes another sip of champagne.

"He was high as a kite," I bleat.

"Probably just shy around you, Candice," smiles Thor.

"No. Not shy. It was his regular daredevil attitude," I counter.

"That's regular for Buff," agrees Kat. "Mindy's his best friend. They were both doing drugs when they moved into the house. Raffi stopped them being homeless, talked their parents into giving them a living allowance. Neither of them qualified for welfare."

"Did I know this?" I trawl across my memories.

"Raffi told me later," states Kat. "That whole house is like a shelter for fucked up people."

"Ollie's not fucked up," states Thor.

"He can't keep a girlfriend," Kat retorts.

"That doesn't mean he's fucked up," says Thor. "And Mai-Lee seems happy."

"How's it possible they'd be living in the house together all this time and not know they were in love?" laughs Kat. "I reckon it's just an easy-to-locate bang."

"No." Thor is adamant as he hands out crackers and brie. "They're getting married. Moving out. They know it's time."

"What?" splutters Kat.

"Buff said you'd asked Kat to marry you," I tell Thor. "That true?"

"No. It's too early, but I hope it gets there." Thor smiles at Kat.

"Me, too," replies Kat.

Thor gets up to the soup and begins ladling it into bowls.

I pip another olive, lean in to Kat. "So Buff was talking about Ollie and Mai-Lee, not you two. I'm glad. It's too soon, Kat."

"I know." She leans in, too. "But the relationship's a keeper, Can." Her face lights up. "That first night," she whispers, "when I woke up and found Thor on me, you were right: I'd been having a dream. About Thor. It was like I'd sensed him come into the room, like I wasn't quite asleep. But not quite awake either. In my dream he was standing naked in my room. She giggles, "Apparently, I even moved my legs apart when I said, *I've been waiting for you, baby.*"

I try to contain my smile. "Do you remember doing that?"

Her face falls. "Kind of. Everything's such a blur."

"It's hilarious," I grin. "A story for your golden wedding anniversary. And does it matter now, anyway?"

She shrugs and feeds me a piece of octopus. "I guess not."

Thor returns and places a bowl in front of each of us. "Ziggy's probably just taking things carefully," he says, then returns for his soup.

"Rejection's hard. I know it all too well." Kat looks glum. "Lots of stuff is coming up now, stuff I haven't thought about for ages. Like every year at primary school, I'd make a new friend in class. The next year they wouldn't be in my class. It happened every year. I figure the parents asked the school to separate us. *Keep my child away from that feral!*" She takes a sip of her champagne. "The thing that kept me in high school was you in my class, Can."

I blink. "Mum went to the school each year and told the principal to make sure we were together."

Kat starts to cry. I join her.

She wipes her eyes. "Ziggy walked me through it. I kept talking about what the other kids felt, that I didn't blame the parents, but he said it wasn't about them, it was about me, and my feelings about it. He got me to shout out all the words describing how I felt when it happened each year. The shouting got louder and louder. I was glad nobody else was there." She blushes. "Very therapeutic. Understanding my confusion somehow softens the blow."

"Understanding is what I don't have about Ziggy," I sigh.

"Maybe you have to look very hard to find the meaning of it." Thor sits down with his bowl and some buttered toast, which Kat dives on. "You can't expect the world to be perfect." He watches Kat delightedly drag her toast through her soup. "Romance brings its own dialect, its own culture. You're mixing your emotions with someone else's, and all their values and expectations and gifts and sore spots. They have to mingle with yours." He sips a spoonful of soup, and I do the same.

"Man, this is tasty! Let's eat it for breakfast tomorrow, too!" I laugh.

Thor's not ready for the mood to be lightened. "There'll be kids raised like you, Kat, for hundreds of years to come. The best you can do is surround yourself with community and be an agent for change. Gradual insistent progress is the only way things move forward."

"Jeez, Thor," says Kat. "It's Saturday night. Live a little, buddy."

Thor grins and lowers his eyes to his bowl.

"What about Ziggy?" Kat asks me. "Is he damaged, too?"

"Unlikely." I shrug. "It must be me."

"You don't know how to do romance right," Thor smiles.

With mock derision I say, "What gives you the right to express your opinion about me, Thor? You've only known me a week."

He smiles. "Just giving you a man's point of view. Looks and brains aside, you can be a little combative."

"He means you're pretty and smart, but you come in punching. It's a little scary." She sees my face. "You didn't used to be this way."

"Hurt by love," I whisper inaudibly. "Ziggy said I was hurt by love."

"Call him," pleads Kat. "Ask what's going on."

"Sure," I balk. "And get rejection slapped in my face. Nothing doing. Besides, I don't need a man."

Kat and Thor start laughing. I concentrate on my soup.

It's only later that I realise the talk has all been about love. None of it centred on the fact that I've found my new career.

# 33

Kat and Thor leave mid-morning. Thor needs a gym session and Kat's working on new designs. The absence of their determined comfort dips my mood impossibly low.

I will not be beaten. I stick on some washing and delve into my work, this time writing some draft blog notes themed *Alone is not Lonely*.

*What is it about finding The One that keeps us living in hope?* I write. *Even when all we've had is failure, we still think there is a person who sees us for who we truly are, who will love us for who we truly are, and that we will find them.*

*That's three impossibilities.*

I decide arranged marriages mean *at least you get married*. Find-your-perfect-match is a recent addition to society in any case.

Yes, my good mood has failed me today. Thor's words return, and I admit I've become too *combative* to be a good choice as a girlfriend. And the energy I've been chugging through to defer my introspective analysis of the Ziggy issue has run dry in the face of Kat's heartbreaking revelations. I get dressed, brush my teeth, brush my hair, and seek respite in my local bookstore.

I smile gratefully as I soak up the ambience. While I love e-books, the thrill of being surrounded by wisdom and imaginings in paper copy always soothes. I stroll from aisle to aisle, stopping when a title or cover captures my eye. The Fashion section reveals books on hairstyles and makeup and how to dress for your figure, but exhibits iconic women flaunting their undeserved and uncommon beauty on each cover. I suspect wandering over to the men's aisle would reveal war and sport and true grit. Beauty versus strength. Yet as we age it reverses: it turns out women are the strong ones, managing children and work and households, whilst men keep their looks longer.

Oddly, the Baby section is next to Fashion. There's a whole shelf on Baby Names, and I wonder abruptly what kind of name Kat and Thor would give a child. Perhaps *Rainbow* or *Dragon* or even *Baby*. I pick up one of the books, leaf through its pages. My hand drags me towards the end of the book; after all I'm still looking for my Z. I stop briefly at Sigmund. Ah, victorious protector, that's right. A variation is, apparently, Zigmund. That's where the *Ziggy* comes from, obviously, so I flick to Ziggy, and fuck! at Ziggy it says *see Zbigniew*. What?

I flick quickly and yes, Zbigniew, which means *reducing anger*, good name for a psychologist, has as a diminutive the name Ziggy. He's Ziggy Ziggy. My heart bangs. What does that mean? If anything? And why look for an answer in a name? Why am I looking for meaning in everything? Is that all I have to point me in the right direction? Isn't the weekend all about not thinking of Ziggy, of reducing my angst about Ziggy? *Go with the flow, Candice, stop fighting the flow.*

Resolute, I stride to Romance. The covers show female author names, and the faces carry the same magnificent features as the Fashion section. Within the pages of both sections' books are the promise of happy lives if we focus on being pretty and enchanting. What happened to other attributes like wise and strong? Anger and despair teeter in my thoughts. I take several deep breaths to level. *Go with the flow.*

I touch a book cover here and there, analysing the match of title to front cover picture, reading the back cover, opening to the last page to find the Happy Ever After. All the heroines are like me, working, wondering, hoping to meet The One, all the stories relying on The Road That Goes Wrong until it takes up enough pages to satisfy our need for the turnaround from ruin to redemption. I sigh. *Love as a redemptive force.* The words form ice crystals in my brain.

I walk back to my car without a purchase.

Just once, I decide grimly, I want to pick up a book and find the Hero turning up right on time and things running smoothly from there. Just once I want to read a book that doesn't *take the reader on a journey of love and betrayal, of determination and the indefatigable heart.* Please. Just once I want a book where there's no twist, no problem to resolve, no injury time. Straightforward, you'll do, all happy. I wince inwardly. I'm that regular heroine, thwarted by love, abandoned by my lack of fortitude. I know for certain the paradoxical situation I'm in is my fault. It can't be Ziggy's, because where have I ever seen such a man? He's got it all going for him, was interested in me, and I screwed up. Even sober I've done something that's turned him off, and I have no idea what that something was. His kiss seemed genuine, then Zero.

As I drive to the Spinster Flat I realise it's not romance we seek but community. Bonding with another person is merely our own personal community. I already have that with my family, colleagues, neighbours, with Kat. Ziggy's not important. Nevertheless, my mind needs answers. What is it that's disconnected us? We can easily make a list. Falling into the pub amidst my dress. Getting drunk at the wedding. Kat's charade at his work. My appointment under a false name.

I've screwed up dazzlingly this time.

Back at the flat Ziggy's book stares brazenly from the table, as if to say *You thought you were learning something when, really, you've learnt nothing at all.* I flip open the cover and the date catches my eye: it's printed this year. I wish I knew what that meant, if anything. Meaning, always searching for meaning. I flop down at the table. Such a small part of our day is spent in the throes of passion and hardly any of it in romance, so why is it a woman's focus? My mind twitches across the ever-evolving face of feminism as I boot up my laptop. I need to refocus on what it is to be a woman.

*We don't often call ourselves feminists these days, it's a given that we'll have our rights supported under law. But we should never forget we were once considered not good enough to have a say in our country, not permitted to hold certain jobs, could not be in charge of a man, did not deserve equal pay for equal duties. Our average pay is still markedly below that for men, and sexual abuse and harassment remain everywhere. We have a long way to go.*

My phone rings. My breath catches at the unknown number.

"Hello, Candice, it's Daisy here. Do you remember me?"

"Of course. How's Rupert?"

"Oh, he's good. Very, very good, in fact." She giggles. It's too much information. "It's Sunday today, your usual gardening day. We thought we'd show you our garden for a change instead of you all meeting tomorrow night. We've asked Laurie and Denise around for lunch, and I'm sorry it's twelve, but it was a spur of the moment decision, and will you come, too? Bring your new man."

*Our* garden? I don't need to ask what Rupert's intentions are about the sale of the units. "Sure, I'd love that. But it'll just be me."

"Oh." This has set her back. Daisy's now had Rupert's remedial romance rehabilitation, and she wants the whole world to be as Happy Ever After as she is. "Shall I invite my brother? He's single."

I laugh rudely. "Remember you said you'd given up men before you met Rupert? That's me."

"Nonsense," she says sternly. "When you least expect it, Mr Right will pop up. I'm speaking from experience."

I censor my reply. "Thanks for the kind offer of your brother. I'd love to come today and get to know you and Denise, but I don't need you to invite your brother. I'll bring my world-famous potato salad."

Thank goodness I have mayonnaise, there are potatoes to dig up, and parsley is rampant in our garden. I'm buoyed by the chance of friendship and community. Ah heck, the partygirl in me lives on.


Daisy's garden is brimming with colour. She tells me she's only lived for a year in her house with the sweet cottage garden out the front. She'd been married for seven years before her husband got itchy and scratched himself on a pretty, young work colleague.

She lived with her brother Zane for six months after the marital home sold until she found this place, with its nifty entertaining area and wide expanse of lawn out the back. Zane is here, despite my request. He's definitely not my Z. He's quiet like Rupert is, or used to be, for now Rupert seems to be the effusive host, laughing and joking and serving up beer and wine in a new polo top and fashionable jeans, calling to his sweetheart in a voice made from sugar to *Get the meat, honey, and I'll fire up the barbie.*

Laurie hugs me warmly and introduces Denise who, despite being seventy-two, still wears skin-tight jeans, a low-slung top, several arm bracelets and a chunky necklace. "This is our very precious Candice. Rupert can thank her gardening plot for Daisy." He chuckles and takes my hand. "She's my best moral support."

Denise smiles as she looks me over. "Immoral support, more like. How old are you, Candice?"

"Twenty-eight."

"Oh, a very bad age. Thirty around the corner and everything you thought to be true no longer holds. All you can do is ride the wave." She glances at Laurie and smiles. "I'm still riding it."

"Perhaps you've reached shore?" I push.

She laughs. "He'll need to convince me to put down anchor."

"I'll let you ride my anchor anytime," grins Laurie.

Time passes pleasantly. Zane is as warm as the sunshine once he has a couple of beers. He's just turned forty and I wonder if, like Rupert was, he's still a virgin. "No woman on the scene, Zane?"

"Actually," he says quietly, "I spent last night with my ex. I want to get back with her. She's not keen." He looks over at his sister. "Don't tell Daisy, she'd be furious. She's been married for five years."

"Oh. Still married?"

"Her husband had an affair, so she had one with an ex-boyfriend to get him back. You get the picture." He swigs his beer.

"And the ex-boyfriend is you?"

"No, the one who came after me. Then she didn't know what to do so she rang me for a listening ear. You know the rest." He swigs again.

I bite back my laughter.

"She's the only woman I was ever really happy with."

"Love stinks," I tell him. "Lies and half-truths and you find yourself singing someone else's song."

He smiles as Rupert clears his throat.

"I'm about to serve up the barbecue but let's get the formalities out of the way first," smiles Rupert proudly. "I'm moving in here. The sale of the units is kind of a blessing, because otherwise we'd be waiting." He and Daisy smile at each other quaintly.

"I'm moving out, too," Laurie nods. "I'm boarding with Denise."

Denise winks at me. She's playing hard to get!

"We were wondering if we could still do the gardening thing," says Daisy. "We could help out each other. Maybe once a month?"

I smile. "Now I have even more friends. Count me in."

"Us, too," Laurie says. "What are we going to do about the flat's garden? Leave it to rot or rip it up?"

"Neither," I say. "I'm going to look after it. The Earth needs to be nourished for its own good."

"Yes," nods Laurie reticently, "that's the right thing to do."

Enough sentimentality. "Come on, Rupert," I smile, "I'm starving, where's this barbecue?"

With nothing better to do we stay into the night. Zane talks to me about his ex. Ziggy's manner has rubbed off onto me, and I find myself slower to judge other people's behaviour. As I leave, he gives me a quick kiss on my mouth and whispers, "Thanks. It's nice to find someone who understands."

I drive home, remembering his lips on mine, and I feel worth something. Powerful. Aware. An agent for change.

# 34

The next day is Monday, and I can stay home and work on my podcast/blog if I want. I don't want.

I go into work seeking companionship, but, unfortunately, it's just me in my section. I take a break from my new direction to immerse myself in my regular work, writing an article about parenting, humorously called *Martyrs and Farters*, when Martin's phone rings.

"Hello, can I speak to Martin?" The voice sounds too sweet for a business call. I have no idea if Martin has sisters, aunties, or a mother.

"Sorry, he's not in. Can I ask who's calling?"

"It's Joy. He left his phone home. I found out when I tried to call."

"You're his sister?"

"His wife."

"Oh. Um. Sorry, I didn't know he was married." *Ouch, Candice.*

"We got married last year when we found out about the baby."

"Baby?" I know this sounds stupid but I am stupid when it comes to Martin. I always pictured him in a grotty little flat eating two-minute noodles and watching sci-fi, not bunkered down in domesticity.

"Men!" she laughs. "He keeps to himself." She sounds like she expects this is typical of men everywhere. "Ryan's three months old. The wedding was at the registry, just our parents and my sister and his two brothers. We didn't want a fuss."

"Uh," I say, because I've lost all proper functioning. It's only when she hangs up that I realise she didn't ask my name. I look at my watch:

it's two-thirty and my stomach's yelping for food. My head says salad sandwich whilst my heart says jumbo double-chocolate milkshake.

I return to the office a half hour later, loneliness chilling my bones. I wonder briefly if Jamie knows about Martin's home life. He should've given this job to him to write. There's a tap on my shoulder.

Kat. "Coffee."

She hooks her arm in mine, humming a little tune as we walk. I steer her across the road to the pub.

"Kat, that song's a little off-putting."

"But I feel happy. It's Monday," she says, as if I must know that Mondays are happy. "I had my second session with Ziggy."

My breath freezes. I'd forgotten that. I buy a wine for me and a lemonade for Kat. She leads me to a booth at the furthest corner.

"This looks ominous." I gulp my wine.

"I asked Ziggy what he's thinking about you."

"Oh, Kat, you didn't."

"I was always going to." She smiles kindly. "I asked if he had a good time on Friday night." She looks pensive. "He said he had *The best time*. I asked if he's going to see you again," her eyes grow wide, "and he said something really odd."

My stomach drops. Never before have I felt so spurned. Being rejected by a psychologist, someone who sees things about you that you don't even know about yourself, feels like the same humiliation as being stripped naked in a public place.

Kat leans in. "He said, *I can't answer that*, and then got on with the session. Which I must say was very liberating. But all the while my brain kept niggling at what happened Friday night. You must ring him, Can. You must ring him right now."

"I'm not doing anything of the kind." I gulp more wine.

"Something's going on we don't know about. Find the answer."

More wine. "Trying to find The Answer is what got me into this mess." There's an edge to my voice. "I was prepared to sleep with a guy after only knowing him for a week! In fact, it was a handful of moments, not even really a whole week. I was still being someone other than me."

Kat laughs. "You nutcase. Parker was a one-night stand."

"Was not," I sulk. "I knew him. He wasn't just some random guy."

"Now you're making up rules. You thought Ziggy was The One."

"First, there's no such thing. Second-"

"You're hurting. I'll ask him more tomorrow, at my next session."

"Tomorrow?"

"He's seeing me every day this week."

I run my finger along the base of the glass. "Isn't that kind of weird?"

"Helpful, more like."

I sigh. "For you, yes. For me, hard."

"Hard is good," she giggles, "if it's the right body-part."

"Kat!"

She quiets. "The only one you can control is you, Can."

We to and fro without resolution. Kat needs a lift home as she's caught the bus all day. She's full of excitement about her therapy, the contracts, Thor. Then she tells me she's going to buy a house.

"I'll have just enough for a deposit on a little renovator's delight. It'll be a blank canvas." She grins. "Thor will pay board. And I've got a job. They needed a receptionist at Thor's gym. It's twenty hours a week. That gives me an income. And I get free use of the gym."

I laugh. "Working *and* working out?"

She looks hurt. "I'm stepping out of past ways. Moving ahead. Aiming for better."

I feel out of step with her progress. "Will the banks give you a loan?"

"There's the new loan that helps people like me." She frowns. "I forget what it's called. I think the government do it. Or something. Thor knows about it." She brightens. "And once my designs start being made, I'll get more money coming in."

When I drop her off, I get out of the car and hold her tightly. She's transformed from waif to wizard in weeks. Thor and therapy were what she needed. I wish it had been as easy for me.

At home I head for the kettle, my head lagging. I spy Ziggy's book again. Damn it, I should've stuck it in the post. I open it to the introduction, sit down at the table, get a crash course on the history of psychology. It mentions something called the Critical Ladder of Universal Expectations, and the kettle is forgotten as I re-define my Vision Quest. The CLUE is what we expect to have satisfied by the world. It's shaped like a ladder to climb. The first rung is Necessities.

> *unpolluted air*
> *clean water*
> *nutritious food*
> *clothes to suit the climate*
> *spending money*
> *a place to call home*

Hmm. The first five aren't a problem for me, but that last one will be soon. I grab paper and write **a place to call home** on it. Doing well so far. Rung Two is Guarantees.

> *feeling safe*
> *being healthy*
> *having enough money*
> *having somewhere to go when things go wrong*

Once again, the last one stings. Harry K's right, I need to save for a house, which means finding a very cheap rent plus a reduction in my frock-buying. I add **having somewhere to go when things go wrong** and connect the two items with a line.

Next is Rung Three: Community.

> *friendship*
> *family*
> *work or other colleagues*
> *a network*
> *partner/close loving relationship*

I have friends, family, fellow workers. Once again, the last one fails. I have Kat but now she's got Thor. I scribble **partner/close loving relationship** quickly and continue.

Rung Four is Worth.

*feeling good about one's self*

*feeling one has a purpose*

*feeling respected*

*feeling loved*

The podcast/blog's given me direction and purpose, but I'm engulfed by self-doubt about respect and love, thanks to the man who promised much but has been so painfully absent. Thor's words return: I don't know how to do love right. Am I combative? Do I drive men away? Make them treat me badly? I write: **Who is Candice Kelly?**

My thoughts congeal.

I'm the price of love. Conceived on a one-night stand, I'm the very public consequence of my parents not being able to keep it in their pants, the brutal revelation they displayed a total disregard for the people they loved. Raised by a man and a woman who battled to make a family from the remnants of their old lives, amid the debris of the shattered lives of Dad's wife and both Harrys.

I have a lead here, but what of it? *Think, Candice.*

My brothers are marvellous. I've always enjoyed their playful love for me. My parents are marvellous, too, a beacon of hope I'll find the love they stumbled across by chance. Hopefully I'll get it right before children, unlike my parents, which is why condoms are my best friends.

I think of Sylvie. Dad's ex-wife doesn't look like she'd suit him. There's no fun in her bones, and she always sports a slightly aloof look, although that might be only towards me. In any case she's officious, self-important, and always looks like she's trying to prove a point. I hardly saw her growing up. She made Dad pick up and drop off Harry K for staying at our place.

Once she married the well-heeled Archer, Sylvie got even more snobbish. Dad, out of guilt, always makes excuses for her. Mum just rolls her eyes. I loved it when Joanna sent all the parents a letter saying she'd have no hesitation *whatsoever* in kicking out "anyone" who misbehaved at *her* wedding. I know this was aimed at Sylvie rather than my parents. Joanna takes no shit. I wish I could be more like her. What this history means for my Worth? Blank. But my Vision Quest has at last taken shape:

> *a place to call home*
> *having somewhere to go when things go wrong*
> *partner/close loving relationship*
> *Who is Candice Kelly?*

I can knock off the first two together. And I have a lead on the last, if only I can capture it. I write a post about *Doing what you can and leaving the rest for later.*

I decide on an early night. I fork cold spaghetti from a can whilst sipping a glass of scotch on ice as I think about Jamie and Clarissa, and Ollie and Mai-Lee. Those relationships have been slow burn. Love at first sight isn't the only path to true love.

I remind myself, again, it's not romance I'm after but a fulfilled life.

I brush my teeth, stare myself down in the mirror, then lay quietly in bed. With sleep evading me I retrace Kat's journey, from the day I met her, the crazy escapades we've had, the secrets she's been carrying like an invisible backpack. She's always been strong, joyous, grateful on the outside whilst she was broken, damaged, shattered on the inside.

Now I know: Ziggy came into my life so he could help Kat, not for my own personal ambitions. I need to be content with finding my Life's Work.

I hope Romance lays in the path somewhere else ahead.

# 35

Unlike last week's plod, the week flies by like a high-speed missile.

Kat texts me every night with news of her sessions with Ziggy. *He says unorthodox method but he's fitting me in @6!* and *Every night on a roll & have to follow it!* It seems she can twist Ziggy around her little finger in a way I can't. Her texts always begin with something like *Wow, this analysis shit is amazing!* and end with something like *You gotta get him in your life, Can!*

I delete each text immediately. She's in good hands with Ziggy and she'll call if she needs me. My best option is to work on the part of my Vision Quest that's healthy: my fabulous new job direction.

But by Thursday night my enthusiasm flags, and I realise my two big dilemmas aren't going away. They need resolution, and the only reason I haven't finalised them is because I've had no idea how.

The first is Ziggy. What did he mean telling Kat he had *The best time*, but didn't know if he wants to see me again? Of course he's not going to tell his client about his romantic life. But he had the best time! The Best Time! Even my poor behaviour shouldn't rate as an issue against the backdrop of *The Best Time*.

I sit doodling on a pad, trying to draw out my feelings. I consult my lists, flick through them dispassionately. Nothing gels. I grab Ziggy's book, but I'm so disheartened about Ziggy that I immediately put it back down. No solution to this dilemma yet. Maybe never.

The second is whether to move. If I move, where to? Another flat would disappoint by way of its less wonderful neighbours. I scribble my options on the doodle pad.

| | |
|---|---|
| *Parents.* | Nope. Too depressing to move home after I've already made a break for it. Besides, they're planning a wedding. |
| *Kat's.* | Nope. She's about to escape the Den of Craziness to live at Thor's, and I am NOT moving into her room, not even for a short amount of time. And if she gets a house, I couldn't imagine living with two lovebirds doing it every chance they have. |
| *Harry B's.* | Nope. Andy could do without a sister-in-law moving in. Especially as they want to start a family. Eeeuw! More non-stop sex emanating through the walls. |
| *Harry K's.* | |

I pause. Yes, Harry K's! Their mansion has plenty of room, and they could do with some help!

Joanna's alone, the kids asleep, when I arrive. K's run to the shops. I waste no time making my pitch. It's a temporary move to get them through till the baby's born. They don't need rent money and they've already got a cleaner, so I'll do the shopping, cooking, washing and general spot tidying. I'll do Simone's school drop-off each morning to give Joanna an easier morning whilst she's feeling spewy. I'll save money for a house and help Joanna. Win-win.

Joanna, the ice queen, bursts into tears. "Oh, Candice!"

I do what I've never done before: I hug her close. "We can be each other's solutions."

Joanna quickly repairs. "You can stay. I'd love the company. And the occasional hand. If you can play with the girls while I take a nap, that would be helpful. But I can manage the rest without a large commitment on your part. I wouldn't have decided on another baby if I couldn't handle it. And you have a life to lead."

"I'm offering to help," I say. "Take it. You must be exhausted!"

"Actually, I'm just hormonal. Tired, yes, but you don't have to hook yourself into mother-work, Candice, when you're in your dating prime. Enjoy yourself before the hard work, fulfilling though it is, begins."

I humph. "I don't know if I'll ever go out on a date again."

She frowns. "Rough time?"

"Yep."

We look at each other for a few uncomfortable seconds. Joanna doesn't discuss personal details and I'm not unpacking the Ziggy saga.

"I think you're lucky with K. He must piss you off often," (she laughs), "but you're a tight knit group."

Harry K comes in the door with his hands full of shopping bags. "Hey, sis, got nothing better to do on a Thursday night than visit an old married couple?"

"Just putting a roof over my head." I laugh at his puzzled expression. "I'm taking your advice, K, saving for a house. Congratulations, bro, you just got yourself a boarder."

It hits me on my drive home that the Z I've been looking for is my Zeitgeist. I pull over and thumb through my phone to confirm it refers to *a dominant belief of an era*. That's it! That's my Z! All the things I'd believed, about myself, my family, Kat, work and colleagues, it's like everything got thrown into the air and came down differently. I'm now in a different era, one of choice and freedom and confidence. My Z is my Zeitgeist. I'm there. And I love it.

At the flat I find a huge display of flowers on my doorstep. My heart quickens against my will as I read the card, but it's from Gene. *Can you forgive me?* I laugh, because the thought it might be Gene hadn't entered my thoughts, well, let's be real now that it doesn't matter anymore, good old Godfrey has such Zero significance in my life that I absent-mindedly screw up the card and toss it into the garden. I leave the flowers on the doorstep; I'll take them in to Mrs Feeble later. That should cheer her up about the upcoming sin of her loving son daring to marry again.

I walk around the flat, quickly planning for the move. My sofa, dining suite and TV/music gear can go to Mum and Dad's until Kat can use them, or until I get a house of my own. Maybe she can also use some of my kitchen gear, too. My treasured knick-knacks will need boxing up and storing. I walk to the dining table and cross off *a place to call home* and *having somewhere to go when things go wrong* with a grin. Yeah, now things are moving. I'm feeling edgy about *partner/close loving relationship* when there's a loud knock.

It's Harry B. Pre-wedding dramas, I presume, from the consternation on his face.

"It's not what you're thinking," he frowns. "It's about you."

The flowers are gone, replaced with a note. I pick it up and see the words, *Sorry, I sent the flowers to the wrong address.* I laugh and open the door, let Harry B pass.

He takes up the whole room. "Who's the note from?"

"Godfrey." I step into the Spinster Flat and close the door.

"Fuck, no, Candice!"

"Don't worry. Got that one fixed." I can't place the expression on his face. "Did I do something wrong?"

We hug, and bad news presses against me. "It's about Ziggy."

I throw him away, horrified. "Something's happened to him?"

He smiles. "Apparently that something is you."

"What do you mean? Wait, how do you know Ziggy?" I'm confused, anxious, frightened.

Harry B looks away. "I told you I've been working out some things lately. I wanted to take this thing with Andy to the next level, but I didn't want to get married and watch it to go pear-shaped. I've got a lot to lose financially." Typical Harry B, equating losing money with losing love. "Dad screwed up his first marriage."

"That was a teenage shotgun."

"But shit happens," he shrugs. "So, Andy and I saw a psychologist for couples counselling."

"A psychologist?"

"Ziggy."

I'm open-mouthed. "No shit?"

"Andy and I wanted to sort through some issues, but I realised I needed to work through the stuff before Mum met Dad. And when she met Dad. And what happened after. So, I've been seeing Ziggy alone."

"What kind of issues?" I'm feeling a squeeze in my chest.

"When Mum told me she was having a baby, I got confused. How could she be having a baby when I didn't have a father and she didn't have a boyfriend? I didn't know about Dad then, of course."

I blink relentlessly.

"K and I didn't want to have anything to do with each other, and we'd been put in the same class. K immediately told me what happened, and I was even more confused. Mum went from no guy to this full-on relationship, pregnancy, everything and suddenly I had a stepfather and a stepbrother. I was the centre of Mum's world and it was hard to share her with Dad and Harry K. I missed Nan and Pop. I missed my old bedroom. We were suddenly living with strangers in a strange house."

I can hardly breath. "I never-"

"Mum and Dad put in a lot of effort to bond us together before you came along. Sylvie was being really nasty." He smiles. "But here's what saved it: you. Suddenly we had this cute little baby girl in our midst. Harry and I stopped fighting, and Dad really became my dad."

I burst into tears.

Harry wipes my tears with his fingers. "Sometimes I'd be sitting on the couch reading a textbook and K would be sitting at the dining table doing an assignment, and you'd stop him, take his hand and bring him over to the couch, make him sit down and then climb up and hug us both. It was good to remember." He smiles and hugs me briefly.

"Oh, Harry."

"I also needed to decide whether to get in touch with my biological father. The old neighbour told Mum he'd moved to South Africa years ago. What's he had to do with my life? He had his chance when he found out Mum was pregnant, and the years since, but unlike Dad he refused to take any responsibility. Of the two dads, I know which I'd choose. Mum and Dad screwed up, but they faced up to their responsibilities every time." He laughs. "In the end you were a bargain. Not only did I get a cute little sister, but you brought me a great father and a pretty good brother, too. You've been one of the gifts of my life."

I hug my beautiful big brother again tightly. "Ziggy wasn't allowed to tell me you were seeing him?"

We pull apart and Harry B grins. "I didn't know he was seeing you! He spoke to me about you at our session today, and wanted to know where it fitted in."

"But surely he knew I was your sister?"

"We haven't talked about you for a long time, and then it was only early on and only setting up what happened in our family. Lately it's been all about me." He smiles. "And we don't share a last name."

I smile. "I told him my name was Agnes at first."

"Agnes?" He laughs loudly. "Apparently you mentioned my name on a date? Anyway, with the wedding decided, we're stopping our sessions. There's no problem with you seeing Ziggy."

I start to cry again.

"Hey, it's not like you need my permission. See whoever you want." He laughs. "Just not Godfrey."

"It's not that. I never understood what happened. He was kind and sweet and then … nothing. I thought I'd done something wrong."

"Set it right, Candice. Don't waste any time."

"Set it right. Yes." Our family story was an important precursor to my ideas about love and, like Harry B, I need to set it straight. I grab my keys. "Go home. I'm going to Mum and Dad's."

He frowns. "What for?"

"A history lesson."

# 36

I pause at my parents' door with key in hand, then knock instead.

Mum hugs me at the door. "Hi, sweetie, forgotten your key?"

"I'm handing your place back to you." I walk into the familiar lounge-room. "It's not my home now. And you're getting married."

She's momentarily crestfallen. "Dad's about to have a shower, but we can have a cup of tea."

"Hi, sweetie," Dad appears and hugs me. "Thought I heard your voice. Let's have some tea."

I squeeze my father tight. He's always been my centre. "I want to talk to Mum, go have your shower."

They signal each other with their eyes.

"Sure." Dad leaves.

Mum puts on the kettle as I ready the mugs.

"Mum, please walk me through when you met Dad, piece by piece."

She smiles as if I'm once again a child.

"I'll start you off," I say. "You've taken your son to high school after getting him through primary school-"

"Finishing primary school was a few weeks off."

"You meet this other parent. He's attractive, chatty, friendly-"

"And great with his son." She makes the tea. "It made me see what Harry had missed." She shakes her head as she stirs the tea. "I was always thinking about what Harry had missed. It drove me crazy."

"But this guy's married. Did you know that first up?"

She's in that moment. "Yes. He said he felt lucky to be the one to bring his son to such an important day, that his wife had to work." She looks away. "I said I wished my son had a dad like him. Or any dad."

"Straight up you both know the score."

She hands me my mug. "I see what this is." Her eyes are on mine. "I knew one day you'd be ashamed of my behaviour. I thought it'd be earlier than this, and I always wondered what I'd tell you." She smiles. "I've felt ashamed of my behaviour, too, more often than you know."

I shake my head. "Mum, never."

She shrugs. "That day is still so vivid. Ashton had nerves of steel with his Harry, and I was a ball of anxiety with mine. I shook his hand when I was leaving because I needed to touch him. Neither of us let go for ages. I had to force myself to walk back to my car. I felt like crying, I was overwhelmed with feelings of, I don't know, gloom. Lust. Certainty. Despair." She holds her hand to her chest.

"If he hadn't called your name, what would you have done?"

"I knew I'd see him at pick-up. I felt surprised and very, very guilty that I was hanging on to that." She shrugs again. "I decided to drive home, do the washing. Or something." She blows across her tea. "Our boys were going to the same school, it would be a very awkward encounter if I acted like a schoolgirl every time I saw him."

"She was too much to pass up." Dad's in his pjs, smiling at Mum.

I feel like I've caught them having sex. "Quick shower, Dad."

He grins. "Didn't want to miss the fun."

I return my attention to Mum. "So he wants to talk. How'd that feel, given you knew you couldn't start anything?"

"I was grateful for even a few more minutes." She smiles at Dad. "Perhaps he was feeling the same way. He wasn't retreating from me, yet he seemed to be a good man, a responsible man."

Dad continues. "This was going somewhere, although I didn't know where. Just another step surely wouldn't hurt. I could back out at any time, I told myself as we got into my car. Then over coffee, well, when we got back to the car-"

"We were desperate to kiss each other," continues Mum.

"Didn't either of you pack condoms?" I ask. "Think about safe sex?"

"I didn't think we'd go that far," says Mum.

"And I didn't want to waste time going to a chemist on the off chance she'd give in," Dad chuckles. "I didn't want to give in to my own need for her, either. But when we met, it was primal."

"Primal." Ziggy's words. "But didn't you stop and think?"

Mum blushes. "We tried. I remember we took forever to start anything, then we each got undressed on our side of the bed and stood looking at each, unable to go further or withdraw."

"We had a shower together and that was that," smiles Dad. They look at each other and laugh.

"Mum, find something to do. I want to talk to Dad on his own."

They both stop laughing.

"Why's this so important suddenly, Candice?" asks Mum.

"Boy trouble."

She smiles. "I was going to take a shower, anyway." She walks off to the bathroom. Now I'm sure I've interrupted something.

Dad gives me a warm hug. "Boy trouble, hey? This the one you wore that half-dress for?"

I bury my head in his shoulder. "Dad, there's something missing from my understanding about how those first moments were for you." I pull away. "How were you so certain that you were prepared to risk your marriage? With a stranger? Harry B was evidence she'd previously made poor decisions, and you'd been caught out the same."

"Your mother was adamant she didn't want an affair, and nor did I. I wanted to be with her, and I wanted to protect her from me at the same time." He shakes his head. "The link between us was one I hadn't felt with Sylvie, and she was the only woman I had to compare it with. We left it simmering. I rang your mother a week later. We decided against meeting up. Another week and we met for coffee. We talked over the possibilities, what it would mean for the boys, how we felt."

"You got to know each other after sex." Like Kat. "And then?"

"The next week I felt an urgent need to call her. She was oddly offhand. She'd found out she was pregnant and had no idea how to tell me. I thought it was my fault for messing her around, so I made a snap decision and told her I was leaving Sylvie. She still didn't tell me she was pregnant. I asked her to keep the faith and I'd call in a few days. A few days! Sylvie was livid, told me she'd already forgiven me and that my loyalty was to the family. I remember she called it *her family*, like I had nothing to do with what we'd made together." His shoulders hunch. "I was that bad guy you read about in novels, the cad who leaves his family in the lurch."

I'm ineffably sad. "I sure did screw things up for you."

"But I didn't know about you when I left Sylvie." He frowns. "I've never regretted you. How could I? You're the best daughter a man could wish for." He gently wipes away the tears that start running down my face. "I can't imagine being without Harry K, either." He shakes his head. "Or Harry B. It's funny how things turn out. Things you should regret that you don't in hindsight."

I'm desperate for his salve. "Is that really true?"

"Yes." He sighs. "When Sylvie told me she was pregnant I couldn't believe it. I was seventeen and felt like my life was over. Facing up to our parents was terrifying. I moved into Sylvie's girlie pink bedroom a few months later. We lived there for a year, during which I tried to make it up to everybody because I felt so stupid. When we got married it was surreal, I was still a kid, and we moved out of her bedroom into a flat because Sylvie wanted our marriage to look normal although we were so excruciatingly young and had this new baby. I had to find a job to support us and Sylvie took Harry to uni with her so one of us at least could get a degree." His face is ashen. "She kept getting stronger and more ambitious and I kept shoring up everything."

I've never thought about what it was like when Harry K was conceived. I'm struck by how much we simply accept life without analysis. "Dad, do you think it's important to travel a path even if it's going to be a dead end, like your marriage was? And did you ever think you might be without Mum or Sylvie?"

He smiles. "The answers only come with time. When I contacted Judith to tell her I'd left Sylvie, we met for lunch and that was when she told me she was pregnant with you. I'd done it again!"

I start to wail. I cry for Sylvie and Harry K who lost their family. I cry for my mother, the good girl who got pregnant during both bouts of casual sex. I cry for Harry B, confused and scared of love. I cry for my father, who followed his heart down its path, both fair and foul. And I cry for me.

He hugs me tightly. "It all worked out okay. Later, Sylvie told me she shouldn't have got so mad, because she was feeling isolated too, like I didn't fit into her life anymore, but she didn't do anything because it was easier to bury it with work and let me do all the family stuff." He pulls away. "She's so much happier now and so am I. When the path is unclear you have to listen to your instinct." He frowns as my wail gets louder. "Heavens! Is this about us or this guy?"

I speak between sobs. "Every time I feel comfortable enough to see what's there, he leaves me guessing. I can't bear it! What do I do, Dad? Isn't it all supposed to be easy once you've found The One?"

Mum appears wet and wearing a towel. She doesn't want to be left out of this conversation. "Life's not a smooth line, honey. You have to build up the picture with each other while the canvas keeps changing. I found it different parenting with a father around. We all had to get used to each other. And the Harrys finished school and we had to start the whole thing over again with you. When you finished school we were swamped with despair. Over twenty years of schooling gives you a routine, and we'd suddenly lost it. That's why you hope your kids go to uni. It gets you used to the fact they're moving out of your life gradually. It's why we left it so long to get married."

My lip wobbles again. "Which is exactly the point. Why gamble on a relationship that may or may not work? Why not just stick to work? I've been working on this extraordinary idea, and it's a shift in direction and that's the only thing I can be sure of. Why risk your happiness by banking on someone else's values?"

"You can never be sure of anything, love," my mother tells me.

I start sobbing again.

"Go get dressed, Judith," Dad smiles, "This needs a father's hand."

Mum wanders towards the bedroom. Dad turns to me.

"What's the real problem here? Something to do with your mum?"

I'm sure my eyes are wide. "Harry B's been to see a psychologist."

"I know."

"And that psychologist just happens to be the man I was seeing."

Dad laughs. "That's hilarious." He frowns. "So what?"

I scowl. "I'm just getting it all straight in my head, finding The One and following the path and how do you know what's the right way to go and why bother-"

"Candice, it's true what your mother said. You'll never know it all." The gregarious Ashton Kelly smiles at me. "Even now your mother and I argue, then we find ourselves laughing together ten minutes later. Life isn't something you get straight. It's an experience, and experiences come with their own lessons." He pulls me to the table and we sit. "Tell me about this psychologist. Does he work for himself?"

I shrug. "I think so. But his parents are psychologists, too."

"Does he have a house or rent?"

"Don't know."

"How old is he?"

"I don't know! I know nothing about him. Harry B tells me he's interested. Ziggy said it was love at first sight, and that's what you and Mum had, and then later he said it wasn't love at all."

"Whoa, Candice. Stay away from any guy who says he's in love with you straight away."

I laugh. "That's a little hypocritical, Dad."

"Is it?" He laughs loudly. "Yeah. If I'd been Pop I'd have warned your mum away from me. Okay, don't listen to any of my advice."

"Dad!"

He shrugs. "Just try him on for size."

"Dad!"

He laughs. "No father means that way! I mean how does the everyday go? Do you laugh together? Is he easy to talk to? The best thing about your mother, apart from how hot she was-"

"Of course."

"There were no games. That was important with leaving Sylvie. I'd been looking after Harry because Sylvie was so busy. I didn't want to lose him because I was a cheat. It wasn't *I've found The One and now I have total happiness.* The Harrys were snitchy at each other, your Mum felt guilty, her parents were mortified."

"They were? Nan and Pop have always been lovely to me."

"Because they're good parents. And you were so cute. It all worked out. You're trying to see the end when you're only at the beginning."

"Yes. Loosen up, darling."

My mother has her pyjamas on. It's obvious she's been quietly listening. I wonder what it's like to wait until you're almost sixty before getting married. How will I feel if that happens to me?

"Will you change your name?" I ask her. "Be a Kelly at last?"

"I'll always be a Baxter. And if I changed my name, Harry would be the only Baxter. He was raised by Baxters until his teens. He'll always be a Baxter, and I am, too. Anyway, you might not be a Kelly forever."

I wince, remembering Kat's voice: *Fuck, Can, don't change your name to Zbigniew!* "I won't ever change my name. It's who I am." And now I know there's nothing left to say. "Thanks for the pep talk."

"Good luck," they murmur as they hug me together.

I break away. "You can get back to whatever I interrupted."

Neither of them stops me leaving.

# 37

Back at the Spinster Flat I walk around like I'm floating in space.

Harry B's exposure of my family's troubled past and the disclosure of the calamity which erupted after my parents' sweet romance have thrown me. I've known my parents' story of illicit intimacy without ever investigating the intricate effect of the impact on everyone concerned. Their Meant-To-Be meeting and the Right-For-Each-Other ending has embedded itself in my brain to create an effect so powerful it's led me down paths I shouldn't have even considered. I was right to conclude I hadn't been at the helm of my life for quite some time.

I lay on my bed, fully dressed, eyes closed, meandering across the many roads that converged to lead me to where I am now, laying on my bed, fully dressed, eyes closed, considering where I am now. Like Harry B, I'm certain the past holds the secret to my lack of direction. I'll solve the riddle of *Who is Candice Kelly?* if I consider all roads that led to me.

I sit at my laptop typing up the soap operas leading to my existence.

1. Harry B's conception during a farewell sex romp between the just-legal Judith and her neighbour's cousin.

2. Seventeen-year-old Judith telling Nan and Pop she was pregnant. How the neighbour was informed.

3. Harry K's conception in an awkward, bumbling back-seat encounter between teenagers Ashton and Sylvie, who thought their affection would last forever.

4. Teenage Sylvie telling teenage Ashton they were pregnant.

5. Teenage Sylvie and Ashton telling their parents they were pregnant.

6. Teenage Ashton, scared, confused and guilty, moving into his pregnant girlfriend's girlie-decorated bedroom to await the birth of his new baby before either of them was old enough to vote.

7. The financially stretched teenage couple's subsequent cheap wedding in a little ceremony in the local park, the birth of their baby, and their move into a tiny rented unit.

8. Teenage Ashton starting his poorly paid job instead of going to uni, because there was nothing else for it.

9. Teenage Sylvie carting around toddler Harry, trying to keep him quiet and engaged while she was at lectures.

10. Sylvie finishing her degree when her son was still in junior primary. How proud and confused Ashton must've been, and what he thought about his own life as Sylvie got a better job than him and started earning more money almost immediately. How Ashton felt when her money could buy a better house than the flat his job allowed them to rent.

11. How Ashton and Judith felt when they met each other and realised here was something precious. What they felt as they stripped naked in front of someone they'd known for only twelve hours, a married man and a single mother. The lid popping off the lust that had been gathering all day.

12. How Sylvie felt when Ashton told her that while she'd been at home working hard, he'd been having unprotected sex in a hotel room with a parent he'd just met.

13. How Ashton felt confessing to Sylvie. How he greeted Harry K the morning after he became a cheating father.

14. How Harry K managed the icy atmosphere. What and how he was told and by whom.

15. How Ashton and Judith managed with minimal contact in the weeks after their night of passion. How Ashton managed Sylvie's mood whilst wanting only to be with Judith.

16. How Judith felt when she found out she was pregnant.

17. How Sylvie felt when her husband of twelve years ran off with The Whore.

18. How Sylvie felt when news broke The Whore had conceived a baby to her husband while he was still married to her.

19. How Harry B and Harry K felt when they were told of the pregnancy. What it did to their opinions of their trusted parents.

20. How the Harrys felt about their new family situation which included a fellow student in their new class.

21. How ashamed Nan and Pop were to find out their wonderful daughter was not only a teenage mother but also the type of woman who would get pregnant to a married man during a one-night stand. How they felt when their daughter and teenage grandson moved out.

22. How the new household managed before I was born.

I lean away. The screen contains an unbearable amount of confusion. A smile slinks slowly onto my mouth. I remember believing, when I was very little, that Harry was another name for brother. I remember wondering when we'd get another Candice or another Harry.

I couldn't understand where Harry K was those nights he wasn't with us. I remember Dad crying sometimes without me knowing why, and how I used to do what my mother did, which was hug him; how Harry B and I slept in with Mum and Dad on some nights when K wasn't around (even though B was really tall); how we had a big celebration dinner when K moved in permanently. I remember the huge sense of loss I felt when K married Joanna and left home; how devastated I was when B bought his house and moved out. I couldn't bear to be without the brothers. That was why I decided to move into my Spinster Flat and lead my lonely life alone.

I pace the flat again, my head spinning with accusations and allegations and adjudications. The early days of my life seemed so carefree but now there's an ominous loss of legitimacy behind my parent's tale. *Who the heck is Candice Kelly?*

I'm the seed that unwittingly prompted my father to make a quick decision to ditch his wife. Based on his fear of losing Judith. Based on my mother's chilly distance. Based on her fretting over conceiving once again on a one-night stand. Shit. I need to speak to someone. If only I knew a psychologist. But at least I have Ziggy's book. I grab it eagerly.

There's a brief run-down of more pop psychology models of last century, and I'm intrigued by something called The Hooami Instrument. Now I'm on the road again. I laugh when I find out it's not named after a psychologist called Hooami, but a test to find out *Who Am I?* It involves a set of questions answered by the test taker, and another set of questions answered anonymously by three people close to the test taker. All the answers are then superimposed over a graph of how the test taker thinks about him/herself and how others think of him/her, revealing a more complete picture. Sounds dangerous! I read the administrator of the test has a filter to ensure there's no harmful fallout of faults the test taker might find too harrowing.

My mind explodes with awareness. That's why I failed the personality test! What I thought was true was just my mental wanderings about who I'd become, not who I actually am. Bugger it. I text Kat, even though it's after midnight.

She texts back, *I'll go to Thor's car and call you.*

"Thor's asleep," she tells me when she rings. "He had an assignment to finish so he got here a half hour ago and woke me up." She giggles.

I don't ask how.

"What gives, Can?"

"I'm in my car," I say, "coming to get you. This requires Buddy's."

"Oh, oh." The only other time we've been to Buddy's when it was shut was when Ben dumped me. "Shall I grab chocolate? Booze?"

"No. Nearly there. I just need you and the sea."

"Because the Earth is a great healer."

Kat always knows when to explain, when to commiserate, when to drink away my sorrows. She wasn't really a beach person, in fact hated the feeling of sand on wet feet. Then one day she showed up at my place and asked Mum to take us down the beach for a swim. She'd found a bikini on special for two bucks, because no woman was the size of Kat. Even on Kat, it was tiny. But we romped in the sea with Mum, a female bonding day, and ate hot chips and sauce and ice cream and drank lemonade because we were only fourteen, although Kat must've thought she was seventeen.

I remember her words vividly: *The Earth is a great healer.* I've always cherished those words in a way I didn't understand, because I had this stupid notion at that time that every family was happy, and she must've meant she was coming down with a cold. It was only later I realised the Earth could heal horrendous hurt in ways nothing else could.

She runs to my car as I slide into her driveway. "Man, if you don't take Ziggy, I'm gonna recommend him to one of the gals in the House."

"Quit it, Kat."

I feel her eyes on me. I concentrate on the road.

We don't talk until we're on the sand.

# 38

"It's spooky here." Kat's voice is child-like.

"No light for the path ahead," I say mournfully.

"Get on with it." Kat's pupils are large in the slim light. She looks more elfin than ever.

"How're you doing, Kat?"

She views me curiously. "We came here so you could ask that?"

"No. But we should talk about you first."

She grins. "I love you. You know that? You're a fabulous gal-pal. You're the thing that's kept me afloat during my old crazy days. It's obvious some deity sent me a few guardian angels. Including Ziggy. But absolutely you and your family. And Thor." She scuffs her shoes in the sand. "Thor deserves better than the old me. I would've hurt him very badly. At the first sign of shit I would've been out of there, you know that. And if there were children involved … well, I want to do better than I had." She smiles abruptly. "Way, way better."

I grab her hand. "I'm sure you will. Are you good now?"

Her mouth purses. "I get the feeling it's going to take me a long time to be good. I'm counting on you and Thor to keep the pressure on. Can we talk about you now? I'm all talked out about me this week."

I jump straight in. "I've always taken my parents' story for granted." I hear whimsy in my voice when really it's pain.

Kat says nothing, just watches.

"My mother was a whore. My father a cheating bastard. I've never really thought about it that way because they've always been so in love, and that made it okay." I pause, but again she says nothing. "I always thought I was conceived in a loving night of heated passion, but instead it was a grubby conception by two people who had no regard for the welfare of their loved ones." I stop, my gaze firmly on my feet, my thoughts lost in the dirty words I've spoken about two people I've always had nothing but respect and love for. I look up.

Kat smiles broadly. "You're looking at this from the wrong angle."

"I've always been looking at it from the wrong angle."

"You ditz! You can't grade your conception on it being a sordid night of sex. Your parents had been searching for each other, and they couldn't wait any longer. You were made in love, Can, a big explosion of love." She laughs. "Where would we be if Ashton and Judith had turned away? They probably lusted after other people before they met, and did nothing about it. But that connection was gold, irrefutable, irresistible. Thank goodness, because otherwise you wouldn't be here. I wouldn't have you or your family. It happened as it did and here we are. It is what it is and that's all what it is."

I blow out a big breath.

"One of the things Ziggy's been leading me through is acknowledgment and forgiveness, and you need it, too. See, I can flip it, look at it from a positive angle. I never told you this, but my father was not my biological father. You know my mother got drunk a lot, and one day she found out she was pregnant, didn't even know who he was or when it happened. She told me this like it was something regular." Kat shakes her head. "Dad apparently came on the scene soon after she found out. So the fact he stayed with a pregnant woman and became my dad, kept my mum from drinking and drugging any more while she was pregnant, is pretty amazing. It was my mum who did all the emotional damage. He didn't stop her, though. But given I wasn't his, I could've been in all sorts of mess if he'd been so inclined."

"I get it." I feel sick, but Kat blazes on.

"See, you can go around and around and not get an answer about who's to blame and who did the right thing and who did the wrong thing. The only thing you can know is that we all make the best decision at the time and it's only hindsight that may convince us we were wrong or right. I'm grateful for my life. If Mum hadn't been doing the drunk-shag special, I wouldn't have been born. I've always felt like I was touched, somehow. Meant to be here. Angels everywhere to show me the way." She laughs a tinkly laugh. "Now I'm taking myself into my future, brave and strong."

"You've always been brave and strong, Kat."

"But now I know it. You've always been brave and strong, too, Can, in different ways to me." She hops up and pulls me to my feet, links her arm in mine. "Who can? Can can. But right now I need to sleep." She giggles as we walk up the stairs. "I crossed paths with Harry B at Ziggy's. His was the appointment before. I know what's going on."

We get into the car.

"The ball's in Ziggy's court," I murmur as I start the engine.

"You and your bloody tennis analogies," Kat laughs.


After I drop off Kat my mind races across a landscape of hurt, regret, panic and surprise, where love turns to humiliation and back again in so many relationships I lose count. Love sure is a stupid sorry ass. There's Laurie's five wives and Daisy's ex-husband and her brother Zane's ex-girlfriend and all my relationships that disintegrated into a pile of rubble.

I feel the confusion in my father's life where he was working in a lowly job and looking after a family when he should've been going to uni and drinking beer and dating a string of lusty women. I trawl across my mother's youth where, having finished high school with top grades, she had to defer her much sought-after university course for a year so she could become a teenage single mother.

Something strikes me as odd: Mum and Sylvie were both at the same university, both single mothers, both dragging their toddlers Harry to some of their lectures. I wonder if they passed each other in the cafeteria or library, maybe smiling at each other's cute toddler, before continuing on to the point where their lives intersected via my father.

What did Kat say? *Flip it!* We're all fine despite the damage. Sylvie got remarried, Mum and Dad are together, they both wound up with good jobs, Harry K has Joanna, Harry B has Andy. Ziggy's fine, too, which is why he's so appealing. But why was such a catch in a pub on a blind date? I calm myself with a recount of Kat's wisdom until I find myself in my driveway. A rescue boat is on its way, but how can I possibly believe it will work out? My breath is shallow. I need the best reassurance I know. I slam my car door, hurry inside to the mirror.

Stripping off my clothes frantically I stride up close, gaze into my eyes. They seem the same almost-brown colour. There's no longer any trace on my neck from Ziggy. I admit I would've had sex with him last Friday night, after knowing him for a week, would've had sex with him last Sunday if I'd confessed there was no boyfriend, or that first Saturday night, if I hadn't smashed myself on free champagne. And there I was, standing in judgment of my parents.

I walk back a step, consider this new information. I see *me*, all together, in my altogether. There's now something remarkably different about me: certainty, truth, comfortableness. Perhaps I wasn't looking for it before, or perhaps I've changed along the way, or perhaps there were things about myself I was too scared to see or didn't want to know.

My father, Ashton Kelly, was always my A. He's the guy who followed his heart, even when it screwed him over, who always tried to do the right thing. Who amended his direction, who loves to love, who's kind and joyful and passionate. All this ridiculous posturing, that All I Want Is Purpose, is plain bollocks. The Z I'm looking for is a healthy mix of purpose *and* partnership. And that Z includes Ziggy. It is what it is. Bring it on.

# 39

I wait confidently for a call from Ziggy all Friday. None comes.

He's working, of course. And he'd be very sure of the situation, so wouldn't feel the need to ring immediately. But as all of us single women know, staying home on a Friday night waiting for a man to call is agony. I drive home early, throw Ziggy's fermenting flowers in the compost; bring in the washing; do a dust, vac, mop; shower and wash my hair. I'm expecting he'll call me, or call in, but the night passes, until at eleven I assume his absence will continue unabated.

Why would a single man with a baited quarry choose to be alone on a Friday night? It doesn't make sense. I hang up my new dress, put on my cutest pjs just in case, haul myself into my Spinster bed and pull the covers up high. I'm still listening for a knock at the door, a tap at the window, a text or a call or something, anything but this silence.

I wake with an emotional hangover and a pillow wet from tears. I text Kat, but she doesn't respond. I stand at my front window looking for solace from the veggie garden. It looks so forlorn. Maybe I'll do some gardening today. The Earth, after all, is a great healer. I boil the kettle, get the milk out of the fridge. There's only a dribble.

My resolve returns. *Must not be like pink balloon.* I toss my uncombed hair into a messy ponytail, stick on my gardening shorts and an old t-shirt, shove my credit card, phone and keys in my pocket, grab a shopping bag, stride purposefully towards the mini mart.

Everything looks different today. The sky is deep purple to the south, the sun hazy, the grey clouds above me cuddling close. I see the trees as if I have Super-Vision, a clear, crisp image of bark and leaf that startles me. I turn the corner and smile shyly at the pub on the right, my memory sparking fondly at my afternoon there. The clouds begin to sprinkle but I keep moving because that's the journey of relationship: the anticipation of the storm, the thrill of the electric charge, the energetic boom, the fade into murky cloud.

When I exit the mini mart, the rain has thickened. The inky sky declares trouble as I step awkwardly on the streaming footpath, my hessian bag of Spinster groceries becoming heavier as its drenching increases. My mobile chimes. I excitedly pull under a tree. Godfrey.

"Oh my God, Candice, can I come over?" He's crying. "You're The One, Candice. I can't live without your smile, the way you are in bed, the way your kiss makes me faint." A childish sob makes me jump. "I'm lost without you to guide my path. Oh, the torment of days without you! You're The One, Candice, I know it now. I've always known it."

Time stills. This, now, is the final straw. I'm not the woman I was two weeks ago, Ziggy or no Ziggy. "You're kidding." My courage deepens. "Didn't you get the message my bucket sent you?"

"Candice! You're The One. *My* One." His voice is pleading. "You're a beautiful angel come to light my path-"

I look at my phone like it's an alien artefact, take a deep breath before holding it back to my ear.

"- and all the diamonds in the world don't shine as brightly as you."

I want to laugh but I don't. I want to hurl my phone in anger but I don't. I want to yell profanities. But I don't. "I've got someone else," I proclaim, even though I haven't.

"No! He can't have you! I'll love you forever! It's always been you."

"Except when you screwed that other woman. And sent me her flowers. And her texts." The silence is long. "I'm hanging up."

He whimpers. "No! Please! They were stupid mistakes!"

"So, you'll be loyal until you find someone else again?"

"Poor me, poor me, poor me," he wails.

I try to be stern, although I want to laugh. "Godfrey, listen. If you contact me again, I'll call the police. Do you understand?"

He starts sobbing again. "Oh no! Oh no, oh no!"

"What the crap is wrong with you? No means no. It doesn't mean anything else. It just means no."

The sobs come to an abrupt halt. "Really?"

"Yes."

His voice finally sounds normal. "Well, he's lucky, whoever he is."

Ain't that the truth. "Delete my number right now. Get it?"

"Okay." The real Godfrey has finally appeared. And disappeared.

I drop despondently onto the damp pavement, my clothes wet and my brain saturated. I close my eyes, sag against the wooden fence, focus on the rain dribbling down my face. I didn't expect my life to be a tragicomedy. I'm scrambling to make sense of where my life went after Homer and his indifference. After Ben and his abandonment. My thoughts drift way, way back to Jake and beyond, to growing up and becoming aware of myself as a member of a species whose behavioural characteristics run the gamut of unspeakable atrocities to loving sacrifice. Where I discovered the confusion of love and the inanity of attraction. Where I hoped to escape the pull of this odd new thing I felt, and to avoid the inherent duties it required of my gender.

Yet somewhere along the way I got hooked. Having a boyfriend seemed as necessary as having a funky handbag. Even Kat has been at the mercy of her hungry hormones, although she's managed to keep her emotions in check. Used to abandonment, she hasn't expected anything more than sex. It's freed her up to revel in her lust then walk away. Freedom everywhere for her. Until Thor.

Romance is a sport. Only you don't know how many players there are, and the rules only solidify as the game progresses. Well, bugger it. Perhaps I am The One. The One for whom there's no match. The One who never meets Mr Right. The One destined instead to be a social media doyen. The One with a worthwhile career. The One with enough nerve to say no to a life of compromise. The One who keeps her contract with herself, who achieves what she set out to do. The One to change the world with her words.

I pick myself up, dust myself off, get back to striding. *Start as you mean to continue.* Yes, that's it. Movement feels good. My self-esteem leaches back in. I remember the Critical Ladder of Universal Expectations. My Vision Quest has been a wonderful boost towards a happy future of Me. My phone beeps again.

*Are you available for a chat?*

Ziggy! Breathe! Remain detached. *Not for 5 minutes. On my way home.*

The response is immediate. *Excellent.*

I start to jog, all previous promises perished, wanting to be home and un-hosed before he rings, turn into my street, past Mrs Snitch's fake lawn and Mr Red's red everything and Mrs Feeble's orange trees and around the fence and down the driveway and I'm searching for my keys in my pocket, because maybe he'll want to come around and I look a sight, need a shower, finally my keys spring free and I look up to see Ziggy smiling under an umbrella at my door. Of course.

"Oh, you're wet," he murmurs delightedly, the tragedy of my fashion sense lost against the curvaceous clingy cladding of my clothes. He holds his umbrella as I open the door, his breath warm on my neck.

"Come in," I say nonchalantly, tossing my keys on the table and carrying the groceries to the fridge. I ponder whether I can do anything with my recalcitrant hair behind the door, but when I stand up he's so close I stumble backwards. He pulls me upright, and for a moment I think he's going to kiss me.

He doesn't. We stand staring into each other's eyes. I can't bear it.

I move away, put the kettle on because I'd kill for a coffee. I shake my hair out casually, bend over and run my fingers through it, hoping I look completely at home with the fact that it's a tangle. I put the band around my hair. Stand up. Stumble back into Ziggy. Turn and glare.

His gaze scans across my wet t-shirt. "You do a wonderful job of primal," he reminds me softly.

*Be strong, Candice.* I put my hands on my hip. "You and Harry B?"

As the words erupt, I realise Ziggy's gained advantage over me once again, this time by knowing our family secrets. I know nothing about him except he works with his sister. Which is my fault, because the perfect time to unpack his family skeletons was at his cousin's wedding.

I wonder:

1. What the CLUE would expect about this, after all, it is the Critical Ladder of Universal Expectations

2. Where on the ladder it would sit

3. Whether I can recover my teetering self-belief.

He says, "We can't talk about Harry or Kat."

"That's fine. I've had enough family analysis to last a lifetime."

He tilts his head. "Want to talk about it?"

I laugh loudly. "No."

He smiles sweetly. "We need to even things up. You should meet my family, whilst sober." His eyes wander across my wet t-shirt again.

"Want a coffee?" I say impatiently.

"I'm not staying."

"You're not staying?" I want to grab him, shake him, scream *Tell me the rules of the game!*

He slashes me with his smile. "Can we try Le Café again? Tonight?"

I smile and blink. "It's a date. Is it?"

He grabs me around the waist but kisses me platonically on the cheek. "Of course it's a date. I'll pick you up quarter to seven."

"I'll meet you there." I'm ready to bail if needed. I have no secrets, he's too clever, and I'm tired of my neediness. Besides, why spoil a new career direction with the love merry-go-round? *Be strong, Candice.*

"Okay," he says. "Make sure you're not late. I don't have much tolerance for being kept waiting."

Isn't that what I told his blind date in the pub?

"Seven at Le Café," he says. He leaves without looking back.

# 40

Emotions are easy now, and you'll find them in any thesaurus: befuddled, bamboozled, bewildered, baffled, confused, mystified, perplexed, puzzled. Forget Z. Now I'm looking for H.

I call Harry K, the Helpful Healer who counsels and protects in his job as a doctor, who is not currently brainlessly in the throes of fresh love, and who hasn't met Ziggy. He agrees to pick me up for a pub lunch, where we spend a couple of hours examining how I turned into the lonely woman who agreed to a relationship with a guy like Godfrey.

For all K's wisecracks, he's a skilled listener. His insider knowledge on the processing capability of men's brains is clearly at odds with the picture seeded in my brain by rom-coms, romance novels and the popular press. Could've saved myself a whole heap of pain by paying closer attention to his advice earlier. "Anyway, Godfrey's just a bad memory now," I finish. "But the real problem's Ziggy. There's something I don't understand, but I can't figure out what it is."

"This the one you know through Kat and Harry?"

"He counselled them, but I met him independently in my local pub."

"I've always told you, don't pick up guys in pubs."

Many times in my youth, when the brothers were both between girlfriends, I'd find a couple of unfamiliar female faces at our breakfast table. The Harrys made the most of their famous pick-up line, *Hi, I'm Harry and this is my brother Harry* to begin chatting with a pair of pretty women. It was only as I got older that I wondered which woman belonged to which brother, and older still when I realised my brothers probably shared more than the isolated back bedrooms of our house.

"You met Joanna at a pub."

"Do as I say, not as I do! Listen, this personality test sounds dodgy."

"The point is it came out wrong. I came out as procedural-"

"Yeah, you are very organised." Harry K smiles appreciatively.

"Instead of creative."

He frowns. "Can't you be both?"

"Apparently not. I'm introverted-"

"Is that where you got that idea from?"

"There's an axis for inner strength/supported strength. The facilitator said that was about being an extravert or introvert."

"Interpretation only. You do have an inner strength, Candice."

"Another axis was emotional or intellectual."

"Again, can't you be both?"

"I didn't write the bloody thing! Last axis was trust: trusting yourself or trusting others."

"Sounds like complete bollocks. Keep a bullshit detector handy with this type of crap. That goes for personality tests, but also men."

I smile. "Personality aside, I want to know what I should expect from tonight. History tells me nothing positive." I perk up. "But it does tell me Ziggy did the right thing when he took me home drunk."

"He did the *legal* thing. Listen, Harry and Kat put in a good word for him, but as a psychologist, not as a boyfriend. I know some great doctors I wouldn't set you up with for all the money in the world."

Unfortunately, true. Career success does not equate to marital success. "I had a wonderful time with him last week and he only ended it because of professional duty. Doesn't that count for something?"

"Yes." He pauses. "It does. But he can be a good guy, keen on you, and still play you like a fool. Guys will stuff around a woman they're interested in to see if she's worth the effort."

"Except when you met Joanna."

He laughs. "Exactly. Her high-handedness hooked me just as much as her honeypot. The thing is not to make it easy for men. Treat this guy with indifference; if he's interested, he'll take your bait. And, after a few months, if he meets your exacting standards, make sure you're stocked up on condoms." He smiles. "Learn from Judith and Sylvie. But don't make it easy. Keep your goodies in your pants for now."

"Harry!"

"I'm being honest. I don't want to see you hurt."

"Okay. Keep my goodies in my pants, treat him with indifference, stock up on condoms."

"But for later." He smiles. "Don't chase simple hook-ups. You need permanency." He pauses. "Think about where you want to wake up tomorrow. In your own bed alone, feeling happy you've made a good start, or glad you didn't walk headlong into disaster."

Harry K drops me home. I'm determined to curb my compliance, strengthen my suspicions, temper my teasing. Ziggy Zbigniew is a Z, it's true but, regardless of whether he loves me or leaves me tonight, I know at last he's not my hero. Because I'm my Hero.

Nobody needs to fix me. When I'm broken, I fix myself. Nobody completes me, I complete myself. I'm the Me I can rely on, The One I was looking for. I don't need to find who I am, I'm already who I am.

Found, not lost. Solo, not lonely. Questioning, not confused.

I go out to buy clothes to suit the new me. I don't wash my hair because I did it last night. I stare down my nakedness in the hall mirror. I decide against make-up, renege and apply a little mascara, scrub it off, reapply it, scrub it off, reapply it, and leave for Le Café before I can change my mind again.

I'll tell you who Candice Kelly is. She's decisive, fearless, strong. Flexible, intuitive, aware. Intelligent. Powerful. Courageous.

A Hero.

# 41

Le Café looks smaller now. I remember being ten minutes early to meet Ziggy for the wedding. Now I'm punctual, not pathetic.

My new clothes are casual. I'm in pants, yes, pants: a new pretty floral pair that hug me right, and a white long-sleeved shirt with no adornment. I'm still whipped up by my chat with Harry K, my brain fuelling a fury of F-words: fired up and fussy about my future, I'm a feisty feminist full of fortitude and facing fate with forthright force.

The maître d smiles kindly. He leads me to a cosy table in the corner where Ziggy stands as I approach. Dammit, he's in a suit. Black suit and tie. Handsome as at the wedding. I feign poise in my casual wear as the waiter pulls out my chair. Ziggy and I sit in synchronicity. He says nothing as the waiter puts a napkin across my lap. His face looks odd, like he's embarrassed or confused or worried.

"Here we are again," I say glibly.

"Yes."

Nothing.

I lean forward. "If you're not going to say anything because of my family skeletons, we might as well call it quits now."

"I'm sorry." He does one of those funny laughs you do when you've been caught out. "Are we drinking?"

"I'll choose." I grab the wine list, rapidly order a bottle of my favourite champagne, six oysters and herb bread.

"How's your week been?" Ziggy asks kindly as the waiter departs.

For a moment I think he's being funny. "The usual."

"And that is?"

The waiter appears with our champagne and two glasses. "Will you be having wine later?"

Ziggy shakes his head. I focus on the waiter removing the wine glasses and opening the champagne. This is difficult when Ziggy looks so good. When the waiter leaves, I find Ziggy's been watching me.

"And that is?" he repeats.

I raise my glass to my lips. "Up and down. To and fro. Here and there." I take a sip.

"I see."

I frown. "What exactly do you see?"

"That it's *the usual*. I thought your week might've been different."

"In what way?"

"A little more like mine."

"In what way?"

"That it contained angst. Concern. Pining." He pauses. "Lust. Certainty." He smiles gently. "Terror. More lust. In fact, plenty of lust and pining and terror, mostly terror. Not a great deal of certainty."

I summon forth Harry K's bullshit detector. "Why?"

"I decided not to see you until I spoke with Harry."

"You didn't rush to your phone after that."

He smiles. "We were taking this slowly."

"You were taking it slowly," I shoot back.

The waiter arrives with our oysters and herb bread. I immediately place half the oysters on my small plate and take half the bread.

The waiter feels the tension. "I'll come back for your mains order."

Ziggy watches me down an oyster. "You're being a little territorial."

I shrug. "Just hungry." I fill my mouth with bread.

He watches me chew. "I apologise for not handling the last date. As a psychologist I have a strict code of conduct to follow. I must move cautiously where a client is involved. Sorry if I seemed offhand."

I shrug again as I swallow, hoping to portray indifference. "Not at all. Men give me mixed signals all the time."

He laughs, sits back. "And you've been so straightforward."

"Do other women find your psychologist's view unsettling?"

He frowns. "I don't have a psychologist's view."

"Sure you do. You know about behaviour, thought processes, personality. I'm sure women find dating you harrowing."

He momentarily closes his eyes.

I start in once more. "Ask me again how my week was."

"How was your week?"

"I worked on my life ladder. I'm CLUEd in now."

"The CLUE, eh?" He smiles gently.

"Yes. And how about the Hooami? If you'd like to enlighten me on anything I don't know about myself, go right ahead."

He pauses. "They're old theories. Tried and tested, but now it's positive outlooks and personal strengths, goal setting, CBT."

What's CBT? Controlled By Therapist? "It was in the book. That was your aim, wasn't it?" From his smile I can tell he's pleased. Now I feel manipulated. I grab my glass and scull half my champagne. His face changes. I can't read it. I slurp another oyster. I feel his hand on mine.

"Candice." There's sadness on his face. "Can we start again?"

"Your blind date was at the pub when I returned for the wedding. I scared her off."

He squeezes my hand. "I'm glad you told me."

I keep breathing. "She was very pretty. If she'd been on time, she'd be here, not me. Fate is a crapshoot."

His eyes capture mine again. "Ask me again about my week."

The game continues. "How was your week, Ziggy?"

He tears his bread into triangles distractedly. "It wasn't the week I envisaged. I'd met this girl-"

I glower. "If you mean me, I'm not a girl."

He looks up and smiles. "I met a *woman*, and wanted to get to know her. There were some boundary issues-"

"What the fuck does that mean?" I say irritably.

"You had a boyfriend and came to see me as a psychologist."

I retract. "Oh. Guilty as charged."

"Not irrevocable. The boyfriend had at last been dismissed but the Harry issue emerged." He rubs his forehead, then looks up at me. "When you told my client Joe that your name was Candice, it didn't twig at all. It'd been a long time since Harry had spoken about you. Most of our talk centred on him. I sorted that out Thursday only to counsel a client yesterday who was working through his anguish over stupidly dumping a girlfriend years ago. She was immediately identifiable as you."

I gulp.

"I referred him onto another psychologist on the basis they'd be a better fit, whilst dealing with the fact I could possibly be in the same situation if the ex-girlfriend were such a heartbreaker. Throw in his revelation she had a new boyfriend and he was rather large."

"Uh, hang on-"

He holds up his hand. "You need to understand I'm only telling you what you already know, because my work is confidential. I couldn't bear the thought you'd begun a new relationship this week."

"Actually, I've had a whirlwind of possibilities," I smile congenially. "None of whom are sitting here with me."

"I see." His eyes hold mine. "Please explain why you don't like *girl?*"

"*Girl* doesn't project us as intelligent adults."

He sits back again and smiles sweetly. "But it's like you calling me honey, or sweetie, or love. Which I'm okay for you to do, by the way."

My hard-edge shatters. What was it Harry K said about taking it slow?

# 42

The waiter returns. "Are you ready to order?"

Ziggy nods. "Stick with success, Candice, order last week's dishes."

I rattle off our order. The waiter leaves.

I frown. "I still can't decide what your intentions are."

He twiddles his glass nervously. "When I spoke with Dad last night he negated all my concerns about you."

Concerns? "You men are confusing." I shake my head. "My ex-boyfriend has been trying to get back together with me, and when I say no, he goes back to the one after me, but does it by accidentally sending her flowers and text messages to me."

"There's an entire dissertation in that one," he laughs. "Perhaps you'd better send him to a psychologist." He leans in. "But let's discuss sweet-talking some more. What you like and what you don't."

The original HeroMan from the pub sits opposite now. "Sweetie and love are fine in a relationship, but not for someone I've just met."

"I see."

I don't know that he does. "Look, women have enough sexism to deal with."

"I imagine it's a difficult life being so pretty." He smiles mischievously.

The femi-sniper in me senses danger, raises the sight-glass. "I think we should institute a Non-sexy Clothes Day for women. See what happens when men are no longer at the mercy of their crackpot brains."

I'm not sure if he's cross or amused. "You might find men can be just as at the mercy of women's crackpot brains. Besides, you could be wearing a sack and still be sexy. You're bewitchingly astute, and you take on life with a steady hand."

"I'm a feminist," I state. "What are you? A masculinist?"

Ziggy's laugh is dazzling, and my resolve teeters again. "I'm not a feminist or a masculinist, if that's even a word: I'm a humanist. A fair deal for all. And a good dose of fun. And love without getting hurt."

I rear back. *Hurt by love.* That's me.

"Let's start again." He smiles. "Again."

I know it now. He's wearing me down with his wisdom and good grace. I steer our attention away from us and whatever-the-heck-this-is. "What do you think about world peace?"

He raises his eyebrows. "A long way off, if ever it comes."

"Why?"

"We're animals. No matter our advances, we'll always fight over resources. And we'll never have enough to satisfy our greedy needs."

I brighten, hoping to make an intelligent impact. "We should invent a way to make dogshit into biofuel. That's a plentiful resource." I sip my champagne coquettishly as Ziggy laughs. Encouraged by my precise and perceptive political prose, I consider beginning a conversation about sweatshops or animal rights or the Earth's ominous need for care. Oh, fuck it. "Let's talk about love."

He grins. "You start."

I fight back. "Tell me what psychology thinks about love. Is it a chemical reaction? Hormonal? Genetic? Satire?"

He pauses. "Psychology sees love as healthy but requiring work. It needs positive interactions, vulnerability, empathy, it needs the couple to change with each other, both must feel safe -"

"Wait, you said vulnerability and safety. Which is it?"

"Both." His eyes are unwavering. "You'll only allow yourself to be vulnerable if the relationship feels safe. With safety, you can bare your true self," he smiles, "and only then can you find true connection."

Damn. He makes perfect sense. I have this with Kat, my parents, my brothers … never with a boyfriend. I stare at the man opposite me, niggle over the sore spot that is my need for him. How can my armed and dangerous Self feel so unexpectedly secure with this man who's given me a rocky road these past two weeks?

Ziggy continues. "You have to be careful. It's easy to be taken for a ride by someone who's pretending to be who you want them to be."

Yep. I can make a list, starting at Jake Holly at one end, with Godfrey at the other.

"Because the trouble is," he adds, "the person reverts back to who they are. That's the way with a lot of relationships. We fall in love with one person, only to find another has taken their place. It's terrifying to find you don't know them at all."

He must have seen this over and over in his daily client list. No wonder he's single. But what's he doing here with me, a woman who's proven herself to be no consistent person at all?

"Being genuine is essential." His smile pierces my heart.

"We could solve a lot of the world's problems if we understood that. If only feeling safe was easy. Then being vulnerable would be easy." I lean in. "You make me feel vulnerable. And not in a safe way."

He squeezes my hand: his signature move flutters my heart. "I was hoping for a very different emotion to that." He smiles kindly. "I feel vulnerable with you, too. More than you know. But I'd like us to move towards feeling safe." He pauses. "What do you think?"

"Perhaps." I keep my voice strong, although he's taken my eyes captive. "Ms Hurt-By-Love here is prepared to listen. State your case."

"Actually, I was wrong about that label. It should have been *Hurt by what you hoped was love.*"

I smile. That says enough. The waiter brings our dishes.

"Please, let's eat as we talk. I'm still hungry." He smiles. "In fact, by now, I'm famished."

I blush. I'm hungry, too.

We begin our food, with him asking questions about Laurie who made the first appointment for me and my other neighbour Rupert and what they mean to me and why I created our own community garden and what their new romances look like. We eat quietly whilst progressing onto examining the general mechanics of love and hate, war and peace. I listen intently as he unpicks the reasons behind the chaos of the world. How all of us are swept along day after day alone on our journeys. How isolated we become if we don't realise others feel the same. How universal are the feelings of abandonment, shame, neglect, worthlessness. How essential is the need to belong. How instead of being lonely we could share our struggles, solve our problems with, instead of against, each other, celebrate our humanness, accept our shortcomings. How we'd all be the better for it, man, woman, child.

And so it is that *The Thing* strikes me. Ziggy's words lull me into a sense of the possible, like I've stepped into another dimension where the potentiality has collapsed, and the world is remedied. With the light let in, I bravely throw down my omnipresent vigilance, prod my feelings. Is it safe to wade into such torrid waters?

The buoyancy feels exquisite.

And with the world taken care of, *The Thing* I now want to do this instant is to go back to Ziggy's place, be alone with Ziggy, immerse myself in Ziggy.

Sorry, Harry K.

# 43

I've never had a dream where I've been stalked before.

I'm awake and slightly scared, the darkened room no comfort, the quilt AWOL. I turn to find Ziggy up on one elbow, watching me. I hope I don't have drool on my face or mascara under my eyes. I smooth the borrowed t-shirt down to cover my knickers and return his smile.

These are the things that happened last night.

1. We were at the restaurant for hours. We talked so much that Ziggy asked the waiter to microwave our food. He eyed Ziggy in horror, returning with our dishes warmed and placed atop contraptions holding a few tea lights beneath the dishes. How romantic is that? We drank one bottle of champagne and yes, we drank it slowly. Over coffee there was a short discussion about whether to call it a night.

2. The night was never going to end there. Ziggy called dibs on his place as we'd been at mine last time. He offered to collect the book later. This sounded promising.

3. I followed him in my car. His house was uncluttered, neat, clean, paintings on the walls, quality furniture. His garden was also uncluttered: a front and a back lawn with some trees and a few shrubs. He did not rush me into bed, nor did he set up seductive music. At one stage we lay looking at the stars from the comfort of a blanket on his back lawn until I thought something ran over my leg. It was only his foot, but the thought had been evoked that there

were living creatures around us, so we moved back inside and put on the all-night music videos.

4. We chose to have a single glass of port and several delicious biscuits from a bakery (the only evidence he'd made preparation). By then it was two a.m. A lively conversation ensued about sex, abstinence, contraception, safe sex, the role of the condom in modern society, and pornography. We discussed our own cautious safe-sex history. He did not reveal his romantic past, so I did not reveal mine. I wondered if this was a psychologist's idea of foreplay.

5. He allowed me to speak of my own conception without comment or analysis. I was pleased our values around safe-sex were the same.

6. He asked me to consider a sleep-over. I countered I did not have my pjs with me. After a very long silence he offered me a t-shirt. I agreed to stay, on the proviso he not seduce me, and repel any of my attempts to seduce him. I told him anything else would be quixotic. He laughed heartily and we went to bed.

"Good morning. How are you?" Ziggy's voice is full of charm.

I rub the sleep from my eyes. "A little freaked out, to be honest, being asked that question by a psychologist first up on a Sunday." I turn my head to the curtains. "What's the time?"

"Ten-thirty. We still haven't had enough sleep. Might need to come back to bed this afternoon," he grins.

I open my eyes wide, call up my control. "I should go home."

His grin dims. "I'm going to start with a shower. Then we'll have breakfast. I'll use the en suite. The other bathroom's next to the toilet."

"I know where it is. Do you want me to have a shower?" I'm wrong-footed. The questions race around in my head: is he hoping for some morning glory? Perhaps he only likes a clean body for his carnal pleasures? And didn't I just say I was going home?

"You don't have to. I like to shower when I get up. It's a routine."

"Okay." There's something undisclosed here, an unnerving undertone I don't recognise. I wonder momentarily if I'm safe. I gather my clothes after watching him shut the en suite door, walk to the other bathroom, decide not to shower. I've seen that shower scene, after all.

I feel remarkably odd putting my clothes from last night back on. I wander into the kitchen, find Ziggy staring into a cupboard.

"Should've bought something special," he tells me. "Sorry."

"Cereal?" I note he's dressed in khaki shorts and a pale-yellow t-shirt. His legs look strong.

"Any of these do?" He points to a row of boxes on a shelf.

I pull one out. "My favourite," I smile, our faces too close. I move away, sit at the table, watch him getting bowls, milk, sugar, spoons.

He sits down, offers me a bowl. "I'm glad you decided to stay."

*It was too late to do anything else*, but that isn't completely true. I was enjoying him, and in any case, I didn't want to go home to my lonely soon-to-be-sold Spinster Flat. "You're good company." I busy myself preparing my breakfast, secretly breathing in his fresh soapy smell.

He says nothing and again I feel tension in him. I watch him carefully with his cereal. When he raises his eyes to mine, I see pain in them.

"What's up?" I ask, worried.

"You're good company, too." He takes a spoon of his cereal. "Are you seeing Kat today?"

"She'll probably be wrapped up in Thor. They'll be exercising, a new thing for Kat." I smile encouragingly and begin my cereal.

He frowns. "She's very thin for a couch potato."

"She's not anorexic, if that's what you're asking. Just doesn't eat much. Too poor." My mobile sounds. And again. And again. I rise to pick it up, and hear it sound again. There are messages from many instead of many from one.

Laurie: *It's Sunday. I'm checking you're not gardening on your own.*

Harry B: *Don't leave me hanging! Did Ziggy contact you?*

Kat: *Well?*

Harry K: *Want me to swing past your place, take you out for lunch?*

I post the same text to all. *Having brekky with Ziggy. Nothing happened last night but a very nice dinner. But don't interrupt me again.*

I hold my phone, waiting for an answer. Everyone is obedient. I place it on the table and recommence my cereal. "Nothing important. So, your sister is your receptionist," I say, steering the chat.

"Sort of," he smiles awkwardly.

"She's sort of your sister?"

"No, she's sort of my receptionist." He sits back, his face bearing a look of distaste. "Here we are, about to have The Talk."

"Uh, um, uh?"

He runs his spoon through his cereal distractedly. "Esther is a speech therapist."

"Oh." I've got an urge to run now. There's something that doesn't fit right, something looming on the near horizon, something threatening to blow this cosy, warm, intimate encounter to pieces. I can't get it straight, why a speech therapist would be doing receptionist duties for her brother. "Why isn't she working as a speech therapist?"

He bites his lip. "She is. She's in the other office."

"She was at the desk when we came out of your office on Tuesday morning. Took the call when I tried to book an appointment Monday."

He flinches. "She does reception for us both, sees her own clients, picks up her children from school three days a week. Her husband picks them up on the other two. He works part-time, too. Mondays she works a full day, takes calls and does sessions, Tuesdays it's a little less."

I feel like I'm in a movie theatre watching a horror film, waiting for the slasher to jump into view. "She's rather possessive of you."

He cocks an eyebrow. "And here's The Talk."

What's he going to say? He's sitting before me, happy, healthy, intelligent, poised, successful, sociable, obviously fine financially.

"I got married at twenty-two."

# 44

"Oh, crap." I sit back, looking around the kitchen for signs of a woman's presence. "You're divorced?"

"No."

I frown at his seeming guilt. "Separated?"

He flinches. "Sort of." He smiles chaotically.

"Sort of?" My voice is venomous. "What the fuck does that mean?"

He takes my hand, squeezes it. "You need to hear all of this. Please. It was an awful time. Both emotionally and financially. That's why Esther is possessive. Doesn't think anyone is trustworthy."

"So -?" I don't know what else to say. Esther is the dog at the gate, protecting her master. What scars does he have? Plenty, by his hesitation in spilling the truth about his *sort-of* separation.

"I didn't want to be a psychologist. I didn't want to be like my parents, analysing everything. I worked as a tennis coach for two years after school finished, then started a straight science degree, physics, chem, maths. Happy."

"A tennis coach. Physics." Hello, Chaos Theory.

"Yes. Working hard, saving to buy a house and all that. Then I met Fanny. Married her after three months together."

I can't help it: I start laughing. "Fanny?"

"Fanny Price." He smarts at my expression. "Not her real name."

I rein in my laughter. "That's a character out of an Austen novel."

His mouth is crooked. "I know now. I didn't know it at the time. That was her little joke."

The despair on his face makes the hair on my neck stiffen. What's he going to tell me? That she was such an obsessive Austen fan she changed her name? No wonder he knew all about Austen's novels.

"For our three-month wedding anniversary she told me to stay out until seven. She had a surprise for me. She couldn't wait even six months to celebrate, she wanted to do something special now."

And she'd redecorated the house in Austen period? I start to snigger at the thought of it, although I know I shouldn't.

He doesn't notice. "When I got home the unit was empty. She cleaned out everything, furniture, crockery, linen, clothes, mine as well, our bank account. All the money I'd saved working hard. Everything."

I freeze as he continues.

"All the wedding presents, she'd left them unopened, saying she wanted to wait until we moved into our own house. I think she probably returned them a few at a time, collected the money. And she took all my stuff, too. The only things I had left were at my parents. Luckily, because we were so young, I hadn't moved everything into the unit. But I didn't even have a bed to sleep on that first night. She left a note, saying *You'll never know why*."

"Wait," I ask, "she sold your clothes? How? Why?"

"Psychopath. Turns out she'd been married before. I was husband number five. Fourth illegal one."

"At twenty-two?" My voice is a screech.

"I don't think so. Her birth certificate said she was born the same year as me, a ploy to give us connection. She had a way of forging birth certificates, so I have no idea how old she really was. Esther tracked her down, because even psychopaths like to play a game, and hers was Austen characters." He smiles, and it's the Ziggy I know. "Hell hath no fury like an intelligent woman with a scorned brother."

"I see why Esther's so protective."

He shrugs. "Fanny was everything a man wanted her to be. She even said she was a virgin. No sex before marriage. She was after wedding presents. She insisted we were happy just with money so we could put it towards a place of our own. That's why she pushed for us to get married so quickly. My family was very generous, because she was everything they wanted her to be, too. She spent a lot of money on keeping herself beautiful. With each marriage she'd leave after three months of being together."

I stare at Ziggy mutely.

"My marriage was adjudged illegal and therefore non-existent. I was a husband without a wife. I was still without my stuff, my savings, our wedding money. She sold everything. She lived like a princess until the money ran out. Then she'd look for the next one. By the time Esther told the police her whereabouts, she'd left the next husband and was onto the next one again. Psychology became a life mission for me."

I can't breathe. "Uh … Oh. Uh …"

He squeezes my hand. "So, sorry if I haven't confessed to an undying love for you. And that I didn't tell you this straight away. It took me six months to recover enough to get back into what resembled a life. I buried myself in psychology in that time, trying to understand my fate. But she fooled my whole family."

"She's in jail?"

Ziggy nods. "Bigamy. Theft. Fraud. Forgery. Impersonation. Everything a man wants in a wife."

"So, your *Hurt by love* diagnosis goes double for you."

He leans away. "*Almost destroyed* is a better description."

"And your psychologist parents didn't pick anything up about her?"

"Mum thought she was looking a little anorexic. Nearly right. Bulimic. Apart from that she was enchanting, compliant, perfect."

"There's one thing I don't understand. You were a tennis coach?"

His eyes crinkle. "That's what you want to ask me?"

"It's just that tennis runs through my life. I played as a teenager." And more, of course, but I don't tell him this.

"We'd make a fine doubles team, then," he smiles.

"And Physics? I studied that a bit at university."

He smiles. "Our connections continue."

I pause. "You didn't pick up any signs she was a fraud?"

"No."

"But you've had girlfriends since?"

"No. It was like I'd been blinded. If I ever felt attraction, I'd shut it down immediately, run in the other direction."

I squeeze his hand in comfort, but my stomach is swirling. How can I manage a wound this large in someone I feel so unerringly deeply for? What capability do I have that will enable me to keep this relationship on track? I may as well walk out now.

He laughs suddenly, and I jump out of my thoughts. "It's why I was so pleased you got drunk."

I blink. "I didn't mean to."

"You were lovely. But I'd had *lovely* before. You were being very protective of yourself. I wasn't sure why. I watched you very carefully."

"Was Esther at the wedding? I don't remember her."

"One of her kids was sick, so her husband came to the wedding and then they swapped. She came to the reception for a couple of hours."

"I was drunk when she got there?"

"You were drunk by the end of the speeches," he smiles. "That's the reason she wasn't sure why you booked in as a client. She questioned me at length about the arrangement, why you'd gotten a man to book for you, why you didn't just tell her you were Agnes from the wedding."

"You seemed resentful that Sunday morning. And she was very abrupt on the phone." I still have trouble getting it straight. "You told me everyone loved me." I sigh. "How old are you anyway?"

"Thirty-three. Ten years since Fanny left. All my energy was put into recovering, finding a routine in life. Get up, have a shower, get dressed, have breakfast. I had to have a routine so I wouldn't stay in bed all day. Then I'd research at the university library. The research saved me. I switched to Psychology, doing my PhD on manipulation and deceit, then Esther offered to go into business with me, said she'd make it easy for me by making all the appointments. That saved me, too, feeling like I was making the world a better place. More truth, less hurt." He smiles. "Dad pulled me aside last year, said I needed to open my eyes again, see what was out there, beyond saving the world, to saving myself."

"He sounds very wise." I put my elbow on the table, my chin onto my hand. "Great first impression I made on him."

"You were an open book once you got drunk." Ziggy laughs. "There could be no lies with you having drunk so much champagne. You told Dad you had a boyfriend who was very pretty and not bad in the sack. You gave him a big suggestive wink." He demonstrates it bawdily, laughs as I cover my face with my hand. "He asked why you weren't spending Saturday night with your boyfriend. You said you were on a mission to find The Truth, and anyway I was making you very horny."

"No!" I peer at him through my fingers.

"Dad asked if your name was really Agnes, and you said you didn't know who you were, but whomever you were was keen on taking me outside for something naughty. And you gave him another big wink."

I lower my face to the table, cover my head with my arm.

"That was when you took me out to the car, and the hickey ensued."

I pull myself up. "I've gotten drunk, embarrassed you, sent my friend to spy on you, put you in an awkward spot professionally."

"I haven't even told you what you said to Mum and her sisters." He laughs at the horror on my face, then squeezes my hand again. "But we did all love you. It's because it's obvious who you are."

I look at my lap. "If only I knew."

"Although the *Agnes* threw me a curveball." He tilts his head. "You told me your life was confusing."

"You said it was what you dealt with every day. I thought you meant with your clients."

"With myself."

Well, shit.

# 45

Ziggy removes his hand. His smile is weary. "I was nervous on our first date. Le Café was Esther's suggestion. Neither of us had been there. The lunch ambience was one of busy eaters and no candles. I was a little side-swiped at the different atmosphere when we arrived for dinner." He blows out a long breath. "Anyway, Esther listened while I rambled on about you. She's very supportive of a relationship."

"I couldn't tell."

"I want to throw myself in with you, but you understand why I've been careful. You're my first … whatever this is … in ten years. I'd like it to be my only. Because-" his voice cracks, "I don't know how I'd deal with another heartbreak."

I take Ziggy in, all of him, the curve of his clean-shaven chin, his hair, currently flat, his eyes dark, panicked, his mouth slightly open as if waiting for words of comfort. No sign of my snappily dressed HeroMan. He's the same as Mum and Dad, all essentially good people looking to dip a toe in the water of love, being swamped by an unforeseen king tide, fearfully finding the fallout echoing through life. The toe all the more nervous when an unexpected second wave arrives.

I smile at his loving, frightened face. "Do you have any slow music?"

His eyes flicker. "Of course. What were you thinking?"

"Something we could dance to. I missed the luxury of remembering us dancing together at your cousin's wedding."

He lights up. "It was quite something." He pauses, then rises to find a record, puts it on a turntable.

"Really, a record player?"

"One of the things I left at Mum and Dad's. Thankfully." He turns, stares wide-eyed. "After deep trauma, deceit, loss, the world looks different. You feel … stupid."

"We're going to take this slow," I say kindly. I walk to him, snake my arm around his waist.

He puts the stylus onto the record, faces me, and we begin to sway. In just a few seconds our hunger surfaces.

"Yes?" he asks breathlessly.

"Yes." My stomach shimmies.

Oh God, he's unbuttoning my shirt, pushing it from my shoulders, kissing my neck, breaking away to pull off his t-shirt. Immediately I close my eyes. Seeing Ziggy naked will be tantamount to casting my eyes on the Ark of the Covenant. I open them to find him stepping out of his shorts and jocks.

Ziggy's no longer a psychologist. Now he's a full-blooded male. Full-blooded is right. With a capital F. Mesmerised, I reach my hands to his hips, draw them delightedly together to his centre.

He whimpers at my touch. "Score even." He pulls my waistband to him, unhooking it swiftly. I can almost taste my heartbeat. There's nothing I want more in this moment than to surrender to the call of my loins, but the whisper in my head is now shouting *You're in too deep!* *YOU'RE IN TOO DEEP!*

"Uh, Ziggy, I'm, uh, thinking-"

He hesitates, his dark eyes upon me. "You're feeling vulnerable? I am, too. But you're not feeling unsafe?"

There is genuine concern on his face. I have only one answer to give.

"I presume you're going to put a raincoat on that thing."

He smiles and pushes my trousers to the floor, wraps his arms around me and unhooks my bra and there we are, naked and brimming with heat. "We're safe, Candice." He runs his tongue around the rim of my mouth and I open my lips to his, trying to conjure up a Candice Kelly who has spunk and competence and an award-winning appetite for moving things forward.

As I run my hands across his hairy chest and up onto his unbearably bare shoulders, the Opposite Reactions team lines up again. The Olympian tug of war between the paramour primed for pumping and the watchdog shouting: *two weeks! two weeks!* rages ferociously.

Ziggy kisses my neck.

I calm myself. "I just want to say, I admire you, respect you, love the man I see you to be, I have feelings for, um, but I don't want to-"

Ziggy softly brushes my hair from my face. "We know what this is. I'm cautious, frightened, but determined to trust the way I feel."

Newton comes bowling in for a second go. *An object in motion will remain in motion unless acted upon by a force.* Ziggy picks me up, forces me to face up to the inevitable. "It's time for primal," his smile whispers.

I get it now, the dichotomy of feeling safe with this man who comes with impeccable references from my brother and best friend, who didn't take advantage of a drunk, naked, attached, crazy woman, versus the vulnerability that necessarily underpins my search for constancy, community, conjunction.

He lays me carefully on his bed, then he's heavy against me, like there's no time to lose. His lips, when they meet mine, no longer ask any questions. Now he tells me the Answer, and I lose my capacity to remain ravelled. He's with me, at me, the air blue with our declarations regarding the unparalleled efficacy of our connecting body parts. I cease being lost, I find the flow and correct my navigation, my heart breaks open with joy and confirmation. In finding myself, I have also found Ziggy, and I ride the pleasure beast that is the icing on the cake of my Quest. Our rhythm reduces all reasoning to rubble, his strength and intent and passion and purpose blowing out now and I find my Z: the Zesty, Zealous Zeroing in on my Zenith with Ziggy Zbigniew.

And to you, here, I say butt out. Some things should remain private.

# 46

Ziggy jumps so loudly that I wake in terror.

"Sorry," he squeals, his breath hard and fast. "Happens now and then. Sorry."

I stroke his chest lovingly. I can almost feel his heartbeat beneath my fingers. He nestles into me, more for his own benefit than mine.

"Ziggy, it's okay."

His voice is muffled in my hair. "I dreamt you were gone. Sorry."

I reach up and put my arm around him. "I'm not going anywhere." I kiss him thoroughly, his hand strong behind my neck, his mouth seeking reassurance. My job done, I relax back, a smile playing on my lips. We're naked and messy and I like what I see, both him and me. The wonder of safe human connection has been an exhilarating shock. Can it be that simple? Kat with Thor, Mum with Dad, Laurie with Denise, Rupert with Daisy, Harry B with Andy, Harry K with Joanna, Terri with MuscleMan, Jamie with Clarissa, Ernie and his girlfriend. The lock and key clicking together.

Now I lose my breath. I've given myself too soon, been swept under the bulldozer of my feelings without protecting myself against future heartbreak if the key decides my lock isn't good enough. "Ziggy, one minute I want to trust this, the next I'm ready to run. I've got my own share of hurt."

He smiles. "And we're going to deal with that. So long as the problems are imaginary, we'll be okay."

Words bubble up within me. "I won't be *everything a man ever wanted*. Your wife might've set me up for failure."

His expression turns sour. "She wasn't a wife." He reaches out and tucks a strand of hair behind my ear. "But I assure you I was a terrific husband. In case we're interested in going that far." He smiles.

"And you're a psychologist. You'll always be ahead of me, knowing more than me, seeing through me."

He shrugs. "My parents, and all my psychologist friends, are able to pull their head in when they're wrong, because we know how dubious the human brain can be."

I believe him. I do trust *this*. I check one last time. "If this doesn't work out between us, I mean, if it peters out or if we find it's not what we expected, can we be kind to each other about it?"

He pulls me close again and kisses the top of my head. No words come and I understand Kat, trying to run from the grasp of Thor, so scared of an ending that she can't manage the beginning.

Finally, he speaks. "It's your mouth, Candice."

I swallow hard. What's wrong with my mouth?

"The words that come out of it reassure me. And when you smile or laugh," he grins, "You hook me. But to kiss it-" he pauses.

I look up at him, trying to gauge what seems indefinable.

"Okay, it's also your eyes," he smiles. "When I helped you up in the pub and you brought your eyes to me, my brain seized. I knew you instantly. You were spirited, warm, pretty but also wary, defensive, guarded." His smile widens. "You felt it too, but you weren't going to make it easy."

Harry K would be proud of me. Got it right first go. "You didn't answer my request."

He shrugs. "I haven't seen anything I don't like. Even your uncertainty about yourself is appealing. It's because you're honest. I need honesty." He glances across my nakedness, grins. "And *primal*."

I remain serious. "You're okay just to throw yourself in at the deep end without any thought I might break your heart?"

The change on his face is dramatic. I want to suck back my words. When he speaks, his voice is strangled. "Do you intend to?"

"Of course not."

He leans away. "I haven't entered into this lightly. I was broken by what I thought was a Happy Ever After. I'm not that man anymore." A frown fleets across his face. "I'm not *throwing myself in* without consciously considering where the roadblocks are for us. But I'm also not going to live my life being scared about investing in a relationship, otherwise Fanny has still won. We're both sensible, intelligent people. You're articulate, outspoken, reliable. At some stage I must decide the value of a relationship with you is worth more than the panic that might rise intermittently."

I flinch, teeter back to level. My misgivings must be miniscule compared to his. "You haven't had any lovers since Fanny?"

"Do I seem out of practice?" He smiles glumly.

"No. You scored well on my PUSSI." I laugh at his expression. "That's short for Physical Union Self-Satisfaction Indicator. We non-psychologists can make up inventories as well."

He smiles quietly. "And I thought you were talking dirty to me."

I smile back. "I thought you'd be desperate. Fast. Ready to blow."

"Looking for quality," he says emphatically.

I nod. "Safe quality you can be vulnerable with."

"Yes."

We smile.

"Harry K, the other Harry, he's a doctor, he's going to be mighty pissed with me."

He frowns. "Why?"

I laugh. "At least we used a condom."

He's lost in thought, and fear squirts into my brain again.

"If your mother thought that there'd be no you. You don't know who we've missed out on because of that condom." He rubs my arm. "Maybe we should think about that sometime."

I sit up like a meerkat. "Wait a minute! Don't go there." I'm astonished at his grin. "What are you saying? No. I'm saying no. That's not … I mean, Ziggy, … no … I-"

He strokes me kindly. "I could be practical here, but I don't want to be. I've wasted so many years. I don't want to wait too long. And I'm saying it worked for your parents."

I should run from the room screaming but I can't be faffed. I'm too happy. Which was why Kat was in a baby fog the first time she and Thor were together, why Harry K has a third baby on the way, why my parents didn't use something to prevent me. The hormones hypnotise us with happiness, beckoning the unsuspecting egg and the all too eager sperm to dance a slow step together into the future. And I'm so glad they do, for without it I wouldn't be here analysing it all.

Besides, knowing Ziggy for two weeks before bedding him is way better than my mother's effort. And a whole lot more cautious than Kat waking up with Thor astride her. And I kept my head, used protection. I'm the ace in the hole. Pun very much intended. But still the questions hover. "It seems so trusting of you to agree to that initial blind date with the woman at the pub, given what you've told me."

He pauses. "Dad said I was still carrying Fanny around with me every day like a winter coat. I asked my friends what first step I should take, and Randall said his wife had a single friend. I agreed, very nervously, to a blind date with that friend. It was the means to get me to that pub to meet you. Fate's not a crapshoot at all." He runs the back of his finger across my cheek. "I really didn't want to go to another family wedding without a date and face all that *When are you going to get back in the saddle again*, like all I'd done was to stop a favourite sport." He smiles. "I had no idea the night was going to pan out so well."

"Taking a drunk cheat to a family wedding?" I laugh. "You were aiming very low."

"Perfect," he smiles. "By the way, Harry's invite says *Ziggy and partner*. After we discussed you, he asked for it back, crossed out *partner* and wrote *Candice*." He smiles happily.

"Is Harry B doing the right thing?" I ask with concern. "I mean, it's not just turning forty, is it?"

"He's very cautious," Ziggy replies. "She seems good for him. She holds him accountable, but gives him his freedom to run his game."

"His game?"

Ziggy smiles. "Harry is a very deep thinker. You know that. Extraordinarily smart. He likes to feel in control of his life. But he bats it away from the public eye with his jokey manner. Andrea gets that."

I admire Ziggy summing up my brother so succinctly. "I don't know anything about Andy. How did she get so smart so young? I'm not that smart and I'm older than she is."

Ziggy shrugs. "Intersection of a number of factors."

He says nothing more and I presume he feels he's said enough about his confidential clients.

"I've been thinking a lot about my parents." I don't know why I'm broaching this with him. Looking for assistance? Filling in a lull in the conversation? "I've always known their history, but it's only now become very real for me. I find myself understanding at odd times how difficult life must have been for them."

"Family," Ziggy smiles, "is an ever-evolving dynamic. It's the learning ground for how to live our lives. Sometimes we learn wrong."

"Kat."

He doesn't respond. "I've seen some hopeless cases, have been privileged to watch them unpick the thread back to where the knot was tied securely, then sew a new tapestry."

I grin. "I didn't take you for a poet."

"There's still a lot we don't know about each other. What we want from life. What we think about things. When I'm allowed to call you sweetie." We laugh together. "But it's all negotiable. We'll work it out."

# 47

The real world, of course, is still out there beyond this paradise, and needs to be addressed.

"My work is changing," I tell him, like it's an important factor in whether he continues with me. "I'm taking on social media for the magazine. A podcast, a blog, and other ideas. Still employed by them, but my articles will be features, and social media will be my main role."

"Wow." I like that he's impressed. "What's its focus?"

I grin cheesily. "All the nonsensical stuff about being a woman."

He smiles. "You're just the one to do it. Can I look it up?"

"Not online yet of course. But I've got a name for it."

"Well?"

"*The Feminist EarthMother PartyGirl.*"

Ziggy sorts it through in his mind, then laughs. "As a psychologist I have to advise you that you've finally hit on your true personality. But you know you've used the word *girl?*"

I pause, running through the title. Dammit, I have! But *PartyWoman* sounds like one of those host-a-party-in-your-home-with-our-product events that I steer well clear of. It seems my love of language has let me down this time. "You got me there. One time when using the word *girl* is fine." I pause. "See, I'm learning to be flexible. Perhaps I should call it *The Flexible Feminist* instead."

"That has other overtones," he runs his hand along my arm.

It's obvious now I've learnt a thing or two from my Vision Quest. But how did I get from confused crazy woman two weeks ago to here feeling so comfortable with this man? And where will I be in two weeks' time? How do I keep the ball rolling on the new improved Me?

"What's that expression?" Ziggy asks.

I smile reassuringly. "Just thinking about living my best life."

He grins. "Those words are from my website."

"I know," I grin back. "I've learnt a lot from you."

"Maybe you've learnt a lot from you."

I think about Kat, how Thor has changed her outlook. But then she's taught Thor too, about toughness and persistence. I see it in all the couples. I know now that we teach each other, sometimes good things, sometimes bad, but learning all the same.

"Yes. I was a damsel in distress. However, nobody saved me but me. I've learned so much from listening, and observing, and reading your book. Getting from A to Z has been an interesting journey."

"From what to what?"

I grin. "Never mind." Time slows, because I finally have answers to two questions, one I phrased at the beginning and one I realise only now that I have been looking for without acknowledgement.

The first is *Who is Candice Kelly?* and it's obvious now. She's loving, lovable, loved. She's safe enough to allow herself to be vulnerable. And she is, of course, her own Hero. The other, which I wasn't watching for, is *Who is Ziggy Zbigniew?* I like the answers to both questions.

"I'm moving out of my flat," I state impertinently.

His eyebrows rise. "Oh?"

"The flats are being sold. Rupert's moving in with Daisy, and Laurie has Denise. We're going to stay in touch."

He frowns. "Where will you go?"

"Harry K's. Joanna's pregnant with their third so I can help her a little, if she'll let me."

"If she'll let you? She's very independent?"

I laugh. "That's an understatement. But they'll give me a room for free in their mansion and I'll take the pressure off Joanna where I can. I can save my rent money for a house."

"A woman who has her own money! I like it." He smiles. "Sounds like a lovely space for us to get used to each other."

"I'm still getting used to me." I frown. "Failing that personality test was an eye-opener."

"You don't fail personality tests!" he says cheerily. "There's no right or wrong answer. You just choose the answer that's right for you."

"And I got the answers wrong! It wasn't like me at all!"

He cocks his head to one side. "Want me to administer another personality test? One that will actually work for you?"

Uh, what? Ziggy marking my answers on an inventory? Finding out my weaknesses? "Not a chance, Dr Zbigniew."

"Come on." He strokes my cheek. "It won't hurt. Here, I'll convince you. Close your eyes."

What now, hypnosis? His expression is so earnest I do as he says.

He speaks softly against my ear. "I'm going to start by asking you a series of questions." His lips fall upon on my neck. "Do you like this?"

I giggle and pull away, open my eyes. "Is that one of the questions?"

"Hmm. Answering questions with questions. Interesting trait. Close your eyes again."

I do. I feel his hand carefully against my breast.

"What about this?"

My breath quickens as his thumb strokes. "Yes."

"Hmmm. Enjoys titillation."

I open my eyes again. "What kind of test is this?"

"You need to trust me." His eyes sparkle. "Remember, I'm a psychologist. Next question is one of my favourites." He moves towards me, lays himself on top. "Do you like this?"

"Oh, yes." I place my arms around his neck. I'd swoon if I wasn't laying down.

His eyes are pools of deep dark longing. "Hmm. Enjoys connection. Body connection. I rate that as an extremely useful trait."

I smile. "I hope you don't administer this test to all your clients."

His lips hover above mine. "You need a special relationship with your psychologist to have this one administered. And then it can only be administered by that psychologist to that one person for all time."

I smile. "What was the next question on your test?"

"Hmmm. Well, it's a non-verbal test. To remove gender bias." He grins. "Are you ready for me to give it to you?"

I laugh. "Oh yes. Give it to me. Very much, give it to me."

I see something in his eyes I haven't seen before, a well of genuine understanding, of a connection so deep I lose my sense of everything, of me, of him, of the room. Is it Ziggy, or have I changed? Has my Vision improved from the success of my Quest? The memory of walking to the shops yesterday morning returns. The clarity with which I saw everything was extraordinary.

Without warning it's like someone's hit the rewind button on my life, images of everyone and everything that's happened in the past few weeks playing out before my eyes. The Vision slows as it flows past Ziggy sitting on my couch, when I found out how I'd acted at the wedding and how he'd acted regardless of how I'd acted, and the intense satisfaction I felt with the respect I'd been given. Being in the depths of shame, I hadn't acknowledged it at the time.

The Vision lurches back to me happily dancing with Ziggy. It's a memory which to date has escaped me fully. On through what it was like sitting in the church waiting for the bride and groom to appear, eating from the plate for two at my local, until finally it freezes on me outside the pub with my hand on the door, the moment before Ziggy enters my life.

"What is it?" he asks, frowning.

I blink, feeling the tension for that woman, unaware of what lies in wait. "I just-" I pause. "It's … everything's so clear now." Now I know it was the WiMPI that failed, not me. What it did, however, was snap me out of my stupor. Bravery steered me through the harsh winds of confusion, landed me safely on shore, just like Kat. And now it's time for one last list of learnings from my completed Vision Quest.

1. Be you. Trust you.

2. Be the creator of your own destiny. Don't leave your future to chance. But when chance asks you to dance, follow its lead.

3. Be sure of your path. If you've gone down the wrong road, get off it as quickly as you can. And don't get lured back onto it. Look for opportunities, even when things go wrong, in fact, especially when things have gone wrong.

4. Love in all its forms is transformative. Make sure the transformation works for you. Love should not hurt. It should feel safe enough for you to be vulnerable.

5. When you don't have a CLUE where you're headed, psychology can help.

Ziggy watches me curiously. "Are you okay?"

"Yes, please, give me the test," I whisper. "Give it to me good."

This personality test turns out to be an interesting one. I marvel at the diagnostic ability of the questions. There's certainly no gender bias, because *Yes* is the only answer given to the questions, repeated over and over again. And not just by the test-taker, but also the test-giver.

So here I am, Candice Kelly the Wondering Woman, finally getting the kind of personality test that is, pardon the pun, right up my alley.

And this time, I pass with flying colours.

# A letter from Joni

Hello everyone!

You might be interested to know I had the title of this book years before I wrote the story. I was thinking how muddled we can get when we try to describe who we are as women. It seemed like fun to write about a woman whose characteristics were as far apart as I could unreasonably get!

I tried to write this book three times. The first attempt was a self-help book, but it felt too preachy. The second was the diary of a school-leaver, but that title felt like it needed a few more years behind it.

Then one day I had a couple of hours to kill with only my laptop for company, and I began the novel again using a thread of consciousness. To my happy surprise, there she was, spilling out onto the page, Candice Kelly, a woman confused and yet aware, scared and yet brave. Watching the unique characters tumble into her world was like channelling some special force. I wrote a thousand words a day for several months, then it was complete. I loved every minute of seeing where Candice went on her journey.

In the end, I reckon Candice has done the three labels proud.

Please enjoy the book club questions that follow. If your group has any comments or queries, you can contact me via my website, jonipage.com. There are extra book club questions there, too.

If you enjoyed *The Feminist EarthMother PartyGirl*, I'd be delighted for you to leave a positive review on social media and / or book platforms.

All the best with your own path!

Love, Joni

# About the author

Joni Page lives in beautiful Adelaide in friendly South Australia with her family. She holds degrees in psychology and teaching, and Honours in education.

Joni lovingly crafts stories about people who are asking themselves big questions about what they want from life. Things don't always go their way, but they are brave and persistent, and they triumph.

Joni is grateful to have been part of the award-winning anthology, *The Sound of Silence: Journeys Through Miscarriage.*

She is an obsessive gardener and a courageous cook.

# Connect with Joni Page

Instagram:      @jonipage_author
Bluesky:        @jonipageauthor.bsky.social
Twitter/X:      @JoniPageAuthor
Pinterest:      @JoniPageAuthor
Website:        www.jonipage.com

# Like some more?

*Swinging Through*, a short prequel to *The Feminist EarthMother PartyGirl*, is available through Joni's website, jonipage.com, for free download.

# Acknowledgements

First of all, thank you for choosing this book!

Big thanks to my husband Sam for his unfailing confidence in me, his boundless energy, and his amazing skills in tech, design and strategy. That man can turn his hand to anything! He really is the best to work alongside. Big thanks to my kids too, for their encouragement, love and listening ears, and for their tech support at trying moments.

Much love to the following: Annie King, who was the first friend to encourage my writing. Catherine Russo, who has kept my writing on point. Megan Scott, for reading entire drafts. Marianne Lewis, Maree A, and Toni for reading my early drafts. Ilona Treijs for sparking my interest in psychology. Brendan Somerville, Anja, Maja, and Sarah for being my gardening gurus.

I learnt about friendship from the best. As well as those already mentioned, here are my truth-tellers - Trudy Sutton, Debra Sarre, Katharine, Tammy and Trish; my funsters - Lindsay Gilchrist, Julie, Michelle, Kim, and Chris; and my mighty ones - Jill Hoopmann and Sandra Tilley.

I am only here in this moment because of the kindness and wisdom of Heather and Dick Begg, Miss Peters, Mr Malone, Christine Beardsley, Erin Bulluss, Mark Le Messurier, Sharon Palm, Max Aberdeen, Graham, and Kerri.

Thanks to Rhonda Bilney for help with the recognition of Kaurna lands. Lorraine, you know what for. Elaine P for changing my life. Keelia for our chats about writing.

Thanks to Steve West for brilliant tech support. To Deb Hall, Maria MN, Sue, and Janine, and everyone who took a lovely interest in my books, massive thanks.

And to my mother, thanks for all the books!

# Book Club Questions

1. What did you think the book would be about when you first saw the title? Do you fit any of the title? What would you call yourself?

2. Candice sorts through her problems by downloading her thoughts into a list. How does this help achieve her new direction?

3. Candice and Kat have very different outlooks, yet they have a solid friendship. Where do they differ and where are they similar?

4. Candice and Kat's friendship is based on honesty, trust and a comforting shared lack of good judgment. Neither has had a successful romantic relationship. In what ways does Kat's relationship with Thor impact Candice's decisions going forward?

5. Both Candice's and Kat's parents behaved irresponsibly. What differing impacts did this have on their children's lives? How have the women successfully lived their adult lives in light of this?

6. What part does Candice's feminism play in her ideas about romance?

7. What impact have the huge number of romances going on around Candice had on her thinking about the place of love in her life, instead of other issues? Is this usual for women?

8. Given the CLUE is a fictional instrument, would you add or take away any items on the ladder, or rearrange the ladder? Make it a different shape?

9. What do you think the "roadblocks" will be in Candice's relationship with Ziggy?

10. What would it be like for the Harrys to have a new stepbrother with the same name at the same school in the same class? Would it make their parent's infidelity worse? Would the fact it was a new school make it better or worse? Do you think there would be much gossip about it between other parents / school staff?

11. Do you think Ziggy and Thor could become friends? In what ways are they similar / different?

12. Where do you predict Candice and Ziggy will be in five years' time?

Some reflective questions follow …

13. Would you be brave enough to do a test like the Hooami, where people give you anonymous feedback? What do you think they would say about you? Who would you like to give feedback to?

14. Candice finds a new sense of direction after her initial failed date with Ziggy at Le Café. Have you ever had something bad happen only for it to lead you down a good pathway?

Want more? Get more! MORE book club questions on jonipage.com

www.ingramcontent.com/pod-product-compliance
Lightning Source LLC
Chambersburg PA
CBHW050609190726
48283CB00007B/2338